T0007066

PENGUIN MODERN CLASSICS
Dada Comrade

YASHPAL (1903–1976) was one of the most prolific and unusual Hindi writers of the post-Premchand generation. He studied at National College, Lahore and became, along with Bhagat Singh, Chandrashekhar Azad, and others, an active member of the Hindustan Socialist Republican Association (HSRA). He began to write while serving a life sentence for his participation in the armed struggle for India's independence. His first collection of short stories, *Pinjare ki Udaan*, was published in 1938. After his release from prison, Yashpal dazzled Hindi readers with the political journal *Viplav*, which he founded and published with the help of Prakashvati, a fellow-revolutionary who became his wife. He wrote more than fifty books, including collections of short stories, novels, essays, a play and memoirs of his revolutionary days.

His two-volume magnum opus *Jhootha Sach* (1958 and 1960), translated into English as *This Is Not That Dawn*, is widely considered to be one of the most penetrating narratives on the partition of India. His novel *Meri Teri Uski Baat* won the Sahitya Akademi Award in 1976. He was a recipient of the Padma Bhushan.

SIMONA SAWHNEY teaches in the Department of Humanities and Social Sciences at IIT Delhi. She received her PhD in Comparative Literature from the University of California, Irvine, and has previously taught at the University of Illinois, Urbana-Champaign, and the University of Minnesota. She is the author of *The Modernity of Sanskrit* (2008), as well as several essays on Indian literature and political thought. She is currently co-editing, with Kama Maclean, a collection of essays on Yashpal.

ADVANCE PRAISE FOR THE BOOK

'Shailbala is like a dream abandoned by all our ideological struggles—struggles of the past as well as of the present. Simona Sawhney's fine translation has once again returned Yashpal's story to that fraught arena where every warrior appears exhausted today—battling, as it were, one defeat after another'—Ravish Kumar, Journalist

'A sensitive and nuanced translation of a daring and unusual novel'
—Vasudha Dalmia, Professor Emerita, University of California, Berkeley

'Yashpal is renowned for his brisk prose and polemical narrative style. With her translation of his political novel *Dada Comrade*, Simona Sawhney has made a remarkable contribution to literary translation in English. Upon reading the novel along with her authoritative introduction, we recognize the challenges of narrating the conflict between the political and the sexual—the very challenges with which the Marxist Yashpal courageously wrestled'—Apoorvanand, Professor, Delhi University

'Bold characters, revolutionary politics, sexual attraction, youthful debates in a hill station's cottage, workers' strikes—in the heady days of the anticolonial movements, leading Hindi writer Yashpal's first novel weaves together the personal and the political in striking new ways. This is novel writing as political as well as sentimental education, with characters who constantly challenge each other, question themselves, and develop through reflections, experiences and interactions. A must read for anyone interested in the intimate history of revolutionary politics in India'—Francesca Orsini, Professor Emerita, SOAS, University of London

YASHPAL

Dada Comrade

Translated from the Hindi by Simona Sawhney

PENGUIN BOOKS

An imprint of Penguin Random House

PENGUIN BOOKS

USA | Canada | UK | Ireland | Australia
New Zealand | India | South Africa | China

Penguin Books is part of the Penguin Random House group of companies
whose addresses can be found at global.penguinrandomhouse.com

Published by Penguin Random House India Pvt. Ltd
4th Floor, Capital Tower 1, MG Road,
Gurugram 122 002, Haryana, India

First published in Hindi as *Dada Comrade* by Viplava Karyalaya, 1941
First published in English in Penguin Books by Penguin Random House India 2021

ISBN 9780143455127

Typeset in Bembo Std by Manipal Technologies Limited, Manipal

www.penguin.co.in

Contents

Introduction

Simona Sawhney

Yashpal

The acclaimed Hindi writer Bhisham Sahni (1915–2003) wrote a beautiful piece in memory of Yashpal after his death in 1976. Sahni recalls the words of someone who had known Yashpal since his childhood: 'In a way, Yashpal descended from the gallows and entered the world of literature.'[1] Although the dramatic turn that is signalled by these words— the turn from a life of militant 'revolutionary' activity to a life of writing—is certainly the most consequential turn of Yashpal's life, something else besides this is captured in these words: namely, the way this second life was born of, and indelibly marked by, a too-close familiarity with death.

This aspect of Yashpal's turn away from militant action is sometimes forgotten when it is seen only as a change in his political orientation. The political change is immensely significant (as I will go on to discuss), and it is captured in a striking way in Yashpal's first—and partly

autobiographical—novel *Dada Comrade* (1941), but the
unsettling and profound impact of having survived, of
outliving some of his closest comrades, also left its mark
on this novel, as it did on many of Yashpal's novels and
short stories.

Yashpal was born on 3 December 1903 in Ferozepur
Cantonment in Punjab. His mother worked as a teacher
in an Arya Samaj orphanage to support herself and her
two sons. From the age of seven to fourteen, Yashpal was
educated at Gurukul Kangri, an Arya Samaj institution for
boys. Here he was introduced to the Arya Samaj culture
of reform coupled with Hindu pride, an intense hatred of
foreign rule, as well as puritanical ideas of sexual abstinence
that he was to reject decisively in later years. In his
autobiography, *Simhavalokan* (literally, 'A Lion's Backward
Glance' but idiomatically, simply 'A Backward Glance'), he
writes about his experience as a student from a relatively
poor family. Though the rule at Gurukul was that all be
treated equally, those who, like Yashpal, studied gratis,
felt disgraced in various ways. He memorably describes
his first and formative experience of humiliation: a painful
experience of shame arising from something that lay utterly
beyond his control or responsibility. In retrospect, he notes
that since that time, he could never remain indifferent to
the disgrace of poverty.

At fourteen, he moved to Lahore for further studies.
He joined the National College of Lahore, founded in
1921 in Bradlaugh Hall by Lala Lajpat Rai. In response
to Gandhi's call for non-cooperation with British rule

(1920), thousands of students across the country left British-run colleges and universities, often putting their future careers and livelihoods in peril. The National College of Lahore, along with the Jamia Millia Islamia (initially established in Aligarh), were two 'national' institutions founded at that time to offer such students an alternative. Students drawn to the nationalist movement flocked to these institutions. Yashpal was struck by the open atmosphere of National College and its difference from the (British) Government universities. Here, not only were students free to express their political beliefs, but they were also, by and large, driven by an intense hunger for learning, particularly for learning about history, economics and political thought. They did not lead ascetic lives, but neither did they care much about fashion and clothing. He makes special mention of Professor Jaichandra Vidyalankar, also an ex-student of Gurukul Kangri, who taught Indian history and politics. Vidyalankar encouraged debate and discussion on all sorts of questions in his classes (including questions of theism and atheism) and a group of politically curious students gathered around him. The seeds of the Hindustan Socialist Republican Association were sown here.[2]

At National College Yashpal met his future comrades Bhagat Singh, Sukhdev, Bhagvati Charan Vohra, Ehsan Ilahi, Dhanvantari and others. They often talked about the failures of Gandhi's Satyagraha and were attracted by the ideals and success of the Russian Revolution (1917). But their political ideas were half-formed yet and in flux; their

list of heroes capacious enough to include Lenin as well as
Mazzini, Nehru as well as Savarkar. Influenced by Giuseppe
Mazzini's 'Young Italy' movement, they started the Naujawan
Bharat Sabha (the Young India Society); one of their first
activities was to hold a defiant public ceremony in honour
of the young revolutionary Kartar Singh Sarabha, a member
of the Ghadar Party who had been hanged in 1915 for
propagating armed insurrection against the British. The
Sabha's other activities included arranging inter-communal
meals for Hindus, Sikhs and Muslims—once some students
even cooked halal and jhatka meat together and served it to
a mixed gathering.

On 8 and 9 September 1928, representatives of
revolutionary groups from various parts of north India
met in the ruins of the Feroz Shah Fort in Delhi to form
the Hindustan Socialist Republican Association (HSRA),
notably marking its distance from Sachindranath Sanyal's
earlier group, the Hindustan Republican Army, as well as
from other militant groups that had been established before
in various parts of north India. According to Yashpal, the
new group marked this distance in two prominent ways.
First, it attempted to break away from the tradition of
'Dada-dom' that characterized the earlier groups. Since
this is of particular relevance to *Dada Comrade*, let me
take a moment to elaborate. Yashpal remarks that earlier
revolutionary groups—by which he means groups that
believed in the necessity of armed struggle against British
rule—had largely relied upon the individual discipline
and charisma of their leader.

The inactive but autocratic leadership of Jaichandra ji in Punjab and J.N. Sanyal in the United Provinces was the result of this same tradition of '*dada-dom*' and we were sick of it. The spirit of democracy had been awakened amongst us. We wanted to centralize regional groups, not under personal dictatorship, but with collective responsibility and leadership.[3]

Incidentally, it was precisely this kind of charismatic but autocratic leadership that Rabindranath Tagore had so powerfully criticized in his last novel, *Char Adhyay* (*Four Chapters*, 1934).

The word 'dada' usually means grandfather in Hindi but in Bengali, it most often means older brother, or more broadly, an older figure to whom one owes deference. This is indeed the way the word is used by Yashpal. His remarks in his memoir, however, indicate that the term had already become inflected with another popular meaning— that of the boss, the thug or even the mafia don. It could thus potentially convey either warmth and affection *or* resentment. This double potential animates the title of the novel, *Dada Comrade*, which can itself be read in different ways. I will discuss some of these possibilities later.

Second, by adding the word 'Socialist' to its name, the group wanted to signal its move towards Marxist thought. It was Bhagat Singh and Sukhdev who proposed the addition of this word, but it received approval from the others as well. Writing about his peers' interest in Marxism, Yashpal notes that though they had not yet understood much about Marxist thought, they had grasped that oppression is fundamentally class-based. He then goes on to make a fascinating and insightful observation:

> We had not been able to fully grasp the scientific truth advanced by Marx, Lenin, and Mao that no power or great man except the people themselves [janata] can break the shackles of the people, or can give them the right of independence and self-determination. Only the people in their collective strength can accomplish this task. [. . .] We wanted to sacrifice ourselves for the mute, oppressed masses, but we had not been able to become part of the masses, *in precisely the same way as Gandhiji wanted to uplift the masses by his personal soul force, and the soul force of a few of his followers.*[4] [Emphasis added]

This is a remarkable passage, not only because it registers a significant site of intersection with Gandhi—otherwise Yashpal's persistent antagonist because of his insistence on ahimsa or non-violence—but also because it foregrounds the tension between individual and collective action that often structures Yashpal's work, including *Dada Comrade*.

Chandra Shekhar Azad (1906–1931) could not attend the 1928 gathering at Feroz Shah Fort, but members of the group were in contact with him, and he was unanimously declared the 'Commander-in-Chief' of the HSRA. Apparently, he was the only one of the more experienced militants who, the group felt, was willing to adopt their new approach. The group performed two notable actions in quick succession. On

17 December 1928, members of the group killed 21-year-old police officer John P. Saunders in Lahore in retaliation for the police attack on Lala Lajpat Rai during protests against the Simon Commission. Then, on 8 April 1929, they protested against the Public Safety Bill and the Trade Disputes Bill by detonating two bombs in the Legislative Assembly in Delhi. These bills were introduced after the South Indian Railway and the Bombay Textile workers' strikes in 1928 and were aimed at the growing labour movement in the country— more precisely, at the widespread communist penetration of labour unions. While the killing of Saunders cannot be seen as anything other than an act of anti-colonial revenge, the protest in the Assembly was explicitly framed as an anti-imperialist act in solidarity with workers. Bhagat Singh and Batukeshwar Dutt, who threw these bombs, did not attempt to escape. They let themselves be arrested and in the months that followed, proceeded to use the courtroom as a venue for publicizing their ideas. We see an analogous use of the courtroom towards the end of *Dada Comrade* when Harish, instead of just defending himself, insists on questioning the fundamental premises of the court and challenging its conception of property and theft.

A year later the secret bomb factory that Yashpal and others had set up in Lahore was discovered by the police and Sukhdev was also arrested. Yashpal went underground. He eloquently describes his own terror during this first experience of living underground as a terrorist. Like a wild animal pursued by a hunter, he says, he fled to his lair— Kangra. While in Kangra, he contemplated his future course of action. It is at this point in *Simhavalokan* that Yashpal takes the opportunity to criticize Sarat Chandra's popular Bengali novel *Pather Dabi* ('The Right of Way', 1926).

> I understood the foolishness of dreaming of revolution, of making bombs on my own while hiding in isolation in the mountains. Only someone without experience can imagine such things, and a good example of this is Sarat Babu's novel *Pather Dabi*. Revolution can only be carried out in midst of people, not in uninhabited areas.[5]

Indeed, the advertisement for *Dada Comrade* published in *Viplav*, the journal he founded in 1938, explicitly positions it as a response to or a rebuttal of *Pather Dabi*. Yashpal thought that Sarat Chandra had portrayed revolutionaries in a way that highlighted only romance and secrecy, neglecting to describe their aims and plans with any clarity.

In December 1929, Yashpal, together with Bhagvati Charan Vohra, placed and detonated a bomb under the train carrying the Viceroy, Lord Irwin, to Delhi for a meeting with Gandhi. The bomb severely damaged the dining car of the train, and two workers were injured. The Viceroy himself was not hurt, but he was certainly shaken by the attack, which quickly received hot publicity. Gandhi unequivocally condemned it, while many others, even in the Congress, were elated by this bold and dramatic challenge to British rule. A famous exchange between Gandhi and the HSRA on the morality of violence took place after this incident.[6] Here, however, I wish to draw attention instead to something that concerns Yashpal in a more intimate way. Reflecting upon his own insistence on planting the bomb on 23 December, despite the misgivings of some of his comrades, Yashpal says that he had assumed he would die, either in the process of detonating the bomb or later if he were arrested. Hence, according to the custom of the group, Bhagvati Charan Vohra had arranged for Yashpal to be photographed in military gear. Such photographs were taken whenever it was assumed that a comrade would die in an 'action'. Yashpal writes that he had begun thinking of himself as already dead once that photograph was taken. Simply by staying alive, he now felt disgraced and ashamed in his own eyes.[7] Hence, he insisted on carrying out the plan on 23 December, rather than waiting for a more opportune moment. Once the action had proved more or less successful—successful enough in that it created a stir and demonstrated that even the Viceroy himself was no longer secure in India—he felt he could live again.

I draw attention to this because I wish to suggest that perhaps Harish in *Dada Comrade* allows Yashpal the opportunity to vicariously enjoy an *alternative* life and death or, more precisely, to bring together two different fantasies. On the one hand, Harish lives the life not of a writer but of a committed revolutionary, a new and different revolutionary, who believes in organized collective struggle and not in individual militant action. Yet, on the other hand, the fantasy of heroic death is not lost either, for in a sense Harish dies in a manner that replicates the heroic death of a Bhagat Singh or a Sukhdev. Indeed, shades of Bhagat Singh may also be glimpsed in other parts of Harish's biography. Narrating, through the character of Harish, the story of another life and a sacrificial death was perhaps a way for Yashpal to bid adieu, not exactly to a road not taken but to a life-and-death he had both survived and forsaken.

If *Dada Comrade* engages, at one level, a decisive change in Yashpal's conception of revolution, at another, it also engages a transformation in ideas about gender, sexuality and desire. The 'new type of girl' introduced in the novel, Shailbala, is not directly modelled on Yashpal's comrade and wife, Prakashvati Pal, but aspects of her story certainly echo events in Prakashvati's life. Prakashvati had left her home to join the revolutionary group when she was just sixteen years old—an event that caused much consternation among the largely male members of the group. Their envy and anxiety were only exacerbated by the evident attraction between Yashpal and Prakashvati and by their subsequent relationship. Despite an intellectual interest in gender equality, most members of the HSRA viewed love and domesticity as treacherous distractions on the path to revolution. It seems unmistakeably evident, moreover, that it was disavowed envy rather than political commitment that prevented them from changing their perspective. Matters came to a head when the central assembly decided to kill Yashpal for this—and related—crimes. He escaped assassination only because he was fortuitously warned by one of his comrades. The HSRA itself split after this deeply divisive incident, and was never quite able to unite again.

After Azad's death in 1931, Yashpal briefly served as the new Commander-in-Chief of the (reconstituted) HSRA, but was arrested the next year, in 1932. He was defended in court by Shyam Kumari Nehru, a niece of Jawaharlal Nehru, and sentenced to fourteen years of rigorous imprisonment. At this point, Yashpal was uncertain whether he would survive the prison term; he was in poor health and prison conditions were unreliable. He offered to release Prakashvati from all commitments, but she remained steadfast in her wish to marry him. In a most unusual move, she petitioned the prison authorities, requesting permission to marry Yashpal. The petition succeeded, and in August 1936, they were married in a civil ceremony conducted in Bareilly jail. This was, by all accounts, the first and only wedding to be conducted in an Indian prison—rules were revised thereafter to prohibit such weddings! As it happened, in the fast-changing politics of that time, a year later, in 1937, the Congress won the United Provinces elections under the new Government of India Act, and ordered the release of all political prisoners, including militants like Yashpal. By the time Yashpal left prison on 2 March 1938, the HSRA had been disbanded. He turned, in his own words, 'from bullet to bulletin'. He made writing his new profession and embarked on a new life devoted to intellectual and creative labour. He had now committed himself to influencing people by narrative acts instead of violent deeds.

Prakashvati and Yashpal made Lucknow their home. Yashpal started a Hindi journal called *Viplav* (Revolt) in 1938, later also published in Urdu as *Baaghi* (Rebel).

A publishing house called Viplav Karyalaya was established in 1941, and a printing press in 1944. These ran under the dedicated supervision of Prakashvati, who, though trained as a dentist, became, in fact, a full-time publisher and manager. In the words of their son Anand, she 'stood by [Yashpal] not as a romantic muse but rather as a more sturdy and pragmatic partner who helped Yashpal find the creative and intellectual space for going on to write seventeen collections of short stories, twelve novels, and over twenty other books of essays, political analyses, and travelogue'.[8] Among the most well-known of his novels are *Dada Comrade* (1941), *Divya* (1945), *Party Comrade* (later published as *Gita*, 1946), *Manushya ke Roop* (1949), *Jhootha Sach* (1958–60), and *Meri Teri Uski Baat* (1974). The monumental *Jhootha Sach* (translated by his son Anand as *This Is Not That Dawn*) is widely considered one of the most panoramic and nuanced novels about the partition of India, the birth of Pakistan, and the early years of the new republic. Yashpal also wrote a famous critique of Gandhi in 1941 titled *Gandhivad ki Shav Pariksha* ('A Post-Mortem of Gandhism') as well as a short book on Marxism simply titled *Marxvad* in 1940. He was briefly arrested again and imprisoned for seditious writing that same year. Though Yashpal's criticism of Gandhi persists in various texts, we should also note that his perception of Gandhi does change—or at least fluctuate—over the years. His portrait of Gandhi in *Jhootha Sach* is far more sympathetic than the one in *Shav Pariksha*—indeed, at moments in the novel, the reader may even detect admiration and reverence

transmitted through some characters. He was awarded the
Padma Bhushan in 1970, and the Sahitya Akademi award
in 1976 for his last novel, *Meri Teri Uski Baat*. He received
news of this last award just a few weeks before his death.

Dada Comrade

Dada Comrade has been called the pioneering political novel
of Hindi literature.[9] It plunges the reader in the turbulent
world of India in the 1920s and 1930s. This is a world shaped
by anti-colonial resistance, by struggles against caste and
class hierarchies, by an irrepressible hope for an egalitarian
future and by rapidly changing conceptions of sexuality
and gender. Today, many readers may question the ways
in which Yashpal conceived of equality, revolution and
gender. Yashpal's feminism, for instance, is not the same
as mine, but that does not prevent me from recognizing
it as *a* feminism: a discourse that wrestled, in its own way,
with questions of gender, sexuality, power and equality. It
is because of his commitment to an ideal of equality that
Yashpal was able to engage so many diverse political debates
of his time: about violence and militancy, the possibility of
justice in capitalist societies, the ethical and political value
of strikes, as well as about birth control, abortion, marriage
and the structure of the family.

Yashpal often dedicated his books to his readers, his
contemporaries, or his fellow travellers. The most striking
example is *Gita (Party Comrade)*: 'This story of yours, dedicated
to none but you!' *Dada Comrade* begins with an invitation to

the reader: 'Come! Let us sit together and think, a way out of this confusion!' What is this confusion, the predicament or uljhan that the novel urges us to consider? Yashpal's preface suggests that it concerns what has conventionally been called the conflict between tradition and modernity. He does not present the conflict in exactly these terms, though he does invoke the 'ages' of humankind, relying on the metaphor of humanity progressively developing from infancy to adulthood. However, the emphasis on the 'new' in the preface as well as in the novel—new thoughts, new ideas, new morality— clearly indicates that the point of conflict is what Yashpal perceives as a widespread *resistance to modernity*. This resistance manifests itself in clinging to traditions and modes of thought that, according to Yashpal, have outlived their use and now serve only to stifle newness.

The example Yashpal gives in the preface is that of sexuality. He wishes to argue that it is important not to repress the sexual; that Indians must learn to think differently about it. In making this argument, however, he provides what I can only read as a rather reductive assessment, not only of the novel's heroine, Shail, but of sexuality as well. He writes that Shail herself is *nothing but* the active yet unfulfilled sexual instinct of the very people who turn away from her—and from sexuality itself—in disgust. Here, it seems Yashpal becomes curiously forgetful of Shail's role in the novel as a woman whose attentiveness to her own sexual and romantic desires provides, as it were, the very ground for her formation as a political subject. She argues about gender hierarchies with Harish, participates openly in political events, defies a beloved and generous father on political grounds, and abandons a life of luxury to follow her ideals. Why then does Yashpal reduce Shail to 'nothing but' the repressed instinct of those who can only see sexuality as the antithesis and undoing of the political? If there is something jarring in the way Yashpal focuses in the preface on Shail as the representative of a particular version of sexuality it may be because it was precisely this aspect of modernity and change that proved the most recalcitrant for Yashpal himself. While he could imagine and portray women as political and intellectual beings—less successfully in *Dada Comrade*, one must admit, than in some other novels, such as *Gita* and *Jhootha Sach*—it was often on the site of the sexual that he too floundered. It is as though he could not fully carry through the project he had himself embarked on: that of narrating the ineradicable intimacy of the political and the sexual. Ultimately, woman's creativity for him remained pre-eminently located in her *procreativity*—one sees this very clearly in both *Dada Comrade* and *Divya*. And following the same arc, her desire can be articulated only in terms of debt or care—it is awakened either by her gratitude or by her compassion for the male. From Ram Vilas Sharma, who wrote in 1954 that Yashpal's heroes dream only of receiving a woman's compassion[10] to Ania Loomba who wrote in 2019 that Shail's pleasure seems to lie only in 'allowing [Harish's] desire to emerge',[11] readers have noted this aspect of Yashpal's writing, albeit drawing significantly different conclusions from such observations. Whereas

Sharma focuses largely on a criticism of Yashpal's male protagonists, mocking their inward and hence, for him, anti-political anguish (what kind of a hero, he seems to ask in a masculinist tone, wants *merely* a woman's compassion), Loomba—like Nikhil Govind[12] before her—draws our attention to the internalization of the political in sexual desire. Yet, they concur in noting that in Yashpal's texts, woman's pleasure seems to lie largely in the experience of her own generosity or compassion. Of course, there is nothing 'wrong' about this—but does it not continue to present a rather traditional image of woman, the same image that Yashpal apparently wished to change? Indeed, we could even go further. In at least two important scenes, *Dada Comrade* repeats a fantasy in which woman's beauty—and heterosexual pleasure itself, whether scopic or tactile—provides comfort and support for the politically active man. In such scenes, sexual pleasure is implicitly positioned on the *other side* of political activity for the male: while political struggle exhausts and ravages him, love and sex fulfil and nourish. The female, on the other hand, is positioned such that she can only enter the field of the political *through* her sexual desire. It is not so much that the sexual is prior to the political for her, but rather that the political is most deeply and clearly sensed by way of the sexual. This pattern may be seen in some of Yashpal's other novels as well, with *Gita* remaining a memorable exception. My point is not that Yashpal should have portrayed men and women in exactly the same way. Indeed, it may even be that Yashpal's work ultimately *privileges*, rather than subordinating, the avowal of the sexual in the field of the political. Nevertheless, the co-conspiracy of the political and the sexual sometimes appears to replicate familiar, constraining and ultimately patriarchal images of sexual difference in his work.

In *Dada Comrade*, Shail seems to participate in political events and activities not because she's a member of Harish's party, but largely because of her friendship with, and evident attraction for, Harish himself. While it is true that she was politically active even before meeting Harish, she usually defers to his judgement and leadership. It is hence the male protagonist who awakens the excitement of both the erotic and the political. This pattern is also true for Nancy, and even for Yashoda, whose attraction for Harish is never spelt out, but is certainly implicit in the very first chapter of the book, and later obliquely reiterated via the jealousy of her husband, Amarnath. Though shades of the maternal are evident in Yashoda's demeanour, an erotic subtext persists. As Visvambhar Nath Upadhyay, an otherwise admiring reader of the novel noted many decades ago, the title of the first chapter, 'A Night of Dilemma' (*Duvidha ki Raat*), signals a dilemma that the chapter can never really draw out of the shadows. Though the chapter does show us how Yashoda is caught between her fear (of Harish, the police, her husband and so on) and her wish to help Harish, it cannot bring to light the deeper and more significant dilemma between her loyalty to her husband and her attraction to Harish. Upadhyay hence criticizes Yashpal for not paying enough attention to the inner world and the emotional depth of his characters: 'It is strange,' he writes, 'that a writer who understood Marxism so well remained indifferent to the *psychic contradictions* of human beings' (emphasis added).[13]

None of this, however, should prevent us from appreciating the ways in which strong arguments against woman's traditional place in the household and even against marriage as an institution are voiced in the text. In an early conversation with Harish, Shail insists that monogamous marriage can mean nothing but slavery for woman, and that within the structure of marriage, two people can never be companions or comrades. Even though at the end she refers to herself as Harish's wife, it is clear that the family she has now chosen to create is no traditional family—it is instead truly a family of comrades (albeit keeping intact a hetero structure). Yashoda's life is not transformed in the course of the narrative in quite the same way, but seen from a different perspective, she perhaps goes even further, since she succeeds in bringing about a radical change in the very heart of the traditional family she inhabits. Once she has assumed a public, political persona, her husband finds it impossible to view her as he did earlier. In one of the novel's most memorable and understated passages, the narrator tells us that when Amarnath now faced his wife, he no longer felt he was her lord; he had become, instead, 'an ordinary person' (p. 170).

Let us linger with Yashoda for a while. If, on the one hand, it is her attraction for Harish that leads her into new territory, on the other, it is undeniably her attraction for Shail that ends up playing a larger role in her gradual transformation. Here, is it worth remarking that we catch our very first glimpse of Shail through Yashoda's eyes, and are instantly swept along by her curiosity: 'In the afternoon a young girl arrived at Yashoda's home. Yashoda herself was not a traditional woman [a woman of the old type], but this girl was entirely of a new type. From the very first sight of her, Yashoda felt both curiosity and attraction.' What is this attraction? In the span of just a few minutes, Yashoda feels an unexpected sense of intimacy: 'as though she had found some old friend from her natal home, whom she had been long awaiting' (p. 32). Without necessarily defining this attraction, we could nevertheless note that desire has found a path here—a path whose trace appears indelibly in the text, even as the text follows it no further. Here, I can't help but mention that Prakashvati Pal herself repeatedly notes how women are drawn to the beauty of other women. In her memoir she writes, 'Tulsidas said, "Woman does not love the beauty of woman". I don't think that is true. Whose mind can remain untouched by beauty and its glow—who would not be attracted to it?'[14] It is sometimes through the initial enigma of such attraction that solidarities among women are forged in Yashpal's work. But such solidarities usually fade away or retreat, instead allowing heterosexual dynamics to occupy centre stage. A prime example is the 1949 novel *Manushya Ke Roop*.

But let us return to *Dada Comrade* and its attempt to rethink and critique traditional family structure as well as gender roles. In a striking passage, we find Shail's friend Robert making a strong case for birth control. Unlike other arguments of that time, his is not based on statist concerns for family planning, or even concerns about women's health and physical welfare. Instead, he makes his appeal in the name of equality. We must conceive of women's equality, he says, in terms of *an equal ability to pursue sexual pleasure*—an ability that must depend on access to contraception. In discussing birth control, Yashpal was responding to a discussion that had been gaining momentum since the early twentieth century. Many early advocates of reproductive control in India were influenced by Neo-Malthusian and eugenic theories: for example, at the 1931 session of the All-India Women's Conference, even the younger supporters of birth control appealed primarily to the health and vigour of the race. This may have been a strategic move. The American activist Agnes Smedley cautioned fellow birth control advocate Margaret Sanger that in India 'it is better not to stress the woman's freedom viewpoint until you have a foothold'.[15] Sanger went on to join R.D. Karve in debating Gandhi on this issue. Gandhi, of course, strongly advocated self-control and celibacy as the only moral means of birth control, and it is likely that in *Dada Comrade* Yashpal is once again staking out his position against Gandhi. At the same time, he is also differentiating himself from those who had not placed the debate squarely in terms of women's own sexual desires.

Surely it cannot be accidental that this argument is made by a former Christian in this novel. While Christian and 'Anglo-Indian' characters often appear as less sexually constrained figures in Hindi novels of that period, here Robert is explicitly positioned as an *advocate* for a different morality, one that the novel endorses. Indeed, Robert sometimes becomes a mouthpiece for the novel to expound political arguments—whether it be the argument for atheism or for birth control. While his Christian past may well have inculcated in him a liberalism and a certain—albeit limited—inclination towards equality (this link between Christianity and equality also appears in Yashpal's last novel, *Meri Teri Uski Baat*), ultimately it is Robert's *rejection* of religion that makes him, for Yashpal, most suitable for such a role.

Robert, however, has other important functions as well: acting as the 'third' whose presence obstructs, and hence fuels, the romance between Shail and Harish, and as the 'fourth' of the quartet that allows Yashpal to stage some of his most 'Europeanized' scenes in the novel. I use this term because I strongly suspect that images from Turgenev's famous novel *Fathers and Sons* (which Yashpal mentions in the preface in a different context), have, perhaps unbeknownst to Yashpal himself, moulded some of the Mussoorie scenes of *Dada Comrade*. We find again an isolated quartet here: two siblings and two outsiders; analogous crossing lines of desire, where one woman attracts both men while the other feels forlorn, envious and outcast; similar scenes of intense conversation interspersed with music; an echo of Bazarov's impending death in Harish's sense of his own grim fate.

I would not have arrived at this comparison had Yashpal himself not written of how deeply affected he was by Turgenev's novel. In an essay written many years after he had read the book, he describes how it gripped him the very first time he read it:

It was forty years ago, but I remember this well. My knowledge of English was limited at that time, but the

very first chapter of the novel seized my mind such that I
would keep reading it till late at night. Other comrades—
Bhagat Singh and Sukhdev—had also read that novel
and we discussed it among ourselves. It seemed to us
that we had found a source of wisdom in the midst of
our mental agitation: the ideas and beliefs that surround
us are not everything. We cannot remain believers and
conformists. We too have the power of discernment
and discrimination [*vivek*]. We will have to become self-
reliant, analyse social conditions on our own, and decide
our own path.[16]

What most impressed Yashpal and his friends was Bazarov's
intellectual self-reliance: the very quality that had drawn
countless readers around the world to this character, as
Edward Said wrote in his 1996 book *Representations of the
Intellectual*.[17] Bazarov, the seductive image of self-reliance,
inevitably, if paradoxically, invited mimetic echoes.

In *Dada Comrade* it is Harish who becomes the voice of
such self-reliance. Not only does he defy the revolutionaries'
prescribed code regarding interactions with women, he
also proclaims—perhaps even more dangerously—that he
no longer believes in the efficacy of underground armed
resistance. This is the final, galling argument that his erstwhile
comrades cannot accept. We learn early in the novel that
Harish has changed, he has become convinced that true
revolutionary work lies in joining the labour movement
and not in targeted assassinations. The labour historian
Ahmad Azhar has recently described this journey of Harish

as 'an obvious allegory for the oscillations of revolutionary terrorism between nationalism and socialism in inter-war India'.[18] What is more vivid, however, about this journey is its decisive move away from sporadic, underground, individual, 'heroic' acts and towards a collective politics of the longue durée. When Harish escapes from his comrades, he again goes underground but now in a markedly different way. He joins his old friend Akhtar, an impoverished and bitter railway worker, and becomes a union organizer.

Akhtar and his wife, Jamila, appear in the novel as representatives of working-class Muslims, just as Yashoda and Amarnath appear as middle-class Hindus and Robert and Nancy as relatively affluent Christians. Here, as in his other work, including his essays and autobiographical writings, Yashpal is keenly attuned to class differences, politics and solidarities. As Ahmad Azhar points out, Harish's interaction with Akhtar merits close attention. From Harish's perspective, Akhtar and his friends are less politically astute than him. He imagines that they do not recognize their true class role; he does. This is what the last lines of the chapter suggest:

> He wanted to wake up Akhtar and seek his advice, but what advice could Akhtar give? Akhtar and his friends knew only two paths: either despair or blood!
>
> Forgetting his own dilemma, Harish started thinking: How can the strength of labourers, indomitable like the lightning that thunders across the sky, be unified and used for revolution? [p. 98]

In the course of the conversation, however, Akhtar has shown himself to be significantly more canny about class divisions than Harish. Not only has he expressed scepticism about nationalist ideals, claiming that nothing will change for labourers even if 'black Indians' replace the British as rulers, he has also pointed out that Harish's dream of workers' rule is unlikely to come true. In this context, the debate on birth control momentarily resurfaces. Betraying his upper-class prejudice, Harish claims that any increase in wages will be useless for labourers if they do not practise birth control. Akhtar's rejoinder is quick and sharp: If they earned so much, labourers would become sahibs, and sahibs don't have large families. In other words, Akhtar rightly and succinctly emphasizes that if poor people have large families, it is *because* they are poor. It is because of poverty that life is more precarious for them, mortality is high, and access to education, health care, and birth control is low— all factors that contribute to large families. He doesn't say all this explicitly, of course, but we may gather that this is the import of his words. Moreover, he seems sceptical of the idea that labourers, *as labourers* within the prevailing system, could ever earn a decent living. Only sahibs could do that, in his view. Harish reads this as a failure of political imagination, but in the last section of the novel, which focuses on the textile mills strike, the novel itself, ironically enough, confirms Akhtar's sense of despair about the political future of labourers.

It does this by moving the spotlight away from the labourers and onto the strike leaders. Yashpal's detailed description of the strike obviously drew on his knowledge of the massive strikes that galvanized Indian labour in the 1920s and 1930s. With the skill of a seasoned ethnographer, Yashpal describes the hot, weary days of the strike, the lack of money, the failing morale of the workers, the management's strategies, the counter-demonstrations and the arguments among the strike organizers. But the narrative cannot be drawn away for long from Harish, Shail and Robert. At one point, Akhtar's friend Rafiq, the only one who seems to be a member of the communist party, does mention 'our party' (p. 191), but the reference is ambiguous—it could also simply mean 'our group'. Has Harish joined the communist party? Yashpal seems hesitant to affirm that. It is Harish, the charismatic, intense protagonist of the novel, who seems to interest him more. This is a Harish who may have moved away from the individual heroism of armed revolutionaries, only to be trapped in the individual heroism that the novel—perhaps because of its own narrative passions and generic constraints—finds hard to relinquish.

In her study of strikes in colonial India, the economist Susan Wolcott writes about the complex networks of solidarity and income sharing that sustained most strikes in the decades of the 1920s and 1930s in India.[19] While in some cases, most notably Bombay and Ahmedabad, strikes among mill workers were indeed led by middle-class union leaders—communists in the former case and Gandhi's supporters in the latter—this was not always the case. Even when strikes were led by educated union leaders, such leaders had significant histories of working with labourers. The

recent translation and publication of R.B. More's memoirs
gives us new insights into the complex relationship between
Ambedkarite and Left politics of that period.[20] If we keep
all this in mind, it seems somewhat strange that Harish, and
even more surprisingly, Robert, suddenly assume leadership
positions in the strike organization. Leaders from among the
workers—such as Rafiq—are certainly mentioned, but one
gets the distinct impression that the plot from here on is
driven largely by the novel's own interest in its middle-class
protagonists. In the world of the novel, Akhtar and his fellow
workers are marginalized not only by the entrenched class
hierarchies of the 'real world', but also by the investments
of the narrative itself.

In the last chapters of the novel, Dada, the leader of
Harish's revolutionary group who is very obviously modelled
on Chandra Shekhar Azad—down to the detail about biting
his moustache--realizes his mistake in sentencing Harish to
death. In an attempt to compensate for his earlier error, he
decides to help Harish. He can only do so, however, by
committing the very crime that Harish had earlier opposed
categorically, and ironically, this earns Harish a second
death sentence he can't escape. If at one level the novel may
be read as staging Yashpal's own fantasy of an alternative
life and death through the figure of Harish, at another, it
is clearly a tribute to Azad himself. Not only does Dada
rethink his earlier commitment to underground terrorist
activity, he also rethinks his earlier masculinist views about
women. It is evident that for Yashpal, these two aspects are
closely linked. He suggests, not only in this novel, but in

other texts as well—including his memoir *Simhavalokan*—
that a fascination with interlinked images of masculinity,
fraternity and violence moulded the revolutionary groups
of the early twentieth century.

Dada's decision to help Harish thus brings into view
only one aspect of his education. We see the other in his
changed relation to Shail. Dada's first meeting with Shail in
the novel appears to be closely based on an interaction Azad
had with the young Prakashvati when he asked her, first,
about Yashpal's whereabouts, and then, abruptly, about her
relation to Yashpal. When Yashpal narrates this incident
in *Simhavalokan*, he says that Prakashvati was by this time
extremely irritated by this interrogation. In response to
Azad's question, 'What is your relation to Yashpal?' she said,
'It is just as it should be. How does it concern you?' Azad was
always addressed respectfully in the group. Yashpal writes that
Azad's not slapping Prakashvati for such an insolent answer
was tantamount to being slapped himself.[21] Interestingly,
Prakashvati provides a rather different account of the same
event in her own memoir, *Lahore se Lucknow tak* (From
Lahore to Lucknow). She recalls that when Azad asked her
about her relation to Yashpal, she sat silently as he growled at
her. 'I could not understand what the matter was and why I
was being interrogated in this manner', she writes.[22]

It is not my intent to prove that one of them is right in
their recollection of the incident and the other wrong. But
it may not be entirely fanciful to wonder if Shail of *Dada
Comrade* had in some way touched and shaped Yashpal's
memory of the young Prakashvati. The novel was written

a good decade before Part II of Yashpal's memoir (which discusses this event) was published. Be that as it may. The more pertinent point is that the friendship of Dada and Shail at the conclusion of the novel signals not only a hope for new political and libidinal subjectivities, but more audaciously, a hope for a rapprochement between the old and the new, a coming together of the two.

In the essay I mentioned earlier, Visvambhar Nath Upadhyay suggests that the novel should have been titled 'Dada *and* Comrade' since it presents glimpses from the lives of both Dada (Azad) and Comrade (Yashpal). In my view, this reading misses the point of the title. The title, I think, suggests that in the old Dada himself—and here we should bear in mind all the ambivalence of this term—we may find a comrade. The novel, I would propose, is not about Dada *and* comrade, or about the conflict between Dada and comrade, but rather about Dada transforming into comrade. In this sense it can be read, as I suggested before, as an homage to Azad, albeit a slightly conflicted one. More significantly, it can be read as a hopeful evocation of the very *figure* of the comrade. Upadhyay recognizes this, which is why his essay ends with addressing the novel itself as one: *'Dada Comrade ko lal salaam'* (A Red Salute to *Dada Comrade*).[23]

At the end of the novel, we see a pregnant Shail leaving her home with Dada. They are prepared to go 'just as they are'. Jodi Dean's recent book, *Comrade: An Essay on Political Belonging*—I am tempted to call it a lyrical anthem—about the term 'comrade' helps us to both excavate and deposit some layers of significance in the book's title that we may have otherwise missed. Dean insists throughout that 'Comrade' designates above all a *relation* and not an individual identity. Let me then conclude this section by citing a passage from her book which resonates with so many of the themes I've been tracking through Yashpal's work:

> [I]n several Romance languages comrade originated as a term for those who share a room or travel together. To be a comrade is to share a sameness with another with respect to where you are both going. Incidentally, these elements of sameness and collectivity point to the difference between the comrade and the militant. The militant is a single figure fighting for a cause. That one is a militant tells us nothing about that one's relation to others. The militant expresses political intensity, not political relationality.[24]

Translation

Tropes of fidelity and betrayal organize not only the discourse of revolution, but also that of translation. Betrayal, however, as we know well, often simply names fidelity to something else. In the field of translation, one experiences this tension in a particularly acute way. Here one experiences two pulls, two claims, each demanding fidelity. Should the translator of a text strive to provide, for the reader who cannot comprehend the original, an experience of reading that, to some extent, is analogous to the translator's? Or should one attempt to find, in Walter Benjamin's oft-cited but still astonishing words, 'the particular intention towards the target language which produces in that language the echo of the original'?[25] In translating, one cannot help but be drawn towards the unnerving, uncanny, but fragmentary kinship between the modes in which different languages signify and symbolize. One finds oneself dazed in the realm of the language forest evoked by Benjamin—bewildered by its subterranean mycorrhizal networks.

In translating *Dada Comrade*, though I was often overtaken by the wish to 'Hindi-ize' English, that is to say, to attempt to produce in English something of the syntax and the cadence of Hindi, I finally ended up rewriting some of those portions. Yashpal's Hindi in this novel, and in most of his work, is a brisk, quotidian language. At times, I made the decision to convey the pace and tenor of this language as well as I could, even if that meant straying a little from the literality—and certainly the syntax—of the original. Translation is an infinite task. I'm sure mine could have been better, but then you may not have read it at all.

Beginning with the titular 'comrade', there are many English words and phrases in Yashpal's novel. Following Gayatri Spivak's landmark translation of Mahasweta Devi's 'Draupadi', I've placed these in italics. Some entirely untranslatable words—for example, modes of address—have been left as in the original. A glossary at the end provides a rough guide.

The Hindi word 'saathi' appears often in the text. Depending on the context, it can mean a companion, a friend or a comrade. I've thus translated it differently on separate occasions.

Finally, Yashpal often repeats the same ordinary words or phrases in close proximity to each other. Sometimes I have kept the repetition, but at other times, when it sounded particularly jarring or odd in English, I have introduced a small change.

Notes

1   Bhisham Sahni, '*Naye Sansaar ke Agradoot*' (Pioneers of the New World), in Madhuresh, ed. *Krantikaari Yashpal: Ek Samarpit Vyaktitva* (Revolutionary Yashpal: A Dedicated Life) (Allahabad: Lokbharati Prakashan, 1979), pp. 33–39, p. 33. All translations from Hindi texts are mine.

2   Yashpal, *Simhavalokan* (Allahabad: Lokbharati Prakashan, 2017 [1951]), p. 53.

3   Ibid., p. 98.

4   Ibid., p. 99.

5   Yashpal, *Simhavalokan*, p. 144.

6   See M. K. Gandhi, 'The Cult of the Bomb', 2 January 1930; *Collected Works of Mahatma Gandhi*, vol. 48, available at http://www.gandhiserve.org/e/cwmg/cwmg.htm; and 'The Philosophy of the Bomb', in S. Irfan Habib, *To Make the Deaf Hear: Ideology and Program of Bhagat Singh and His Comrades* (Gurgaon: Three Essays Collective, 2017 [2007]), pp. 205–217. This document was almost certainly written primarily by Bhagvati Charan Vohra, though Yashpal and others, including Bhagat Singh, may also have contributed to it. It was credited to 'Kartar Singh, President, HSRA'.

7   Yashpal, *Simhavalokan*, p. 240.

8   Anand, 'Introduction', in Yashpal, *This Is Not That Dawn*,
    trans. Anand (New Delhi: Penguin, 2010), p. xiii.

9   Visvambhar Nath Upadhyay, '*Dada-Comrade: Nayi Naitikta
    aur Soch ki Pehel*' (*Dada Comrade*: The Beginning of New
    Ethics and Thought), in Madhuresh ed. *Krantikari Yashpal*,
    pp. 78–85.

10 Ramvilas Sharma, *Pragatisheel Sahitya ki Samasyayen* (The
    Problems of Progressive Literature) (Agra: Vinod Pustak
    Mandir, 1954), p. 119.

11 Ania Loomba, *Revolutionary Desires: Women, Communism
    and Feminism in India* (London and New York: Routledge,
    2019), p. 119.

12 Nikhil Govind, *Between Love and Freedom: The Revolutionary
    in the Hindi Novel* (New Delhi: Routledge, 2014), pp. 134–157.

13 Upadhyay, '*Dada-Comrade: Nayi Naitikta aur Soch ki Pehel*', p.
    82.

14 Prakashvati Pal, *Lahore se Lucknow tak* (Prayagraj: Lokbharti
    Prakashan, 2019), p. 25.

15 Barbara N. Ramusack, 'Embattled Advocates: The Debate
    over Birth Control in India, 1920–40', *Journal of Women's
    History*, Volume 1, Number 2, Fall 1989, pp. 34–64, p. 37,
    available at https://doi.org/10.1353/jowh.2010.0005.

16 Yashpal, 'Turgenev', in Kunwar Pal Singh ed. *Yashpal:
    Punarmulyankan* (Yashpal: A Reevaluation) (Delhi: Shilpayan,
    2004), pp. 519–20.

17 Edward W. Said, *Representations of the Intellectual: The 1993
    Reith Lectures* (New York: Vintage Books, 1996), p. 15.

18 Ahmad Azhar, *Revolution in Reform: Trade-Unionism in Lahore,
    c. 1920–70* (Hyderabad: Orient Blackswan, 2019), p. 57.

19 Susan Wolcott, 'Strikes in Colonial India, 1921–1938,' *ILR
    Review*, Volume 61, Number 4, July 2008, pp. 460–84.

20 Satyendra More, *Memoirs of A Dalit Communist: The Many Worlds of R. B. More,* translated by Wandana Sonalkar and edited by Anupama Rao (Delhi: LeftWord Books, 2020).

21 Yashpal, *Simhavalokan*, p. 329.

22 Pal, *Lahore se Lucknow tak*, p. 29.

23 Upadhyay, '*Dada-Comrade: Nayi Naitikta aur Soch ki Pehel*', p. 84.

24 Jodi Dean, *Comrade: An Essay on Political Belonging* (London, New York: Verso, 2019), p. 152.

25 Walter Benjamin, 'The Task of the Translator', in Marcus Bullock and Michael W. Jennings ed. *Walter Benjamin: Selected Writings,* vol. 1, *1913–1926* (Cambridge: The Belknap Press of Harvard University Press, 1996), p. 258.

Dada Comrade

Come! Let us sit together and think, a way out of this confusion!

Two Words

Dada Comrade is presented in the form of a novel. Because of its form, this creation becomes part of the field of literature. Before this, when I wrote *Flight from the Cage*[1] and *The Struggle for Justice* (*Nyaya Ka Sangarsh*), I had hoped to find a place in some corner of the literary field. I received success far beyond my hopes, and for that, I thank my readers.

My book *Marxism* (*Marxvad*) was part of the task I had assigned myself for the *Viplavi* (Revolutionary) *Tract*, but there is more to *Dada Comrade* than this 'task'—namely, the wish to provide an opportunity for my creative inclination or to make an attempt on the path of art.

The appreciation I received for what I had attempted in an artistic spirit in *Flight from the Cage* certainly fuelled my enthusiasm. However, lovers of art and literature also have a complaint against me—that, I give art a minor and propaganda a prominent space. I don't wish to present an *appeal* against this verdict. I am content that I am able to clarify my intentions through my work.

Instead of confining art within its own detached field, why do I attempt to make it a vehicle of emotions or ideas? . . . My desire is not merely to lead a private life but rather to enrich society. That is why, even while connecting with art, I cannot understand art only in terms of private satisfaction. I think the aim of art is to provide fulfilment in life. Instead of the artistic attempt going astray and exhausting itself in striking poses in the ether, would it not be better for this attempt to offer progress to society and a foundation for new art?

Even before the book's publication, friends who had read some parts of it counselled me: 'This is your first novel, and it is truly worthy of an introduction by some well-known litterateur!' I am grateful to my literary friends for their advice and good wishes. I also know that my own words cannot offer either the critical evaluation literary friends may provide, or the advantage of being introduced by them. Nevertheless, my own feelings can best be expressed in my own words.

Contrary to my usual practice, I must present my defense of this book. It is not for me to say how successful *Dada Comrade* will be as a literary creation. Critics and readers will speak about that. This defense relates to the ideas that have been presented, under cover of literature, in the form of *Dada Comrade*.

From the perspective of contemporary common beliefs concerning conduct in our society, these ideas will seem terrifying and revolutionary—exactly in the manner that Galileo's assertion 'The earth is round and it moves' was terrifying for the geographic knowledge and belief of its time. Robert's ideas and Shail's conduct in *Dada Comrade* cannot claim to provide a prescriptive 'remedy' for the prevailing difficulties and conflicts in society—they are simply an attempt at diagnosis. The aim is to point out the anomalies and contradictions in the prevalent conditions of society as well as in its consequent conduct and moral beliefs.

It is evident that at every step we encounter opposition between contemporary conditions and ancient moral beliefs about conduct. The question is: should we suppress this awareness by ignoring the contradictions we experience and their causes? Should we erase the changes that have occurred in our conditions and return to antiquity in order to preserve our ancient beliefs, or should we harmonize society's conduct and moral beliefs with our new conditions?

Several 'isms' are in conflict in the world today: capitalism, Nazism, Gandhism, socialism . . . At the foundation of this conflict of ideas is the attempt to reconcile conditions, situations and beliefs. Only the harmony arising from this conflict of discourses will provide the basis for a new human civilization. As human beings, we cannot ignore this conflict. Our concern about the result of this conflict is not just sentimental, it is rather a concern about our own life and the life of society.

We must reflect upon the following question: when, as a consequence of the growing age of human society, the swaddling cloth of its infancy starts oppressing its body, would it not be better at that time to create for it an extensive cloth of new ideas? Must we constrain its body such that it fits within its old limits? This is the question that *Dada Comrade* invites you to consider.

Some of those who love good conduct will see shamelessness in Shail's behaviour. From the perspective of the ideal, they will find the presentation of such a character repulsive. It may be that Shail cannot gain their sympathy, but who is this Shail? The Shail of *Dada Comrade*, being nothing in herself, is simply the unfulfilled but alert and active instinct of those who wrinkle their noses and brows in revulsion. This human instinct is constantly at work in society. The increasing population of this nation and the world is irrefutable proof of this. To keep trying to fulfil an instinct one considers repulsive, while also criticizing it constantly—isn't this the burden of today's 'traditional' conduct and morality?

If the aim of moral conduct and ethics is to lead the human being to a better order and to progress, then we must acknowledge that this aim cannot be attained by our current moral and conduct-related beliefs. That this instinct constantly scorches human beings with embers of lust, that it continually torments them with guilt—can human beings find no solution for this?

Like other powers of nature, the human being's creative instinct is also a power. Man has brought under his control and put to use the unvanquishable powers of nature: water, wind and electricity. Can he not, then, find a natural path for his own creative power and thus prevent the source of life's joy from becoming a source of peril? The question is simply about changing moral ideas in accord with changing conditions.

Let alone others, I suspect the sentiments of even some old revolutionaries will be hurt by *Dada Comrade*. They might think that this is an attempt to lower the dignity of revolutionaries, but that is not my intent. In this context, I am reminded of Turgenev's novel *Otse-Sini* (*Fathers and Sons*).[2] On its publication, it was the revolutionaries who hurled the most abuse at Turgenev, but ten years later, this very book was considered representative of the revolutionary spirit. Not the individual but a spirit is the instrument of revolution, and the revolutionary is not a spirit but an individual. The aim of revolution is attained not by attachment to individuals but by fidelity to a spirit.

I should also thank a few people. First of all, let me thank Dr Prakash Pal.[3] Because of working ceaselessly, night and day, last September I suffered from ill health. Taking the entire burden of *Viplavi Tract* on her own shoulders, she made it possible for me to go to Mussoorie for four months. The peace and ease of Mussoorie gave me the opportunity to write *Dada Comrade* and *That World* (*Vo Duniya*). I plan to present *That World* soon to my readers.

I am also indebted to my host in Mussoorie. I wrote the book there and discussed it with him for hours. Though he was not completely in agreement with the book's ideas, he nevertheless advised me to publish it, so that the conflict of ideas might become publicly manifest.

—Yashpal
May Day, 1941

Notes

1   *Pinjare ki Udaan*, earlier translated as *Flight of the Caged
    Imagination*.
2   Yashpal writes 'Otse-Sini' (literally, Fathers and Sons), but
    the title of the novel in Russian is '*Ottsy i Deti*' (literally,
    Fathers and Children).
3   Prakashvati Pal, Yashpal's wife.

A Night of Dilemma

Yashoda's husband Amarnath was lying on his bed and looking at the newspaper, waiting for sleep to descend. The servant had also gone to bed. Something rattled in the kitchen downstairs. 'That stupid Bishan must have left something uncovered,' Yashoda thought, irritated. Though unwilling and drowsy, she had to get up. She went down the stairs to the kitchen. Put water in the bowl that the cat was licking and rattling. Thought it wise to check the bolt of the drawing room door before returning upstairs. How could one trust a servant! When she turned on the light switch, she saw the door was firmly bolted.

Yashoda had just put her hand on the light switch to turn off the light when she heard the sound of quick footsteps on the stairs outside along with a knock on the door. The visitor had seen the light through the window. She had no choice but to open the door. Sleepy and disgruntled, Yashoda asked, 'Who is it?'

In response came the knock again, now with a hint of authority.

Yashoda had barely unlocked the door when it was thrust open. A man swiftly pushed himself in and closed it behind him. 'Excuse me . . .' he said.

Seeing an unknown man entering so forcefully, Yashoda, in fear and surprise, could scarcely ask 'Who?' when the man took out a pistol from the right pocket of his coat, held it in front of Yashoda's face, and threatened in a low voice: 'Silence! Or I will shoot.'

A rising cry of fear was blocked in Yashoda's throat, and her body trembled. She stood in shock. With his left hand the visitor bolted the door but his right hand kept the pistol in front of Yashoda's face. His watchful eyes were also on her.

Signaling towards the door inside, the visitor said, 'Let's go. Please turn off the light.'

Trembling, Yashoda went towards the inner room. Reaching inside, the visitor said, 'You may turn on the light.' With trembling hands Yashoda sought out the familiar space and turned on the light.

The visitor's pistol was still aimed at Yashoda, but now his voice and expression turned a little soft and compassionate.

'I have not come to harm you,' he said. 'I would not have troubled you, but I had no choice. Just let me sit here for a few hours. As an Indian, I make this plea to you.'

His manner lessened Yashoda's fear. She noticed that he was still breathing rapidly. It seemed he had been running. Fine drops of perspiration were visible on his brow. He was young. Nor did he seem a terrifying person. He had a turban on his head, and a slight moustache was sprouting on his face. Intertwining and clasping the fingers of both hands, Yashoda asked in a low, frightened voice, 'Who are you?'

Casting a sharp glance at Yashoda's face the visitor responded, 'You must have heard about the revolutionary party? We were in prison. Today we were being taken to Amritsar for the second trial. Our friends attacked the police and allowed us to escape. There was no other place . . . I saw the light in your window and came here. If I keep wandering around, I'll certainly be arrested. If I'm caught, I'll be kept in prison for my entire life! I will leave in the morning before dawn. We are not robbers; we are fighting for the freedom of our country.'

Yashoda could not say a word. Her anxiety had not yet subsided. Right or wrong, duty or crime—she could not understand anything. She could only understand this: a man escaping from the jaws of death had landed at her feet to save his life. The fog of stupor cast over her mind by the sudden attack of fear gradually began to clear. Still clenching her fingers, she kept looking at the youth. The very man of whom she had been so fearful was now begging for his life. In her imagination she saw: several people, armed with swords and guns, coming to kill him. He wants to save his life, he is crouched at her feet, hidden within her aanchal. She could not say anything. She looked mutely at the refugee. The pistol that had been pointed at her forehead just a few moments earlier was now dangling from the youth's hand. Seeing her quiet, the youth came a step closer and said in a low voice, 'I will just sit here.'

Taking a deep breath, Yashoda worriedly gazed at the youth, looking at him carefully. Trying to reassure her, the youth said again, 'I will just sit here, you have nothing to lose. You go and rest.'

In a trembling voice Yashoda asked, 'May I ask him?'

The youth compassionately agreed, 'All right.' But then, hesitating, he said, 'I am already here. He will perhaps be anxious. Let it remain quiet. Better not to make any noise. Anything can escalate the matter. I will leave in the morning. At that time you will be able to explain everything to him. There will be no harm then. You go and rest.'

Yashoda thought for a moment . . . he is right, he is here already. Now how can he be thrown out? There is no option but to remain quiet. For some moments she remained standing, withdrawn in her sari, eyes downcast, then with an air of acceptance and helplessness she nodded and walked to the staircase. As soon as she stepped on to the staircase, the light downstairs was switched off. Her feet were trembling and her heart was pounding as she climbed the staircase, but a feeling of resolution had come over her—now this will have to be borne.

Amarnath was still looking at the paper. Hearing a sound in the room he asked without lifting his gaze, 'You've come?' With a feeble 'Hm . . .' Yashoda lay down on her bed. She felt hot because of her heart's agitation. In her mind's eye, she saw the same scene: several people armed with swords and guns pouncing to kill the youth, gasping for breath he falls at her feet and hides within the aanchal of her sari. A forceful emotion rose in her heart and found no release. She felt disturbed in mind and body.

Looking at the clock below the electric table lamp Amarnath said, 'Ten-thirty!'

To hide her unrest Yashoda turned over. 'Why, what's wrong?' her husband asked in a worried tone.

'Nothing . . . sometimes this happens when I climb up the stairs,' Yashoda responded and covered her face with her hand. At times she suffered from anxiety attacks. Knowing this, her husband asked again, 'You are not feeling anxious, are you?'

'No, it's just that the light is bothering my eyes.'

Amarnath turned off the table lamp and lay down. In just a few minutes his deep, even breathing indicated that he was sound asleep. Restlessly, Yashoda again turned around. She lay in the darkness with her eyes open. Along with her husband's steady breathing, she could hear the ticking of the clock and her own heartbeat. In her imagination she saw again the scene of armed men pouncing on the young man, the doors of her home suddenly opening, and the pistol appearing in front of her. Then the sounds of her husband's breath, the ticking of the clock and her own heartbeat would fade and she would once again hear the voice of the youth who sat downstairs. How he had showed her the pistol at first! His frightening appearance and then his fearful eyes, seeking protection! She thought: he must be trembling with fear sitting in that room downstairs.

She felt she had been thirsty for a long time but had not thought of drinking water. Quietly getting up, she took a glass and filled water from the pitcher. She had not yet taken it to her lips when it occurred to her: he must be thirsty, how breathlessly he had come running to the door . . . he must be thirsty!

Filled glass in hand, she slowly and soundlessly went down the stairs in the dark. Reaching the room she turned on the light. She saw that the youth was vigilantly staring, pistol in hand, towards the door from where he had heard the sound of her steps. When the room was lit, he lowered the pistol. Without saying a word Yashoda handed him the glass of water. Looking at her gratefully he drank the water in one gulp.

Thanking her in a low voice, he was about to place the glass on a small tripod table near him. Seeing her extend her hand, he gave it to her in an embarrassed way. Taking the glass, Yashoda went out of the room. In a few moments, she brought back some more water and placed the glass in front of him. This time there was an even deeper gratitude in the youth's eyes. Drinking half the water, he placed the glass on the table.

Yashoda thought: he must be hungry, he will surely feel cold at night, and could one spend the entire night sitting on a chair? But what could she do? How could she make arrangements noiselessly, by stealth . . .? Holding the rail of the staircase, she stood thinking for some time. Then it occurred to her: what if her husband wakes up or Maaji is startled! Suppressing a deep sigh of helplessness, she again climbed up the stairs and quietly lay down. A few minutes later she realized that she had not drunk any water. A cool shiver ran through her as she drank, and with it came the thought of the hungry youth downstairs, shivering with cold. She became restless again and could not restrain herself. Stepping lightly in the darkness, she went to the storeroom. Carrying a thick cloth to spread on the floor, as well as a pillow and a blanket, she started descending the stairs very carefully.

Meanwhile, the light in the room had been switched off again. Yashoda was balancing her load with both hands. For a few minutes she stood there, uncertain, then the youth fumbled for the light switch and turned it on. Seeing her thus burdened, he spoke with deep gratitude and embarrassment, 'There was no need for this. You should not have taken the trouble . . .'

Placing the bed cloths on a chair, she left. When she returned a few minutes later with some food on a plate, the youth had made a small bed for himself next to the sofa. Putting the plate on the tripod table, Yashoda turned and asked softly, 'Would you need anything else?'

Yashoda's behaviour had given the youth courage. Coming close, he pointed to his clothes and said, 'It would not be wise for me to go out tomorrow in these clothes; I will be recognized. It would be a great help if you could give me a dhoti or some old piece of cloth to wear and four or five rupees before I leave in the morning. If possible, I will try to return your things.'

After a moment's reflection, Yashoda said, 'He wakes up at about six in the morning. The servant will also come downstairs to clean. Maaji wakes up even earlier. She will also come downstairs to bathe.'

Crossing his arms across his chest, the youth said worriedly, 'The roads will be absolutely deserted before six, it would have been easier in a crowd . . . yes, if I could get your servant's clothes, it would be better.'

Climbing the dark staircase once more, Yashoda reached her bed. It was not midnight yet. Now her anxiety had lessened. Apprehension had taken its place. The fear of being attacked had given way to the fear of consequences, which weighs more on the activity of the mind than on the rhythm of the heart. Sleep was miles away. A young man, she thought, such a gentle boy, separated from his home, his life in danger! . . . People wish to catch him and imprison him for life, they want to kill him . . . he is fleeing to save his life. How courageous he is! He has left his home and put himself in danger for the sake of the country. Scenes of Congress rallies appeared before her eyes. She saw thousands of people raising slogans and carrying flags. When Mahatma Gandhi came to the city, she had watched the procession from her rooftop. She had seen several other processions as well. Her body would thrill listening to the slogans. Victory to Mother India! Long Live Hindustan! *Vande Mataram!*

Her husband Amarnath supported the Congress. He was the secretary of the neighbourhood Congress Committee. He took great interest in the elections. Large pictures of Swami Dayanand, Tilak and Gandhiji hung in their home. Yashoda had deep reverence for Gandhiji. She knew that the Congress and Gandhiji wanted Indian rule in the country. A kind of enthusiasm would fill her heart when she saw large processions and meetings. She knew that the government and the police were displeased by such events. Processions and meetings that demanded Swaraj were met with batons and bullets; people were imprisoned. Such pieces of news brought her fear and sorrow.

Yashoda had also heard that there were people who fought for the country's freedom with bombs and bullets. The government either imprisoned or hanged them. These people were terrifying and fearless. They hid in forests and continued to battle against the government. They became a topic of discussion only when one of them was arrested or when news of some disturbance appeared. Various amazing and frightening stories were heard about them. She could not see anything of that sort in this youth. Even though he had a pistol in his hand, he was helplessly begging for his life to be protected. Despite being several years older, he was just like Yashoda's own son, Uday, who was also helpless, and in need of his grandmother's and mother's help. Her own son was sleeping safely close to his grandmother but the son of another mother, in escaping the hideous jaws of death, had fallen into her lap.

. . . In the morning, before six, the roads are quite deserted—the youth's helplessness echoed in her ears, but what could she do? Her heart beat wildly hearing the sound of footsteps on the road. At times she heard the steps of several people, and became even more frightened.

From the window to the right of her bed, she could see a part of the road. In the light of the street lamps passersby could be seen. Her gaze was fixed in that direction. Hearing the sound of several men on the road, she looked closely and saw a group of uniformed policemen with guns on their shoulders and large electric torches in their hands. They were casting light from these torches on dark parts of the road and on the homes they passed. Yashoda's heart started pounding. The closer the footsteps drew, the faster her heart beat. It seemed they were hammering forcefully on the door of her home. Her eyes closed, her breath stopped and she no longer felt anything.

When she regained consciousness, the sound of the policemen's footsteps had receded into the distance. She felt as though the claw clutching her throat and strangling her had been removed. Taking a deep breath she shook her head and tried to focus on remaining conscious. She looked at the clock. It was almost one. She recalled that the youth had asked for some clothes and money . . . the streets are deserted before six in the morning! Then she thought of waking her husband and taking his counsel in this matter. What could she do alone? Turning around she placed her hand on her husband's arm but then she thought: what if he is startled and utters a loud exclamation, or panics after hearing her tale! . . . Suppressing the wave of emotion rising from her heart, she withdrew her hand.

Gazing at the beams on the ceiling she was lost in thought. What should she do . . . she felt confused. Eyes closed, she called out to God repeatedly. In a crisis, He is the only helper. Praying fervently she surrendered herself and the youth to God's protection. Gradually, she became convinced that God was taking care of both of them. She kept her mind focused on Him. Her lips and mouth were dry again and she rose to drink water. She looked at the clock—it was already two-thirty.

Again she got up from the bed. Her body was weary, but she gathered herself, aware of the danger and the youth sitting downstairs. Again she went to the storeroom. Opened the trunk with extreme care. She was afraid that Maaji, sleeping in the adjoining room, might awaken at the slightest noise. Took out a man's dhoti, a shirt and a coat. Then returning to her room, she opened her own cupboard cautiously. Taking out a small box, she saw that she had eight rupees in small change and some notes. She took out a ten-rupee note and the change. Going down the stairs she entered the room. The youth rose and switched on the light. He was spending the night sitting up, wrapped in the blanket. Placing the clothes and money on the table, Yashoda picked up his glass and was about to leave to get more water for him.

Addressing her, the youth said, 'It would be better if I could have the servant's clothes, so I can leave at the crack of dawn.' Bowing her head in agreement, Yashoda left and after searching for some time, she returned with some dirty, disheveled clothes which she placed on the tripod table along with a glass of water.

Satisfied, the youth said, 'This is good. I will leave at a quarter to six.'

Taking a deep breath, Yashoda turned to leave. Pausing, she asked, 'There isn't any fear now, is there?'

'It is hard to say, but these clothes will help immensely. If I could also get a basket or an old canister, that would be good, but please remember, do not ever, even by mistake, mention my stay here to anyone, however close to you that person might be. That will put you in trouble. To give refuge to a prisoner on the run or an absconding revolutionary is a crime by law, and you could be imprisoned for five to seven years. I will make sure that no one sees me leaving this house. In case I am caught again and you are questioned, you must flatly deny everything. It must be about three now, I will leave before six. I will always remain indebted to you for the trouble you have taken and the sympathy you have shown me. Not only I, all the members of our group and those who support us will also be grateful to you. After I am gone, please make sure that the clothes I leave behind are burnt immediately.'

In the silence of the night, the clock in the drawing room struck three. The youth was standing with his head bowed in gratitude. Thinking he had nothing more to say, Yashoda turned to leave. The youth spoke again, 'At a quarter to six please come down and bolt the front door.'

Yashoda returned to her bed. In the darkness, her eyes, turned to the ceiling, saw the same scenes over and over again: the Congress processions, the youth confronting her with a pistol, his fearful pleading for his life. . . . When her husband moved in his sleep, she would look at him, or at the clock. At times she felt that the hands of the clock were moving too slowly, and at other times, that they had suddenly leapt over several minutes.

A faint sound of someone singing came from the street. She looked at the clock, both hands were joined at four. In the distance she could hear the indistinct crowing of cocks. The sound of a strong stream of water falling in an empty bucket came from a neighbouring home. She could hear sounds of throat clearing and coughing in Maaji's room. Then Maaji's voice softly humming, 'Awake and rise, O traveller, for dawn arrives . . .'* Maaji would sing her devotional song in the morning very softly while slowly, lovingly, caressing Uday's back. For Uday the song was a lullaby, bringing sweet sleep, but for the traveller caught in the grip of terror, it was truly a message to rise and leave.

It struck five. Yashoda became aware that her guest, the recipient of her sympathy and compassion, would soon be gone. Why should he not stay a little longer? Why could he not be liberated forever from danger and fear? The hands of the clock seemed to be racing now. She saw from her window that the first glow of dawn had suffused the sky, but she still kept thinking that it was too early yet for the sun to rise, that the streets would be deserted. She could also now hear the sounds of the committee sweepers on the street and crows on the trees. All too quickly, it was a quarter to six. There were just two or three minute to go. She rose to go downstairs. She had barely stood up when she heard the newspaper man calling: 'The Escape of the Bus-Case Prisoner! Today's headlines!' With a shock she fell back on the bed, but quickly gathered herself and went downstairs.

---

* *Uth jaag musaafir bhor bhayi*—a devotional song attributed to the saint-poet Kabir.

The youth was waiting for her, wearing the servant's dirty clothes, a rag tied around his ears. He stood up when he saw her. 'I have no words . . . the compassion you have shown . . . may you be blessed!' He spoke in a liquid, moved tone, but his gaze had already uttered more than his tongue. Opening the door, the canister held close, he swiftly descended to the street.

Seeing him leave, Yashoda's heart was in her mouth, and she trembled exactly as she did when Uday bent over the low terrace wall. Bolting the door, she watched him from the window as far as her eyes could follow. Shivering with cold, drumming the canister under his arm, the youth kept walking as though unconcerned. Even when she could no longer see him, her petrified gaze remained fixed in the same direction. Then, when she saw other people walking around in the street, she remembered: she must immediately clear the drawing room of all his things.

A Girl of the New Type

The middle class is a strange mix of people of varied conditions. Some of these people are accustomed to beautiful bungalows and cars but modestly describe themselves as part of this class. Others, even while living a life as precarious as that of manual labourers claim to be of this class on the strength of being educated and decently clad. It is the people belonging to the middle class who are most concerned about national politics and social reform—more than people of the upper class, occupied with their manifold selfish pleasures, or of the lower class, never free from the struggle for daily survival. Amarnath Babu was an indisputable member of this class. Every day, in order to experience his link to society and the nation, he would look through the four-paisa newspaper before his bath, as he shook off the night's lingering drowsiness.

Amarnath's neighbour Girdharilal was a clerk in a bank. Instead of spending four paise in order to know the news, he would walk over to Amarnath's home in the morning, datun in mouth, and a two-and-a-half-year-old baby in his arms. In doing so, he thought he was also helping the child's mother while she swept the house. 'What's the news?' he would ask.

Both men profited from this arrangement. Girdharilal was able to read the paper and Amarnath got the opportunity to defeat Girdharilal in debate and demonstrate his own political wisdom. Whether because of his radical ideas or discontent with his situation, Girdharilal was a staunch leftist, and Amarnath Babu a supporter of the non-violent policy of the Congress—that is to say, of Gandhian ideas. Every other day the two would debate political events. As far as Yashoda was concerned, this was simply a diversion for Amarnath. Usually she would derive contentment merely from hearing her husband speak enthusiastically and laugh loudly, but that day she listened carefully. Amarnath too was happy that the revolutionary accused of armed robbery and murder had escaped police custody and saved himself. He even had sympathy for the revolutionary who, in attempting to escape, had been shot and killed, but he could not bear Girdharilal's assertion that this was the only true path, and all else mere hypocrisy and dishonesty.

He argued heatedly, 'What have these revolutionaries managed to do in twenty-five years? Even in the course of a century they would not be able to bring an awakening to the country like the one Gandhiji brought in a decade. After all, compared to the government, what can a few bombs and pistols accomplish . . . Indeed, how can these little fireworks possibly harm a government whose armoury is so vast? Of course, it's a different matter if the point is simply to burn and perish like moths.'

Yashoda was listening to all this as she bathed Uday and helped him dress. Uday was no less affected by the news. Banging his wooden stick repeatedly he said, 'Bhabhi*, I will take a gun and go.' Sometimes he wanted to go and catch the escaped dacoit; at other times to fight those who were pursuing him. Yashoda tried to explain, 'Ok, you can go, but at least wear your clothes.' She wanted the child to be quiet so she could hear the debate but he wouldn't listen to her.

Yashoda did not like it when Girdharilal could not provide an adequate rejoinder to Amarnath's remark. In an irritated tone, Girdharilal said, 'So when you Congress people are garlanded as martyrs after spending three months in prison—is that more heroic than these people ascending the gallows?'

Yashoda was listening keenly; she felt some relief on hearing this. Amarnath could not laugh at this taunt, nor respond by raising his voice as was his habit, but it was also difficult for him to accept defeat. Finding himself incapable of holding back, he retorted, 'There is no less courage even among robbers and dacoits!'

Slapping his forehead to demonstrate his amazement, Girdharilal asked, 'Bless you, do you really consider these people robbers?'

Amarnath had now gathered himself. 'When did I say that? . . . But you cannot deny that these people's actions

---

* *Bhabhi*: literally, sister-in-law. The child is perhaps addressing his mother by a name he has heard others use for her.

obstruct the Satyagraha launched by the Congress. Gandhiji has said so many times that just once he should be given full opportunity. Are these people wiser than all those big national leaders—are they bigger than them?' For some time the debate continued in this manner.

Girdharilal had become irritated; to escape from responding, he put the crushed datun in his mouth, picked up the child and prepared to depart.

To express her sympathy for Girdharilal, Yashoda called from the window, 'Why don't you wait, Bhaiya? Let Lallu drink his milk with Uday and play here for a while. And you too have breakfast before going.'

The invitation to eat breakfast before bathing had no practical import but it wiped away Girdharilal's resentment at being silenced in the argument. Everyone knows that Yashoda does not talk much, but she is good-natured. Amarnath was also embarrassed about his harshness. Pleased with Yashoda's opportune thoughtfulness, he added his assent: 'Yes, Girdhari, why not have breakfast here with us?'

Taking the child in his arms, Girdhari accepted the gesture of reconciliation and, his mouth stuffed with the datun, said in a garbled voice, 'Id will be doo lade,' and left.

Wearing his outdoor clothes after bathing, Amarnath was wondering which new insurance client he should meet today, and through whom. Yashoda placed the breakfast plate in front of him and reproached him lovingly, 'And what is wrong with you . . . needlessly scolding Girdharilal!'

Looking at his wife with the pride of victory, Amarnath responded, 'That ass—pretending to be a revolutionary!'

Yashoda wanted to ask: Don't you have any sympathy for these revolutionaries? But such a new question, one she had never before asked, and which carried, hidden in its folds, the momentous secret of the previous night, could not escape her lips. Raising her large eyes and looking at her husband, she said, 'The poor man has escaped with his life . . . what will happen to him if he is caught?'

Finishing his glass of milk, Amarnath wiped his hands and responded, 'Once they escape, these people are not caught. They have elaborate arrangements. Who knows in what sorts of hideouts and forests they live.'

Yashoda breathed a sigh of relief and was silent. Whose word could be more reliable than her husband's? Even if he did not think well of the revolutionary, at least he had attested to his safety!

Yashoda began reading the newspaper regularly. Even though she did not find the one piece of news that most drew her interest, she read much else in the process. Her practice of reading had almost ceased after her marriage. At times her mother-in-law would ask her to read from the *Bhagavad Gita* or some other book, but that was rare. Her household chores were neverending. After passing the middle grade from Arya Girls School, she put her learning to use only in reading and responding to letters from her natal family or in reading the occasional novel by Premchand or Sharat Babu. She was not particularly drawn to reading or to keeping contact with the wide world through the window of words. Reading for her had been merely a diversion to be innocuously pursued in one's spare time. Her world had been confined to taking care of Amarnath Babu's body and his home. Since his birth, Uday had become the focus of her worry and concern. After all, what is the life of an Indian woman beyond this? But now that she had started reading the newspaper daily, this appeared as an essential task too. She began to experience a connection with the world that surrounded her.

Almost a month had passed since the event.

One afternoon, a young girl arrived at Yashoda's home. Yashoda herself was not an old-fashioned woman, but this girl was absolutely of the new type. At the very first sight of her, Yashoda felt both curious and attracted towards her. The girl's sari was made of khadi, but she wore it in an entirely new manner. The sleeves of her sweater ended just at the shoulder. She carried a large purse in her hand, such as European women carry. After some brief, initial talk, the girl asked, 'Are you a member of the Congress?' Shaking her head Yashoda said, 'He is a member.'

'Well, why don't you too become a member of the Congress? Do men have a monopoly on all good actions? After all, educated women like yourself should also do something!' Saying this, the girl took out a receipt-book from her purse and with it two other books. Opening the receipt-book she said, 'You must become a member of the Congress.'

Yashoda knew that many women worked in the Congress party; they went to marches and meetings, but she was not acquainted with them. Nor had she ever felt it necessary to make such acquaintances. Inwardly sympathetic towards them, she remained silent. She looked at the books lying in front of her—one was titled *Women of the World* and the other *A Life of Captivity*.* Yashoda said, 'I find no respite from my household work.'

The girl responded with some intensity: 'If you remain imprisoned at home, how will you find respite? Apart from the kitchen and children, one should also have one's own life!' Yashoda liked the girl's words and her liveliness. Without further ado she gave four annas and took a receipt for membership in the Congress. Seeing that she was quiet, the girl said, 'Why do you remain totally enclosed at home in this way? You should meet others sometimes. Work among other women. Today is Monday . . . will you have some time on Friday? Please come to my home that day. You will meet some women . . . I will come at this time and take you.'

The prospect of going to other people's homes is not as simple for women as it is for men. They are aware of considerable responsibility in this regard. At this invitation from an unfamiliar young girl, Yashoda looked at her intently. The softness and inexperience of youth was evident in her clear wheat-coloured and rather long face, but there was also an eagerness suggesting intimacy in her manner of speech and gesture. Self-confidence gleamed in her large eyes. In her, one saw not the beauty that provokes torment but an attraction that abides in memory. Compared to men, women understand better where lack of shyness means

---

* Sachindra Nath Sanyal's book *Bandi Jeevan* (1922).

fearlessness and where it becomes shamelessness. A man usually reasons, but a woman reaches her own conclusion by intuitive perception. Yashoda did not feel the need to ask anything. The girl introduced herself on her own.

'My name is Shailbala. My house is on Nisbat Road. I am studying for my MA. My father's name—you might have heard of him—Lala Dhyanchandji. I want that we, women, should also do something.' Pointing towards the two books, she asked, 'Will you read these?'

On Yashoda's expressing assent by nodding her head, Shailbala gave her the books, gathered her bag and prepared to go, as though her task was over. And now, just like a working man, she should leave.

In that half hour, without having said anything significant verbally, Yashoda began to feel a sense of closeness with that young girl—as though she had found some old friend from her natal home whom she had been long awaiting. Taking Shailbala by the hand, Yashoda led her upstairs and with loving insistence invited her to eat something.

Yashoda came down to the door to bid Shailbala farewell. Just then Amarnath Babu returned home. Until Shailbala started her car and drove away, Yashoda kept looking at her fondly. When she had gone, Amarnath asked, 'What brought her here?'

'It's Shail,' answered Yashoda matter-of-factly, as though there was nothing new about Shailbala visiting her. Why didn't her husband recognize her?

Amarnath asked again, 'Yes, but how do you know her?'

Calmly arranging her aanchal on her head, Yashoda said, 'She is very nice. Why don't you come upstairs?' With that, Yashoda went upstairs.

Yashoda read both the books in solitude, and with great attentiveness. She did not mention them to her husband. It was not that she thought of hiding anything from him. She simply assumed that this was her own affair—just as in the daily routine of a woman's life there are several matters that have no connection with the husband or with other men.

On reading these books, a new feeling began to rise in her mind. She experienced the desire and enthusiasm to do something, but there was no path for her. She had never spoken much. While sewing, knitting or doing housework, if she ever thought about anything, it had to do with the unexciting burden of the household. Now her sensibility was different. Forgetting that burden, she now realized the attraction of movement and progress. Her vision was no longer limited to the narrow enclosure created by Amarnath Babu, Uday, the kitchen and the pantry. She began to see: beyond the four walls of the house, there is another world where Shail lives. There are so many important tasks in that world. She waited impatiently for Shailbala. She was her only intimate friend who knew what occupied her. In her invisible life, in deep shadow was that youth—the one who had spent the night in the dark little room, had worn the servant's clothes and then walked down the street, drumming on an empty canister.

On Friday when Shailbala seated her beside herself in the car, and driving the car herself, took her to her own

home, Yashoda felt as though she were going to a new
world, just as she had felt after her marriage when she
departed for her husband's home. At that time, because of
the overwhelming intensity of the event and the occasion,
her consciousness and awareness had been largely numbed;
today, she was amply attentive. She was aware of a light
thrill of joy. She was going towards a more complex world.
Even after reaching Shailbala's house, her glance did not
go towards the form and grandeur of the house. She was
looking only at Shailbala's unabashed agility.

In the drawing room a young man was waiting.
Taking both the books from Yashoda, Shailbala gave them
to him. Then, leading him to a corner of the room, she
said something to him in a low voice, and then addressing
Yashoda, she asked her to follow her towards an inner
door. Crossing a veranda, she took her inside a room. Here
another youth, sitting on an armchair, with several papers
placed in front of him on a small tripod table, was quickly
writing something. Hearing the sound of their steps, his
pen paused; he looked intently towards the door, and
taking out the cigarette from his mouth, he stood up and
said, 'Please come!' Pulling up the other armchair close, he
invited Yashoda to sit.

There had never been an occasion for Yashoda to sit
close to an unknown man, but she did not think of that
now. She was watching in astonishment: was this not the
same man!

Yashoda could not recognize him, but she suspected it.
The hair on his head was uncut and he had a light beard

and moustache. He was entirely a Sahib—complete with suit, collar and necktie. Not paying attention to Yashoda, the youth placed his hand on Shailbala's shoulder and said, 'Listen!' He led her out to the veranda, and returned within half a minute. This time, gathering the papers scattered on the table, he smiled and asked in a courteous tone, 'How are you?'

Yashoda no longer had any doubt. Sighing in relief she asked in response: 'There is no fear now, is there?'

'There is always fear. When you invite fear yourself, how can you complain? But yes, not like that night. That was not fear, that was death . . . you gave me refuge and saved me,' the youth answered with a smile. Yashoda's heart melted. The scene from that night awoke in her memory. She kept looking silently at the floor.

The youth asked again, 'Did you talk at home about that night's incident?'

When Yashoda shook her head in refusal, he said, 'And what's the need, don't say anything. The husband is a god, to be sure, but there are scores of other gods too. It is best to let each remain in his own place. Here, neither Shail nor anyone else knows that that night I took refuge in your home. Nor is there any need to tell them. And only Shail knows your name and address. I asked that you come here today. The rest will depend on your own wishes. We need your help, but we cannot force you. It was only because of my personal debt and reverence for you that I became eager to drag you into this difficulty, or perhaps I should say, into this honour. It certainly isn't necessary for you to wander about with bombs and pistols, as we do, or to spend your life hiding behind walls. We are forced to live this way because of particular circumstances. You could work with Shail. She is only a young girl yet. If you took care of the work, we would get more assistance. Everyone here calls me Harish.'

Looking towards the door, Harish called, 'Shail!'

Shail was waiting for this call. The tapping of her high-heeled shoes was heard, and then Shail entered the room, smiling. There wasn't a third chair for her to sit on. Without any embarrassment, Shail attempted to sit on the arm of Harish's chair, but slipped and reached his lap instead. In an exasperated tone, Harish exclaimed, 'What an animal you are!' And pointing towards the table, he said, 'Sit there!'

'Oh, there is no room for us anywhere!' Shail spoke reproachfully, getting up and seating herself on the table. For some reason this unusual behaviour—which would usually be considered indecent—aroused no antipathy in Yashoda. She simply smiled, as though it were nothing but an innocent joke.

Addressing Yashoda, Harish spoke, 'Now you have understood everything. You have read *A Life of Captivity*. Those are events of times past, but the same events persist today in new form. We want to remain alive—whether as a person, a community or a nation. For that, the first requirement is to have control over our means of living. We should have the opportunity to use and develop our power. Only then can we lead our lives as human beings. We do not have those rights and opportunities

today, either in our capacity as individuals or as subjects
of the country. All around us, daily, we see trouble in the
lives of people. The reason: our power and ability find
no opportunity and become useless. When a country is
oppressed to benefit another country, how can the people
of the oppressed country find any opportunity? If we are
alive, it is only like animals that spend their lives for the
benefit of others. It is this condition that we must oppose.
We can only be successful in our aim if we can spread this
awareness all over the country. Wherever there are such
men—in Congress, or elsewhere—they will be part of
our group.'

'But, Bhaiya, Dada and BM say that the Congress
is totally useless. We should not maintain any contact
with those sorts of people. Such contact will bring us no
benefit—only the danger that our secrets may be leaked,'
Shail questioned, resting her hand against her chin.

'I know what Dada and BM say, but you and I have
brains in our skulls too. A pistol has come into our hands, so
is it necessary to kill someone or the other? What will come
of this?' Harish replied in irritation.

Shail spoke again. 'BM says, your methods will turn
the people away from the party's work and towards the
hypocritical campaign of the Congress.'

'The Congress campaign may indeed be turning
hollow, but the people don't want it to become hollow,
nor do they think of it as hollow. It is our misfortune that
the leadership of the Congress has passed into such hands.
You tell me,' Harish asked, leaning forward, 'what will we

be able to achieve by a secret campaign where we confine
our strength to a mere handful of men?'

Pulling the aanchal of her sari over her shoulder, Shail
said, 'You say: widen your field. Those people say: don't
become too familiar with others lest you become useless for
our work.'

Harish did not respond. He was staring at the wall, sunk
in thought. Yashoda looked from Shail to Harish. She was
trying to understand this debate. Looking at Harish, Shail
asked, 'Should I bring tea? Will you eat something too?'

Without lifting his head, Harish spoke, 'Yes, yes,
please do.'

When Shail left the room, Harish looked at Yashoda and
said, 'Such is the nature of this work. One has to relinquish
attachment and love. Not just for our family: we must
relinquish love even for our comrades.' And then he smiled,
changed the topic and said, 'This is perhaps a minor matter,
but I had said that I would return your things. I don't know
where those clothes are, but here is your money . . .' Taking
out eighteen rupees, he placed them in front of Yashoda.

Seeing Yashoda lower her eyes in embarrassment, he
said, 'Don't take this if you don't want to, but you will still
work with us, won't you? Otherwise, I might carry the
burden of your debt until I die!' Noting that Yashoda for
her part said nothing, he spoke again, 'Why don't you work
among women? Once women adopt a project and make it
their own, no power can destroy it.'

Shailbala returned carrying tea and some food on a large
tray. Placing the tray on the table, she sat down on the

carpet near Harish's feet. Shifting a little to make room on her chair, Yashoda said, 'Please come here.' Shail silently signalled her refusal, indicating with her hand that she was comfortable on the floor.

Seeing Shailbala pour tea and shell eggs, Yashoda said, 'Now, please allow me to leave.'

'Will you not have a cup of tea?' Harish asked.

Looking at her, Shail spoke, 'Perhaps you abstain from such things?'

'Then why don't you ask for a separate cup of tea to be brought for her?' Harish interjected.

Indeed, Yashoda did abstain from such things, but to have a separate cup of tea brought for her would mean acknowledging her own difference from these people. She did not like this feeling of difference. She replied, 'No, there is no need for that. As it is, I do not drink tea, and it would be better if I left now.'

Harish commanded Shail, 'Go, take her home.'

Lifting her cup of tea to her lips, Shail said, 'Can't the driver take her?'

Shaking his head in refusal Harish said, 'No, you go yourself, I am here for another hour yet.' Shail stood up to take Yashoda home.

Yashoda thought: how this proud and sharp girl dances to the command of this youth. Is it possible that she too may have to follow his orders similarly in the future?

When Shailbala returned after dropping Yashoda home, Harish was sitting lost in thought, his face clasped in both hands. Seeing her, Harish said, 'Shail, I am going.'

'Where, somewhere outside?'

'I'll have to go because of BM's letter that you gave me,' he answered, looking at Shail.

'But how dangerous it is for you to travel! If those people want to meet you, why don't they come here? Are their lives in greater peril than yours?' Her voice was growing more plaintive. 'I would say, don't go,' she said, tugging at the threads hanging from the loose end of her sari.

Looking at her in surprise, Harish asked, 'What are you saying? . . . I should disobey the party? . . . Dada has called me.'

Shail sensed that her words had betrayed a concern for Harish that went beyond what she might feel as a member of the party, as though she had crossed the limit of normal civility. Yet, even now, she had been unable to say all that she wanted. She kept tugging at the threads of her sari.

'What if they gave you a wrong command? . . . Perhaps the command is not Dada's.' Pausing slightly, she spoke again, 'BM's words make me suspicious. I didn't want to say this, but . . . he was saying about you . . . why do you continue to stay here? He had even forbidden me to meet you. I said, everyone is the same for me. . . . I did not like his behaviour. . . . I think he envies you. He was saying—Harish's work now consists only of smoking cigarettes, making tall claims and setting up a girls' party.'

Biting his thumb, Harish sat with bowed head for some time. Then he asked, 'What did you not like about his behaviour?'

Bowing her head, Shail responded, 'I don't know . . .'

'What do you mean . . . why don't you speak?' Harish asked with irritation.

'How you rush to bite! . . . what can I tell you? Men just want to swallow up a woman.'

'Is that what I want too?' Harish asked angrily.

'Don't you know about your own self, what you want! . . . Why do you ask me?' Shail responded, looking into his eyes with a smile.

'You have known BM for a long time. If my coming to your place causes trouble, I will not come. I will find some other shelter.' Harish then began thinking quietly.

Shail became serious. 'Should I follow only BM's wishes? Is my own mind nothing?'

'What are you getting entangled in, Shail!' Harish asked in a weary tone. 'Is your being a girl the cause of all this trouble? And there was also talk of your marriage, what became of that?'

'You think, I will get married and the trouble will end,' Shail spoke reproachfully, but then, embarrassed by her own words, she quickly changed the topic, 'You also believe, don't you, that a woman should become the property of someone or the other? That men should magnanimously continue to give one another the chance to enjoy absolute authority over the woman each owns? BM says as much to me—"Become someone's or make someone your own." You tell me, what does it mean to become someone's or to make someone your own? To make someone your own means nothing more than belonging to someone, in such a way that a woman retains nothing of herself. If a woman must belong to someone or the other, then what can her independence possibly mean? Perhaps she only exercises independence in choosing her master once, but a slave she must become.'

Shifting in his chair, Harish asked, 'Can't husband mean companion rather than master?'

'What nonsense! If a woman must be bound to one man—and according to the conditions of society remain subordinate to him, dependent on him—whatever name one gives to that relation, in fact it is nothing but woman's slavery. As for companions—one can have any number of them. But would you tolerate a woman who had many husbands?' Shail asked.

Laughing, Harish responded, 'This burden is not mine to bear—whoever wishes to bear it, let him worry!'

Shail made a face. 'This is the trouble. A man can never see a problem from a woman's perspective. Her greatest misfortune is that she must give birth to a child, which is why he remains anxious to establish his mastery over her, as if she were a piece of land.'

To further tease Shail, Harish spoke in a casual tone, 'Let him who wishes to further his lineage engage in these arguments. As for me, I have been freed from all such debates.'

'There is so much more to life than children and the protection of the family,' Shail turned her face away.

Without hesitating Harish replied, 'But that is the same for man and woman.'

'It certainly is, but it is the unfortunate woman who is instantly punished!' Shail spoke on the spur of the moment, but then the weight of tradition pressed down upon her and she became embarrassed. To divert Harish's attention, she quickly asked, 'There is some time yet before your departure, isn't there?'

'There is, but how long can I stay here like this? What will your family say? My train is not till two in the morning,' Harish said, reluctantly preparing to get up.

Looking at the watch on her wrist, Shail spoke. 'It is only half past eight. In this cold, where will you wander about till two in the morning! That is not right. Why don't you eat, and then I will take you to the front door. You can say goodbye to Father at that time. I will open the garage door in the meanwhile. Come upstairs again through that door and then you may leave in time for your train.'

Harish looked at her in astonishment. Bowing her head, Shail said, 'You don't understand your situation . . . what danger awaits you at every step.'

'And it doesn't await you?' Harish asked.

'What of me? If I must, I will face a few more insults. I have heard plenty before—so let there be a few more! Come sit, come to the dining room, nobody but Father will be there at this time. Why don't you become an engineer again? What was the name of your firm? . . . Jeremy and Johnson! Do you know what Bhuaji was saying the other day? . . . What a nice young man he is! I thought, if you only knew what kind of a nice man he is, you would probably die of fright!'

Harish laughed. 'So, Bhuaji approves of me? Will she arrange your marriage with me?'

'Yes, as it is, you are quite good looking! . . . Get up, you are just hiding here. What will the servants and others say?' Shail spoke, giving Harish a push on the shoulder.

Harish felt something new in body and mind. Since accepting the life of a revolutionary, he had thought of woman as something outside his chosen path. Though he had come close to Shail several times, he had not considered her as a young woman but only as a fellow-member of the party, who was different from other members merely in appearance and apparel. But today his mind was repeatedly alerting him: this is a young woman, bearing within her the source of life's sweetness, of companionship and happiness. Don't you recognize her? His mind was saying: you are not just a machine of the revolution, you are also a human being.

In the dining room, Shail's father was sitting alone at the table. Entering the room, Shail said, 'Father, Mr Shukla is leaving. I said to him, why must you leave without meeting Father? He should eat with us before going. After all, it is dinner time.'

'Come, come!' Father spoke with affection and regard, 'You are in that firm, that . . .'

'Yes, indeed, Jeremy and Johnson.'

'Who is the banker for your company—Central Bank?'

'No, Imperial and Lloyds. These companies don't deal with local banks. We don't have many branches here as yet. We are established in UP, CP and Bombay.'

So as not to give Lala Dhyanchandji an opportunity to ask further questions, Harish rambled on about how foreign companies are taking over business in the country—and in the course of this discussion, dinner came to an end.

After taking Harish out through the front door, Shail immediately went to the garage. Harish too had just reached there when Bhuaji called Shail from her room for some medicine. Signalling to Harish to sit quietly in the car, Shail went upstairs. After giving Bhuaji her medicine and talking to her for about twenty minutes, she switched off the light in her room. Then, turning on a zero-power blue light, she slowly, silently, climbed down the stairs and took Harish to her room.

Pointing towards the neatly laid bed she asked Harish to lie down while she sat on the sofa-chair nearby. Coming close to her Harish said, 'I have not come to ruin your sleep. You sleep, in any case, I'll have to leave. What if I fall asleep and don't wake up in time . . .?'

'Don't worry, I will stay awake,' Shail answered.

'But you don't have any practise!'

'How would you know, how many nights I have spent awake in this room, simply staring at this clock.'

'In the discipline of love?'

'Perhaps . . . , you know the path of one discipline, I may know the other! Don't remind me of all that. Why don't you lie down?'

Sensing a blend of tenderness and authority in Shail's tone, Harish sat down on the arm of her chair and asked, 'May I sit here beside you?' Shail shifted to one side and made room for him.

For some time, both sat quietly, in absolute silence. Looking at the clock on the dressing table, Harish asked, 'Is the clock not working?'

'No, no, it is working, it just doesn't make noise—like women!' Pressing her lips together, Shail laughed.

Bowing his head, Harish said in a somewhat troubled tone, 'Your manner suggests that you are carrying some deep burden of sorrow. To hide it you always try to laugh, as though you were carefree. Perhaps you are criticized so much because your behaviour is unusual and uncommon. People think that you attack society, but to me it seems that you yourself are in pain. I am amazed that you are ready to face the perils of revolution and at the same time you dream passionately of the world of love. As for me, you know my situation: it is not in my fate to create the world of love and dreams. As a companion, if I wish to share your sorrow, that will hardly bring you any peace. But you have done so much for me that I want to come close to you and look inside your heart. You know very well that my life will be quite brief, but the desire for life beats in my heart too, and there may be very little time for it—sometimes it rises in an intense and terrible way, only to be defeated. In my life, only experience of the joy of others can bring joy to me. If I ask you for just this, would it be too much? You know my life is like a sealed vessel that will one day be consigned, unopened, to the river . . .'

'Enough, let it be!' Shail interrupted. 'One should not say such things. Look, it is very cold, and if you fall sick, there will be more trouble.'

Shail's tenderness gave Harish more courage. He persisted, 'Don't worry about that. Nothing will happen to me. You speak.'

Placing her chin on her palm, Shail asked, 'What is to be gained by that? You will either think of me as a fool or begin to hate me. I will lose your sympathy as well.'

'Does my sympathy have any value for you?' Harish asked, looking at her in the dim light. 'If so, my sympathy will only increase the more I am able to know you.'

'And what will you gain?'

'Knowledge itself is a gain. To learn of the experience of others is also an experience.'

'What others experience—I don't know,' Shail started speaking, 'but love has been in my life ever since I became aware of the world, and perhaps it will never let go of me as long as I live. When I was a child, I loved according to my capacity. As I became more mature, the scope of love also increased—that is to say, I became desirous of both giving and receiving more love. Whenever that desire can't be fulfilled, I am filled with disappointment and anguish. When one has failed, fallen flat on one's face, and been humiliated, one may even wish to die! Indeed, some people, disappointed in love, do die, but I couldn't. In the future, I think, I will not let my hope soar so high that on falling I would fear death—but I find myself helpless.' Shailbala was speaking while tugging at the button on Harish's sleeve.

Seeing her fall silent, Harish said, 'That is about the future. I was asking about the past.'

Placing her hand on his arm and looking into his eyes Shail asked, 'Why are you asking? Such questions are asked by those who must decide whether I am worthy of them or not. But you are not faced with the choice of accepting or rejecting me!'

Harish answered with a suppressed smile: 'That is why you can speak freely to me. I am not here to determine your value according to my needs. I can only see what you are, insofar as you are a part of society. Your personality is apparently flourishing, yet it suffers secret torments, and society suffers those torments through you, in your person. That is why I wish to understand that pain. If we want to know about the condition of society, we cannot examine its pulse or use a microscope to study it. We can only learn about society by the experience of people in society. I am especially fortunate that I happen to have come so close to you. If I were to speak frankly—I feel a connection to your joy and sorrow. . . . Why are you silent? It is already ten . . . I am here for just four more hours . . . I can't hope to experience such intimacy with you ever again. Please speak!'

'Then listen!' Shail said. 'I must have been about twelve or thirteen years of age then. I was studying in class six or seven. A boy lived in our neighbourhood—he was very beautiful. On his way to school one day, he gave me a letter. Girls are usually annoyed when they receive such letters, but I was not. If someone likes me, wants me, why should I respond with anger? He wrote many letters. I used to feel happy reading them. You can imagine what kind of letters a boy of fourteen or fifteen would write. But for me, his letters meant that he loved me, and by writing letters to each other, the two of us were secretly doing something of which no one else was aware. Perhaps you could say: this insignificant act made us feel that we too were something. It is by experiencing one's sense of being and discovering one's personality that one finds happiness and self-respect, one finds satisfaction . . . You will say I have embarked on teaching you psychology, but what can I do! If I have a chance to write an essay for the MA exam, it will be on this topic.

'Other boys, the sons of Father's friends, used to come to our place as well. Father has always allowed me to be free. Because Mother had passed away, I stayed close to Father. I could talk to everyone. One day a boy was teaching me a tune on the harmonium. We were laughing a lot. At that moment the boy who wrote letters, entered. He did not like this. Later, he scolded me about it. I never spoke to him again . . . love ended.

'I began to think: why did we fight? The answer was: I wanted love to widen my life, and he, by placing restrictions on me, wanted to limit my life for himself. See, even a boy of fourteen–fifteen wished to consider me as his property.

'After that, I noticed other boys. You tell me, how could I not find agreeable that which is agreeable? How could I not experience desire or love for it? Any boy who happened to be in view seemed ideal to me at that point in time. When I was in class ten and in the first two years of college, I read many novels. Several portraits of life appeared

before my eyes. . . . Then, I became acquainted with
another boy, Mahendra. He was the brother of a friend of
mine . . . very good-natured and good-looking. If I did not
see him, I became restless. On my way back from college in
the afternoon, I'd see my friend home so that I could catch
a glimpse of her brother. If I found an opportunity, I'd go
again in the evening. When his letters came, I'd read them
ten, twenty times over. I'd stay up till midnight writing
to him. Who knows why my independence and pride had
vanished! During that time, I encountered scores of boys,
they tried to come close to me, but I did not even notice
them. Both of us had decided that we would be companions
for life.

'He would come to our place. We would spend hours
together. At that time, we lived in our other house. The
sound of his footsteps on the stairs made me tremble. As
long as he stayed, I felt alive—the moment he left, I was
dead. The Congress was in full force in those days. I was
always among the girls who led pickets and demonstrations,
so a crowd of patriotic young men would gather at our
home. Whenever Mahendra visited, there would be
sidelong glances; he would be taunted because his father
was a government officer. I could not bear to see him
insulted. I told him: I will come to see you, you should not
come here. Or, try to come at a time when these people
are not here.

'I would go to his home, rest my head against his
chest and weep. He would console me. Once he came
to my place, very upset. At his home, another battle was

raging. Negotiations were underway for his marriage to the only daughter of a wealthy landlord. The entire family was ranged against him. Seeing him upset and sad, I took him in my arms to reassure him. He stayed in my room all night long . . . we forgot ourselves. On regaining my senses, I wept bitterly. He said: "Don't worry, we'll go away somewhere" . . . but I was not ready . . . how could I leave Father? And then there was my own situation. In the Congress, and elsewhere, people knew me. He said, why don't you take a medicine—it will release us from anxiety. He brought me a packet. The medicine gave me a high fever.

'Doctors came, one after another, with bottles of medicine. For the first few days, I did not take their medicines. Later I did, but they did not make any difference. Mahendra would often come, sit close to me, take my hand in his and cry. He said it was all his fault, but not for a day did I feel anger towards him. Yes, I felt sad if he didn't come. For some days my condition was such that the doctors were not sure if I would survive.

'There was no dearth of sympathetic young men. One of them was your BM. There was another leader of the youth, you know him . . . ".Khanna". I don't know why, I was always suspicious of him, but because he had been to prison twice, I had to bow my head in reverence to him. From the very beginning, he was envious of Mahendra. I was still bedridden when he became eager to make me his life partner. I was anguished by his words but could not easily reject the honour he gave me. While I lay in bed, he would kiss my feet and say: "How great you are!" But at the same time, I had to listen to an entire epic of complaints against Mahendra. This mental agony, added to the physical agony, was driving me insane. I tried to make sure that the two of them never met. I respected both in my heart—that was my problem. At Mahendra's home, the situation had become unbearable for him because of the question of his marriage. He would tell me what had happened at home, and I would tell him: you should get married. I wanted him to find happiness in some way, but still, his refusal to marry someone else brought me peace.

'He did not come for many days. Then one day he came and told me—he was getting married. Only a sound of shock escaped my lips. Afterwards, when I regained consciousness, he was no longer there.

'Some days later I got a letter from him. He was married, and he could not bring himself to face me. My condition deteriorated. I wanted to go and see him, just once, but I did not have the strength. In the midst of all this, Khanna told me many times that he had found his life's companion in me . . . the two of us would walk together in society and in the realm of politics. As I remained silent, he would sit by my pillow and shed tears on my brow. Eventually, I had to admit defeat. Holding his head against my heart, I cried. The doctors attempted to save me by treating my illness while I aggravated it by contracting these maladies of the heart.

'Seeing Father's moist eyes, I was determined—I would turn my heart to stone and quietly treat my disease, but I failed. In the end, for Khanna's sake, I vowed to try and regain my health. After six months of severe dedication, I became fit to get out of bed. My life now was "infused-with-Khanna", but Mahendra was still with me, like a shadow. Till this day I have not been able to forget him, nor will I ever forget him. Every evening, resting my head in Khanna's lap, I would dream of my future life. Khanna had pulled me out from the grave. I became his, but sometimes when I would close my eyes, my arm on his shoulder, he would ask, "Do you still remember Mahendra?" . . . How could I lie!

'One day, he made explicit that which had been implicit. He asked, "Will you marry me?" I responded, yes.

'Then he asked—"You did not give your body to Mahendra, did you—only your heart?"

'My breath ceased. I could not respond. I could feel his quick, hot breath on my brow. After a brief pause, he asked in an alarmed tone, "Your body as well?"

'I trembled, but I did not have the courage to lie. Bowing my head, I indicated assent. For some moments I was in a semi-conscious state, but when Khanna's arms suddenly relaxed their hold, I was shaken. Opening my eyes I saw—his fair face had withered. I tried to gather myself and sit down, but I could not . . . Impurity of the heart can be forgiven, but not of the body . . . and this same Khanna used to say that he loved me with his soul, but in fact he wanted sole right over my body.'

Shail lifted her eyes and looked at Harish. Attempting to smile, she asked, 'Am I very wicked?'

Placing both hands on her shoulders, Harish answered, 'What are you saying? Someone with such courage can never be unworthy.'

Biting her lip, Shail gazed at the facing wall. A few moments later, addressing Harish, she said, 'And this same Khanna maligned me by calling me promiscuous. Now BM does not want me to talk to anyone except himself.'

Surprised, Harish asked, 'Why?'

'Precisely. I have not been able to understand . . . Yet, what must one understand? The tradition of man's sole protection and authority over woman! He wanted me to leave my home and go with him . . .'

Suddenly, covering her face with both hands, Shail bent over. Seeing her head trembling, Harish bent low and asked, 'Are you crying, you crazy girl? Is this the extent of your independence and self-respect? You have been so courageous—why cry now?'

Wiping her cheeks, wet with tears, Harish held her close to him, her head resting on his chest. His voice became tremulous. He said, 'I swear, I will die if you weep.'

For some moments they kept sitting. Then looking at the radium hands of the clock, he said, 'Shail, it is half past one . . . I have to leave. You close the garage downstairs.'

He held her close to him once more in a farewell gesture, then left quietly without waiting for an answer.

Central Assembly

This particularly constricted street in the city of Kanpur is largely populated by people of the lower class. In that house of the old type, where electric wire had not reached even in 1931, the doors did not have English hinges but were fixed with traditional axles. The roof was tiled.

Eight young men were waiting. One was sitting against the wall leaning on his elbow. To his left a candle was burning on a piece of brick, and the youth sitting next to it was reading a book by its light. Near him, a youth lying flat on his back was reading a newspaper. Two comrades* were talking to one another in Bangla. The youth sitting in the centre was especially strong and robust. Taking out the cartridges from a pistol, he was cleaning it while talking to a young man sitting next to him.

---

* *Saathi*—also carries the non-political sense of 'companion' or 'mate' depending on the context. I have translated '*saathi*' as 'comrade' wherever appropriate. Where the English word 'comrade' is used in the Hindi text, I have placed it in italics.

Of the two youths talking in Bangla, one moved forward
a little, and addressing the one in the centre, said, 'Dada, see
it is eleven . . . we shouldn't miss the three o'clock train.'

The youth reading the newspaper gathered up his paper
and said, 'Ok, then you start . . . it doesn't seem he will be
able to come.'

The youth with the book, placing his finger on the page
he was reading, spoke, 'I had already told you—after four in
the evening no train arrives from there.'

The second Bangla-speaking youth adjusted his blanket
and asked, *'But has he been informed?'*

In response the book reader spoke vehemently, *'Of
course. I did inform him myself.'*

Dada looked at both of them in turn. Realizing his
mistake, the youth said, 'I meant to say, was he properly
informed?'

The book reader repeated what he had said earlier,
'The information was given three days ago. I gave it to him
myself.'

Dada looked at everyone and asked, 'So then, what
should be done?'

The youth with the newspaper threw it aside and
sat up. 'There must have been a problem on the way, so
he wasn't able to come. It is also very difficult for him
to travel.'

The book reader laughed and said with a taunt, 'Indeed,
if his heart isn't in it!'

Dada said irritably, 'But in this matter it was essential for
him to be here . . . we should talk in his presence.'

The dark-complexioned Bengali comrade blinked his large eyes in worry and said, 'But we cannot come here repeatedly. From here we will go East.'

The other Bengali addressed his companion: 'Akhil! You say what you have to about Bengal. These people can discuss their own matters some other time.'

Akhil was a thin, young man—distinctly of the East Bengali type with his spare frame and dark complexion. When he tried to speak in Hindi, the natural seriousness of his face appeared all the more intense. Finding it difficult to express his feelings, he said, 'What do you think about our future plan? . . . It is very tough in Bengal. There is harsh police control. And if we don't do anything at all, it will all come to an end. The older leaders only talk big; they've been caught in the games of the Congress . . . we can't do anything because we don't have an *expert* in *explosives* in our midst. As for the young men, the communists are pulling them away . . .'

The book reader laughed and interjected, 'And the one with the *explosives* holds on to the key and keeps everyone on their toes!'

Dada, biting his lips in worry, looked at the candle. Twin reflections of the candle shimmered in the dark brown pupils of his eyes.

Just then a voice was heard from the staircase, 'Caution!'

Dada lifted his head and asked, 'Who?'

From the stairs the voice came, 'nine-nine-eight-eight.'

Blinking his alert eyes in relief Dada said, 'Let him come in.'

In a few seconds a young man entered, wearing the blue clothes of a coolie of the railway engine house and wrapped in a cheap blanket. Upon seeing him everyone welcomed him, but the manifest forms of their welcome differed. Without saying anything, Dada merely nodded his head, which meant, 'You have come.'

Akhil looked at him with shining eyes and said, '*Oh, you have come after all.*' The other Bengali youth laughed and said in Bangla, 'Come, come, Harish.'

The newspaper reader looked towards the book reader and said, 'BM had given up hope.'

Looking at Dada, BM spoke, 'The train arrives at four o'clock, what took him so long . . .?'

Lifting his eyes and looking at Harish, Dada asked, 'Where were you? Why did you not meet us after your arrival? Did you not know that you were to reach here by nine?'

BM looked at his Bengali companion and said, '*He will give some nice story.*'

Harish had sat down, leaning on his arm. Annoyed by this taunt, he spoke in anger, 'Do you mean I was out for a leisurely stroll?'

Dada scolded, 'Why don't you speak plainly?'

Looking at Dada, Harish responded, 'Did he speak plainly? . . . Did you not hear that! . . . Does he mean I make excuses?'

Dada was silent. Except for Dada and BM, all the others began saying, '*No, no, no!*'

The youth sitting near Dada laughingly pointed towards Harish's clothes and said, 'Hey, what is this disguise you're in?'

Dada repeated his question, 'But where were you all this time?'

'I am coming directly from the station, Dada,' Harish replied.

The newspaper-reading youth asked in surprise, 'But which train arrives at this hour?'

Harish said, 'I did not come by passenger train. Ali, you know how difficult it is for me to board a train at that station. I had found out that at 2:15 in the morning a goods train carrying coal was to leave for Mughalsarai. More than half the wagons were empty. Wearing these clothes and going by way of the tracks, I slept in one of the wagons. You know the pace at which a goods train moves. It has just reached; in fact, it stopped at the very end of the station. I got down and came here straight from the station.'

Hearing his explanation, everyone withdrew their complaints. Akhil looked at his companion and gave his approval, 'Well done, very good!'

Ali asked, 'You rascal, didn't you feel cold at night?'

'My bones stiffened,' Harish said, 'but not as much as they would had the police cast a glance on me.'

The youth sitting next to Dada said, 'Ali, have you read that story from the *Hitopdesh*? A jackal wandered into the city. Running in fear from the dogs, he fell into the dyer's vat of indigo colour. When he emerged he had become blue. When the jungle animals saw him, they were afraid and bowed in front of him and that jackal became the king of the jungle.'

BM exclaimed in pleasure, '*Hear, hear!*'

Dada looked at the youth sitting near him and scolded, 'Jeevan, can't you desist?'

A bit embarrassed, Jeevan looked at Harish and said, 'Dada, I did not mean anything by it; isn't that so, Harish?'

Ali slapped his thigh and said, 'No doubt about it! Harish has scared away those police animals, but what can he do when his fellow-jackals begin to howl? He will have to join the chorus after all.' He laughed. Ali, Jeevan and Harish looked at each other and smiled. BM twisted his lips a little and pretended to smile. The others may not have understood, or they did not pay attention.

Akhil said, '*Now comrades, let us come to the point.*'

Dada said, 'Yes . . . but some important matters must be decided before we determine our future plans. Without resolving these matters, we will not be able to do any serious work.' Dada was trying to speak very calmly, but because of the suppressed excitement in his mind, his nostrils quivered slightly and a tremor was apparent in his tone.

Having heard Dada and observing his demeanour, the two Bengalis looked around, trying to understand the situation. Finishing what he had to say, Dada turned his gaze to the wall facing him. A struggle of emotions was still manifest on his face. Harish looked in surprise at Dada, Jeevan stared at his fingernails, BM at his book and Ali at BM.

Renouncing home and family, opposing colonial power, facing indifference from the nation, dealing with constant fear of death and keenly aspiring to put their lives at stake in doing whatever they could for the nation—these shared purposes and feelings had bound and united the revolutionaries in a deep bond of friendship and singleness of aim. This was a bond of such affection and compassion that it surpassed the bond between brothers born of the same womb or between lovers blinded by love—yet in that simple bond of trust, a twist had now appeared. Because this change had become evident, each person sensed that his own position was now unstable and insecure. For a moment, a fearful silence descended, as happens when one suddenly hears an extremely sad piece of news.

Not understanding anything, Akhil asked in a low voice, 'What does this mean?'

Without responding to him, Dada addressed BM: 'Speak!'

Biting his fingernail, BM said, 'Why don't *you* speak, you know everything.' Except for Jeevan, everyone else was looking at BM. He felt their intense gaze on him.

Lowering his eyes, addressing BM and keeping his agitation in check, Dada spoke again, 'Why don't you speak; after all, how will this matter be resolved?'

In a hesitant tone BM answered, 'It is not my personal matter.'

'But it is you who have discovered everything,' Dada said.

Gathering courage, BM answered, 'But you know it too.' Pointing the book in his hand towards Jeevan and Ali, he said, 'They also know.'

Dada's lips quivered. He was about to speak when Jeevan said in an emotional voice, 'Let me just say it, Dada.'

Exhaling his agitation, as though he had been freed, Dada kept his vacant gaze on the floor and said, 'Speak!'

To calm the emotion in his voice, Jeevan drew lines on the mat with his fingers and started speaking, 'This is the problem—Dada has received some complaints. It is essential to place them before you. If our comrades start working against the discipline and goals of the party and try to form their own separate parties, then how can the party work? We will be killed in vain without accomplishing anything.'

Jeevan's frightened looks and his opening words turned the mood in that tile-covered shed even more apprehensive and grave. Dada's gaze was fixed on the flame of the candle. Its reflection was dancing in the pupils of his eyes. The suppressed agitation of his mind had reddened the whites of his eyes. It was as though a fiery conflagration on the distant horizon had caused a slender flame of fire to leap in the bloodshot sky. Everyone else was looking at Jeevan's bent face and tear-filled eyes.

Burdened by this heavy duty, he paused for a few moments to catch his breath, then started speaking, '. . . It is about Harish.' He uttered these words with particular difficulty. 'The complaint is that he is working against the party. Instead of assisting the party, he is advising people to assist in the work of the Congress and especially in the work of the communists. By asking them to participate in the Congress movement or in other public work, he wishes to keep those away from the party who could help in our secret work. The party is in economic difficulties at present. Some of our men are stuck in various places. Because we don't have money for fares and other expenses, we can't get them out of these dangerous places and send them elsewhere. For many days now, they have been surviving on mere handfuls of parched grain. Harish was given the plan for an armed robbery in Amritsar and asked to make arrangements for it, but it is said that he intentionally put it off. Apart from this, there is a complaint that he squanders the party's money. He wears expensive clothes, eats in posh restaurants, drinks alcohol, travels in cars and has illicit friendships with girls of ill repute.'

Dada interrupted, 'Why don't you speak plainly?'

Jeevan said with some embarrassment, 'The complaint is that one girl, who has been helping the party and who wanted to leave her home to work for the party, has been forbidden by Harish to meet other party members or to leave her home, so he can keep her as his lover. He tells people that the work of the party is futile and that its members are stupid . . . they don't understand anything. Dada and others are not educated, they don't study . . . the work of the party should be carried out in a different manner.'

Jeevan fell silent. He took out a handkerchief from his pocket, wiped his eyes and blew his nose. Tears had not fallen from his eyes, but his eyes were red.

When Jeevan finished speaking, all were stunned. Taking his eyes off the candle, Dada kept looking at the floor in the middle of the room and was silent.

Harish felt that everyone was waiting for his response. Shock and apprehension made every pore of his body vigilant. Looking at Dada's face and his lowered eyes, he said, 'I am amazed that such a monstrous web of deception has been woven and placed before you.' His words were particularly reassuring for Ali and the two Bengalis. No change was seen on Dada's or BM's face. They looked at Jeevan again in the hope of hearing something further from him.

Harish again spoke, 'Regarding some matters, I might have a different opinion, and, in that case, we can discuss such matters here, but to say that I dissuade people from sympathizing with the party, or that I am trying to create my own separate party, or that I describe other members of the party as stupid—this is simply false. I have been branded as someone who wastes the party's money, who is depraved. If these complaints arise from envy, there is no cure for them. If they arise from mistaken impressions, those can surely be removed. The first accusation is that I wear good clothes. The clear explanation is, I must wear clothes that are suitable for the kind of society I have to enter, otherwise I will not be able to meet those people. I could not have worn a suit and come here by a goods train, nor could I wear these blue clothes of coolies and go amidst high-society people.'

Akhil looked at Dada and the other comrades and shaking his knee in satisfaction, said, '*Yes, that is right*, that is right.'

'Moreover,' Harish said, 'I don't spend the party's money on these things. I take the necessary amount from my personal acquaintances.'

BM looked at Dada and asked, 'What does it mean for a party member to have personal acquaintances? If the public is sympathetic towards a party member, it is because of the work of the party. Everyone should have the same facilities in the party.'

A sharpness entered Harish's tone. 'I understand all these matters, but clothes are not worn for the sake of clothes. If any other member of the party needs these clothes, he may use them. I am ready to give him the clothes . . . Now if I wish to meet someone . . . that man invites me to a restaurant, should I say to him, I am an absconding revolutionary, please meet me under a tree in the darkness of the night? Don't I have to make an impression on him before I introduce myself, and if he willingly bears the expense for the restaurant, what does the party have to lose . . .?'

Ali and the other men showed their approval by gestures of acceptance. BM asked, 'In the month of November, how much was spent for the parties at Nishat Hotel?'

Harish had become exasperated by now. He said, 'Sir, this is how it is with the factory . . . if you ask three men to make picric acid and guncotton all day . . . they vomit all day because of the pungent gas and suffer from dizziness . . . the picric acid gets so deeply absorbed in their hands that whatever they touch turns bitter; . . . when they can no longer even retain their balance, then, in order to fill their bellies and refresh their minds if they happen to go to a restaurant to eat omelette and ice cream and are therefore considered guilty of a crime—well, then, I can say nothing! . . . And then, there remains the matter of not allowing a girl to meet others because I wish to make her my girlfriend—sheer nonsense! If someone doesn't want to meet another person, I can't forcibly tie them together by the neck. This is a personal matter. If someone doesn't like another person's behaviour, what can I do about that? And if I think that instead of leaving her home, a girl can do the party's work better by remaining at home, then she should be left there—one shouldn't wander around with her simply for one's own pleasure.

'The girl you are referring to—I know she can be of more use to the party right where she is. If she were more useful away from home, it would be a different matter . . . And lastly, there remains the question concerning our manner of work—I understand the concern. We should once again think about this. Until now, most of our energy has been spent on armed robberies and a few political assassinations, but this in itself is not our goal. Our goal is to end the oppression of the country and win for it the right to self-determination. After all, what is the meaning of Swarajya? Till now our entire endeavour has been to make secret societies. By living far away from people, hiding in caves and basements, we can neither win the cooperation of people nor provide leadership to them. These pistols, revolvers and bombs—in a way, they are not just obstacles in our path; they are, in fact, swallowing us up . . .! Our entire energy is exhausted in a single armed robbery, conducted with the aim of obtaining more arms or carrying out a political assassination. What do we gain by this robbery? . . . We lose the sympathy of the people. After each robbery or assassination, some men are inevitably captured and our organization suffers some disintegration. Fifty or a hundred of us cannot gain Swarajya. Only the united endeavour of the people can bring about Swarajya, and we are so distant from them. Sometimes people throw a word of praise at us as though we were skilled acrobats or jugglers . . . but the leaders heap abuse on us and try to keep the people away from our influence.

'For the past thirty years, we and our comrades have been experimenting with this method. We have made so many sacrifices, but the people remain just where they were before. Have we been able to *approach* the people? We should change our technique—instead of becoming martyrs, we should think more about the consequences of our attempts. For this, deep study is essential. We should examine: what has Russia done? . . . By infiltrating the Congress, we should organize other kinds of public movements and agitations . . .'

Interrupting him, BM said, 'This is the problem. You want to change the tradition of the revolutionary party. There are many other organizations that are involved in social and economic work. The work of the revolutionary party is armed political revolt. Surely counselling people against this amounts to breaking up the party, doesn't it?'

Akhil nodded his head and said, 'This is not right. This is *serious*.'

Ali asked, 'Yes, true enough, but what is the aim of the party?'

When Harish began defending himself, he had felt that the sympathy of those present was with him, but what he said about the work of the party caused a change in the attitude of his companions. With all his strength, he clarified his position: 'This does not mean breaking up the party. If the party thinks about its own programme, will it break apart? Then, you say that I am creating a new party. Where is this new party? . . .'

BM said, 'The real problem is breaking up the existing party. When it breaks, new parties will definitely emerge.' Some others wanted to speak, but Harish said excitedly, 'If I tell party members to study, to think about their field of work and to widen it—does that amount to destroying the party?'

Akhil, BM and Ali all wanted to speak, but looking at Dada, they stopped. Dada turned his eyes towards the candle and said in a heavy voice, 'I neither know about these new matters of study and modern techniques nor am I concerned about them. For all this time, I have fought and fulfilled my duty, and in future too, I will continue to fight. As long as I am alive, no one can touch me—I know this. I do not enjoy being a commander, and I did not join the party in order to be one. All of you placed this burden upon me. I have always worked in consultation with others that is why I am called stupid and illiterate. . . . And now I am to study! I understand killing and being killed. I don't have time for more than this. Now big people with BA and MA degrees have entered the Party, let them take over the leadership . . . let them study and follow their techniques. . . . Excuse me, until now I did what I could by following the counsel of others and my own judgement . . . now I am not concerned with anyone.' Putting his hand in his pocket, he further added, 'I will keep this one pistol with me, for I have no wish to swing like a dancing monkey on the hangman's noose should the police catch me. As for all the other weapons, I will duly return them. They were bought with the party's money and belong to the party. . . . Now they have come to teach me to study and learn new techniques!'

Dada's anger spilled over in the form of tears. He wiped his eyes with the corner of his dhoti. The rage that could have been appeased in facing the enemy and shedding blood had now turned its destructive heat upon his own self as he saw his companions, intimate as his own two hands, part ways with him, and he took this as a sign of his own weakness.

Harish understood very well the impact Dada's words would have. What made him most anxious was that his intention was being entirely distorted. Gathering courage, he spoke again, 'I am sad that I am being misunderstood. I have never said anything against you or any of our comrades. I am not concerned whether someone is literate or illiterate. By study, I don't mean reading a handful of English books—I am talking instead about our own goal. That is why we have yet to learn a lot.'

Dada did not say anything. He gazed again at the burning candle, but Akhil, spreading both hands, gesticulating in an attempt to compensate for his limitations with the language, said, 'What must a revolutionary learn? . . . Only *sacrifice*. One must simply learn to die for the nation, to die for the *motherland* . . . learn to die by one's own hand . . . what is the need for further talk?'

Without looking at anyone, Dada said, 'You may continue this debate another time. But please excuse me. Take charge of what belongs to you . . . I am not interested in learning anything now.'

Ali said, 'Dada, what are you saying? . . . How can the party exist without you? You are the oldest and the most experienced among us. We have all come together with you at our centre . . . What are you talking about?'

Steadying his voice, Jeevan said, 'Everything can't be done according to one person's opinion. Please listen to others as well.'

With a deep sigh Dada answered, 'Now I don't want to listen to anything. The man whom I trusted so much, with whom I faced death so many times—when he starts talking in this manner, how can we work together anymore? . . . Many a times Harish and I have disagreed, quarrelled, but this is different. This is a matter of principle. He no longer has faith in me.' Dada wiped his eyes again.

Moving forward a little, Ali said, 'Dada, Harish did not say that he doesn't have faith in you. He has simply placed a new idea before the party. We may accept it or we may not.'

Harish spoke again. 'I only want to say that in view of the goal before us, programmes and campaigns often need to change. In Russia, the movement for independence first took the form of terrorist acts. At that time the common people in Russia had no connection with such acts. Lenin understood this weakness of the Russian revolutionaries. He counselled them not to destroy their energy in political assassinations but to create among the people a consciousness of their rights by engaging the questions that occupy ordinary people.'

Shaking his hands and his head Akhil said, '*No, no, we don't want this Russian bosh* . . . no, we don't need this.'

BM laughed loudly and said, 'Exalted Sir! We have not yet escaped the slavery of the British and you are already condemning us to be slaves of the Russians!' . . . Pointing towards Jeevan, he asked, 'What time is it?'

Jeevan looked at his wristwatch and said, 'One-thirty.'

Akhil said in a worried voice, 'Time is passing by . . . we must talk about our future work . . .!'

Taking over from him, BM said, 'What future work? When we don't even agree on what our work is, how can we talk about future work? Only those who agree may discuss work. If you want to change the party's programme and talk further, then we should leave. Dada doesn't want to have anything to do with that either. If we continue to work in the old manner, then what about those who have lost faith in that method—what will they do?'

A stunned silence descended on the hovel. A sharp saw seemed to cut across Harish's mind and heart. In the folds of this manipulation he sensed deception and conspiracy, but he was caught in the web. It was not possible for his self-respect to break it. Fighting back his tears and with lowered eyes he asked, 'So should I go away?'

There came no response from any side. Avoiding each other's gaze, everyone was looking away. For a long time, no one spoke. Then Jeevan's thin and unsteady voice was heard, 'If you don't have faith in this programme . . . how will you be able to participate in it wholeheartedly?'

Thinking of the grave consequences, Ali quickly said, 'But for now you will surely participate in this programme, won't you?'

In a tone of helplessness Harish said, 'I am participating, am I not?'

Both the Bengalis and Jeevan looked at Harish with enthusiasm. He too felt that the fearful crisis had passed. At that very moment, BM, looking at Dada, asked Harish, 'Will you participate in an armed robbery?'

In a distressed but firm tone Harish said, 'I am against that . . . the aims of the party are harmed by that.'

Still looking at Dada, BM asked, 'So?'

This tiny word placed before everyone an inescapably sorrowful consequence. Dada was motionless. Jeevan took a long breath. Akhil shook his head, '*No hope*. There is no way out.' And his companion also shook his head.

Again that stillness. Not seeing any other option, Harish bowed his head and said, 'As you wish . . . If you ever need me, I'll come again.' Clamping his lips with his teeth and rising all at once to hide the tears in his eyes, he climbed down the stairs.

Harish was walking, his lips clamped under his teeth. He was afraid lest the agitation in his heart burst out as tears. His head was dizzy from the unexpected attack. He was walking on, as though unaware, along the same path that he had taken from the station. Just as a cart-horse walks along the familiar practiced road, Harish's feet kept moving on the familiar path. Crossing the lane, he reached the deserted bazaar and kept walking.

Hearing a loud admonishment, he turned around—a red turban and a long loose brown coat. A policeman.

After some choice and weighty abuse, the policeman asked in an angry and authoritative voice, 'Where are you wandering about?'

Harish responded, changing his demeanour according to the situation, 'Nowhere, Sir!' His voice was trembling in fear.

'What are you doing here . . . did you go to the liquor shop?' The policeman scolded.

'Sir!' Harish said.

'You scoundrel, have you been drinking?'

'No, Sir!'

'So then you had gone to your mother's . . .!' The policeman used extremely vulgar language that would have enraged any respectable man.

But Harish was not a respectable man at that time; he was a drunk coolie, a criminal. Whining, he said in a trembling voice, 'Sir!'

'Off to the police station!' the policeman threatened. 'You scoundrel, after drinking you plan to break into someone's home at night!'

Harish again responded in a whining tone, 'No, Sir, I am a poor coolie . . . I was just going home.'

Accustomed to hearing this kind of entreaty every day, the policeman's heart had turned to stone. 'At two o'clock at night poor men don't wander about in the streets! Those who wander are wastrels and thieves! What do you have . . . show me!'

Harish had a pistol tucked in his waist. If the policeman saw it, he would be in serious trouble. Taking a step back in fear, he shook out his blanket and said, 'Sir, I have nothing on me . . . only seventeen annas. I went to the liquor shop but it was closed.'

'If you have nothing, then let's go to the police station!' The policeman was evidently angry; taking Harish along, he started walking. Caught in a quandary, Harish walked behind the policeman, flattering him and begging for forgiveness.

The policeman heaped more abuses, 'Do you imagine yourself to be my father-in-law that I should let you go home! They are all like you. If I let everyone go, whom should I fine—my father-in-law?'

Another policeman on duty appeared in front of them on a bicycle. Harish was now silently repenting: it would have been much better if he had managed to escape the first one. Now he had to contend with two. Both policemen greeted one another. The one with the bicycle asked, 'What's going on?'

The one on foot pointed towards Harish and said, 'This scoundrel was wandering around at this time of night, who knows in search of what. I am taking him to the police station.'

The one with the bicycle said, 'Well, at least we accomplished something!' Pushing his bicycle towards the first policeman, he said, 'Just hold this, Bashir!'

Bashir understood his companion's intent. He turned to Harish and ordered, 'Hey, hold that bicycle, what are you staring at?' And then said to his friend, 'Pandit, give us a match! It's so damned cold, let's light a bidi.'

The Pandit policeman took out a matchbox from his pocket with his left hand and gave it to Bashir, and stringing his caste-thread over his ear with his right hand he moved towards the gutter.

Bashir lit the match and started smoking his bidi. Harish propped the bicycle against an electric pole, shoved Bashir with all his force on to the other policeman, took the bicycle and started pedalling furiously. He had passed just one electric pole when he heard the sharp sound of a policeman's whistle. He immediately turned into a nearby lane. From there into a second one, then a third. He was cycling recklessly. Soon he faced a road again. Beneath an electric pole he saw a policeman with a red turban and a brown coat, standing alert with a whistle in one hand. Riding very slowly now he came directly to the policeman.

'Salaam, Havaldar Sahib! Why are they blowing the whistle, Sir?' He asked the policeman.

Without looking at him the policeman answered, 'Who knows, it comes from the southern direction.'

'I got scared,' Harish laughed in a polite way. 'Has a riot occurred somewhere?'

'Where are you going?' the policeman asked.

'I am going to the "8-Down"—I have engine duty. It leaves for Calcutta at three. Aadaab, Sir.'

'Aadaab.' The policeman turned away.

Harish reached the station. He put the bicycle aside. The train for Allahabad was just departing. He boarded it.

Upon Harish's departure, the stillness of despair and hopelessness filled the hovel once again. Akhil was the one to break the silence. Firmly pressing the fists of both hands under his armpits, he looked at Dada and said, 'Now what?'

Shaking his head, Dada spoke while looking at the floor, 'Now, please give this central *charge* to someone else. I cannot handle all these complications. I will do whatever I am told to do, or else I will go away to the mountains. I am a soldier . . . I have nothing to do with these discussions and debates.'

No one accepted this. Looking at the comrades, BM said, 'The one who objected to your being *in charge* has left. Now why do you say such things?'

Everyone said, *'No, No!'* in a determined way and nodding their heads, gave their approval to what BM had said. Ali took a deep breath. Perhaps he wanted to say something, but then judging it to be unnecessary, he slowly exhaled and without speaking, bent his head.

Moving his head to indicate his relief, Akhil said, 'And now . . .?'

Drawing a line with his nail on the binding of the book he held in his hand, BM said, 'Before deciding on our future plans, it is essential that we take stock of the present situation. When we have a *member* of the party who is *in charge* of an entire state, who has a special status in the party, who is familiar with all the *actions* of the party, who has the distinction of having participated in a couple of special *actions*, who is attempting to make his own separate party, who wants to keep to himself the *connection* with other members in his state by painting Dada as stupid and useless, who has amassed considerable money in the name of the party—how much damage can such a person inflict on the party! . . . The most worrisome question is this: what will come of the kinds of relationships he has with girls? Will we now have to take on the task of providing abortion pills? Whatever might have been said so far against the revolutionaries, no one questioned their morals. And then who is responsible for the money that has been taken and squandered in the name of the party? Whomever we contact in Punjab about money says, 'Harish took it.' At the very least, we have lost Punjab. We dare not show our faces there as representatives of the party. Before proceeding further, please think about all this. Until this problem is solved, we cannot do anything in Punjab.'

Akhil's Bengali companion said in a serious voice, '*But Punjab is very important!*'

Ali looked at BM and said, 'What do you mean, should Harish be shot?'

Everyone was shaken. Only Dada remained calm.

BM said, 'It is you who must decide. I have simply presented the situation to you.'

Looking at BM, Ali said, 'But you alone know what he has done so far, and what its impact is.'

'It is another matter if you accord him greater significance than the party,' BM responded.

'No, no, nobody is greater than the party,' Akhil raised his head and said in a decisive tone.

Looking at his fingernails, Jeevan said, 'But now he is no longer working for the party.'

'But he is not indifferent to the party either. In fact, he is capturing the field of the party,' BM responded.

Akhil shook his head and said, *'Shoot him!'* His companion agreed, *'Yes!'*

Ali asked, 'Is it advisable to give such a dire turn to a mere difference of opinion? Whatever BM has said about money and girls, that may well be true, but Dada, why don't you go there once and see for yourself?'

BM said, 'I can't take the responsibility of taking Dada to Punjab—given the state in which Harish has run away from here . . . and that all *connections* are with him.'

Biting his moustache, Dada lifted his head and said, 'Let's see who dares to raise a hand against me. I will go . . . Harish . . . luxury is a bad thing. This quarrel about girls! . . . This happened once in 1917 as well.'

Akhil said, 'No, this is not enough, we must be able to trust our men. *Shoot him!*' His companion agreed, *'Yes—yes!'*

Dada counselled, 'This is a very serious matter.'

BM asked, 'Do you mean that it is dangerous?'

Dada looked sharply at him and said, 'It is not the danger . . . I am not afraid of anyone . . . but if you decide, then it will have to be done.'

Akhil and his companion again pressed, *'Yes—Yes.'*

'What do you say, Jeevan?' Dada asked.

'Whatever you say.'

'I don't say anything, you give your vote.'

Jeevan said, 'Whatever the party decides.'

'The party is in front of you,' Dada was irritated now. He looked at BM.

He responded, *'Shoot!'*

Akhil's companion said, *'Yes, shoot!'*

Without lifting his head, Jeevan said, *'Yes, shoot!'*

Ali was next. He looked at Dada and said, 'I accept the decision of the *majority.*'

After a few moments of silence, Dada said, 'He will go to Punjab.' Then looking at BM he asked, 'Who is the other man you need?'

'Jeevan!' BM responded.

Looking at Jeevan, Dada asked, 'Do you accept?'

'Yes!' Jeevan responded, raising his eyes.

The Labourer's Home

The passenger train from Haridwar stopped at Lahore station. Travellers began descending on to the platform. A coolie from the *railway workshop*, wrapped in a blanket, and with a couple of tools in his hand, exited towards the railway line. Seeing the man take the wrong way, a policeman stopped him, 'Hey, where are you going . . . Show me your ticket!'

Returning, the coolie pleaded abjectly and showed his ticket.

'Is this the way? . . . Where are you going?' The policeman questioned again.

'Sir, I will cut my way through to the quarters from here. From the other side it is a long detour.'

The policeman left him, and the coolie, singing a ghazal—

Cast a glance at this hidden flame of anguish as you leave;
See how someone's youth turns to ashes as you leave[*]

---

[*] Ghazal by Fani Badayuni (1879—1961), (*mal-e-soz-e-gham hae! nihani dekhte jaao*). The verse is slightly misquoted in the original Hindi text, which suggests Yashpal may have been writing from memory.

—walked across the railway lines and on to the roads that twisted amidst the factories behind the station.

December days. The winter of Lahore! On the roads covered in smog, one could barely see a few yards ahead in the glow of electric lights. Smoke pierced the eye. Beneath the electric lamps, in the smoke- and fog-filled air, rays of light spread out like small triangular tents for some distance and then disappeared. The young coolie walked along the road, humming. On reaching dark corners, he would turn around and run his gaze over the patches of light spread here and there along the road. On approaching closer to the mill quarters, he stopped to light a bidi, and for some time kept staring at the road behind. Not seeing anyone following him, he dove into the line of quarters.

The youth stopped in front of one quarter. A tattered sack curtain hung over the door. He rattled the bolt.

'Who is it?' a voice questioned from within.

'Akhtar, open the door! It's me,' the youth replied.

'Who?' another voice came from within.

'It is me . . . Sardar!'

Sardar was the same youth whom we came to know in Kanpur as Harish.

The door opened. Upon entering, Harish bolted the door and said, 'Salaam Bhabhi! What is Akhtar doing . . . has he fallen asleep?'

'May you live long! May your youth prosper!' The woman blessed him. She was wrapped in a red phulwari (a khaddar dupatta embroidered with silk thread).* She was wearing a salwar and kurta of thick cloth. Because of the severe cold, she had covered her nose and mouth with her dupatta and kept shrinking into her clothes. Sensing a deep sadness in the woman's voice, Harish asked, 'Bhabhi, what's the matter?'

Wiping her eyes with her dupatta, Bhabhi responded, 'What can I tell you, my brother! I don't know what has come upon him since this evening. Returning home at dusk, he said to me—you take the girl and go to the village. He has brought a bottle of liquor. He insisted that I go. I said, you may kill me, but I will not go. He has also brought a butcher's knife from somewhere. Showing it to me, he said, "If you are so stubborn, I will indeed kill you!" . . . I said, go ahead! I will not leave you. Since then he has been sitting in a corner, wrapped in a blanket, with his knife . . . the bottle is with him.'

'He drank some?'

'Not yet,' Bhabhi wiped her eyes. 'But who knows what he's thinking. When Munni came to him lovingly, he shouted at her. Said, "Take her away"!'

'Hmm . . . well, let's go in.' Saying this, Harish went in.

There was a shed-like room beyond the small yard. On one side of the door was an earthen stove. Some jars and tins were placed before it. On the wall to the right some clothes hung on a rope fixed with pegs, and on a cot below lay a torn and dirty quilt. A small kerosene lamp placed on

---

* This parenthetical explanation is included in the original text.

the stove cast a reddish light on the floor and smoke on the ceiling. A few sparks from burnt firewood could be seen in the stove. On the floor near the cot, wrapped in a blanket, sat Akhtar.

Harish came in and called, 'Akhtar, my brother, what's the matter?'

Scratching his trimmed beard, Akhtar lifted his head and asked, 'Sardar? . . . Come and sit, Sardar!'

'What has happened to you?' Harish asked.

Drawing a deep breath, Akhtar lowered his head and spoke, 'Sardar, will you do something for me? . . . I trust you.'

'I am ready—whatever you say,' Harish said, sitting beside Akhtar.

'Will you accompany Jamila and the girl home? It will be dangerous for you, but it is just four miles from your own village. How will anyone recognize you now . . . can you do this much?' Akhtar asked, looking at him.

'Let's forget the danger . . . why are you sending Bhabhi away?'

'You must take them and leave right away,' Akhtar insisted.

'At least tell me, why? I am very sad that you are hiding something from me . . . have I ever kept anything from you? . . . Where is the knife?' Harish asked. Jamila was sitting by the stove, her chin on her knees, looking worriedly at the two friends.

'Hmm . . .' Akhtar drew a deep breath and looking at Jamila, he said, 'You go out for a bit.'

Jamila stood up, but tears fell from her eyes.

'Stay, Bhabhi!' Harish admonished and then, addressing Akhtar, he said, 'You don't have faith in Bhabhi? Had she been that kind of a person, would I be sitting here?'

'You don't understand, it's that kind of a matter!'

'All right, Bhabhi, you go out to the yard for a minute,' Harish said. Jamila went to the courtyard, weeping. Harish put his hand on Akhtar's shoulder and said, 'So now tell me.'

Akhtar bit his lips, drew a deep breath, and spoke, 'The head mistri* has ruined my life. It was my turn to become a *fitter*. For three years he has been blocking my promotion. Last year, during the month of Baisakh, I begged and pleaded with him. You see, now that I'm getting old, it is difficult to work so hard. . . . Then this daughter was born. I already have a son. We could manage if I got a promotion. Both Zahoor and Harnam Singh, who had joined with me, became fitters two years ago. They are paid sixty or seventy. And I am still at twenty-six! That bastard . . . he always files some false complaint or the other. He asked me for eighty rupees. I pawned Jamila's nose-ring for forty, borrowed forty from the same moneylender and gave him eighty. The moneylender kept charging five rupees interest each month, which became thirty rupees. The head mistri makes 250 each month, plus fifty or sixty on top of that . . . now when my turn came, he said, "What have you ever given me?" . . . The jobber's nephew, the Brahmin's new

---

* A worker—overseer.

boy, joined hardly a year ago—he has been made a fitter.
You know why? . . . He has brought his newly married
wife from the village! And she goes to watch over the kids
playing at the mistri's home and there that bastard . . . the
mistri . . . he plays with her . . . he grabs so many women
from the line . . . do you understand! One goes to his home
to sweep, another to wash clothes, another to watch over
the kids . . . you understand? I can't bear this humiliation,
Sardar! Our own kids starve to death . . . we fill the bellies
of these scoundrels and on top of that, this disgrace! You
take both of them to the village. The mistri goes once to
check on the engine in the evening. Today I will finish off
the scoundrel . . . and then a Kashmiri and then . . . I have
no wish to be arrested. I will put an end to myself, you
understand, don't you? . . . You are my only friend . . . You
are a brave man . . . You understand . . . that is why I trust
you, you know.'

Harish nodded and asked, 'And Bhabhi? . . . Have you
looked at her eyes? She will die weeping.'

'You have also left your home, don't people in your
family cry? You tell her, she can join them.'

'You talk about me, Akhtar, but did I leave my family
for my own honour?' Harish asked. 'And have you forgotten
the time when you fell sick? For a whole year Bhabhi took
care of you by washing people's dishes . . . does she not
have any claim over you? You would have been put in jail
or hanged a long time ago. Do you remember, when you
had lost your job in the railways, and you stole that purse,
how bitterly she wept? . . . If she had not reformed you,

what would have become of you? And you will leave her to her tears? . . . Are you not ashamed! And why have you bought this bottle? Without it, you lack courage . . . but after drinking, you will commit murder! And then what will become of your children?'

'It is just this thought that makes me weak, Sardar! That is why I bought this bottle. Since Jamila came, she has never let me drink . . . You know how she forced me to quit. After a long day at the factory, I would go with the other labourers to the liquor shop. She would come to the factory door and wait. The other labourers would laugh. I used to feel so embarrassed. I would come home and beat her. In a drunken state, I beat her a couple of times. Then one day she said to me: "Good, beat me! But beat me while you are sober. At least you'll know that you have beaten me." She showed me her bruised body. I felt great fear. I touched her body and swore: I will not drink again . . . and then I never did. Before that, I must have sworn on the Holy Quran twenty times and still continued to drink,' Akhtar said, with a deep sigh.

'You see now? She is freezing to death outside. Listen to her crying! . . . Bhabhi, Bhabhi! Come inside!' Harish called.

Jamila came inside. She started crying bitterly. Harish looked at Akhtar and said, 'Aren't you ashamed? . . . Now you console her!'

Akhtar looked at the ceiling and sighed, 'When I think of that scoundrel of an *engineer*, my blood boils, Sardar!'

'Let the mistri be, I will take care of him.' Gesturing towards Jamila, Harish said, 'Just look at her! If he doesn't come around, let go of the quarrel. I have to die in any case, so why not for you? Why should your children be ruined? For me, it will be difficult to survive now.'

'Really? Why?' Akhtar asked.

'It's just that my comrades have turned against me.'

Akhtar bristled. 'Is that true? Then you must stay here!'

Jamila was still weeping. Harish said, 'Bhabhi, I haven't eaten for two days, and you are needlessly crying. Here, take these . . .' He placed Akhtar's knife and bottle at Jamila's feet, and repeated, 'Bhabhi, I haven't eaten for two days, are you listening? . . . Now no one will ask you to leave.'

Jamila started sobbing uncontrollably.

Harish said to Akhtar, 'Get up, drink a glass of water, give some to Bhabhi and some to me as well . . . you must stop her crying.'

Akhtar kept sitting and said, 'Be quiet now, Jamila, let it go.'

But Jamila could not stop. Harish gave Akhtar a push, 'Get up, and give her a glass of water.' Akhtar laughed at the push. 'Oh, let it be, *yaar*!'

Harish didn't back down, he said threateningly, 'Get up, give her some water to drink . . . and ask for forgiveness.'

'Ok, Boss . . .' Akhtar got up. He filled water in a tin beaker. Going up to Jamila, he said, 'Here, drink this, it is your brother's command. Now stop, this is enough!'

But it was as if Jamila did not even hear him, she kept crying.

Harish gestured to Akhtar that he should touch Jamila's feet.

Akhtar laughed and said, 'Ok, Madam, I fall at your feet, now drink this water, why do you want me to get thrashed? And if this isn't enough, then here . . .' Akhtar touched Jamila's foot with his hand.

Jamila exploded. 'Don't tease me! Enough, I will not live here now.'

'So, you heard that?' Akhtar turned to Harish.

Harish stifled his laughter and again gesturing towards Jamila's feet, asked Akhtar to touch them.

'So, should I place my head on your feet?' Akhtar laughed and asked Jamila.

Showing her anger, Jamila slapped away Akhtar's hand. 'Enough, I have said it: don't bother me! I won't live here now.'

'Ok, then don't live here, I will also go with you, but drink this glass of water, otherwise you will see my dead . . .'

'Be quiet!' Raising her face in fury, Jamila threatened.

'Drink this glass of water! Otherwise, I swear . . .'

'I swear I will die if you swear!'

'Whose oath is bigger: yours or mine?'

'Enough, I don't know!'

Harish was laughing. He said, 'All right, Bhabhi, you have to drink, I swear upon myself, upon God, upon the Quran, upon the whole world!'

'Yes, now everyone is after me!' Jamila said, wiping her tears and taking a sip from the beaker.

'No, no, you must drink all of it,' Harish repeated.

'And what if I can't?' Jamila was annoyed.

'Then I must swear again . . .' Harish threatened her.

Somehow, Jamila forced herself to drink the water. Harish said, 'Yes, now let's talk about food. I am really starving.'

'Jamila, come to your senses! Tell us, what have you cooked?' Akhtar asked.

'I have cooked stones! What did you bring home? Munni went to bed crying for dal.'

'While you were wasting money on alcohol, you scoundrel!' Harish scolded Akhtar.

'Now don't remind me of that,' Akhtar drew a deep breath.

'I mixed gram and wheat flour with salt and made some rotis,' Jamila told Akhtar.

Searching his pocket, Akhtar said to Harish, 'You wait, I will buy a bit of meat curry. How will you eat dry roti?'

'Bhabhi, don't you have some jaggery?' Harish asked.

'Yes, indeed, I also gave Munni some jaggery with her roti . . . And there is some ghee as well, let me mix it in . . . And let him bring some curry . . . But how will you eat the curry from the market? . . . It will have just a few scraps of meat in it.'

'Such airs!' Akhtar said. 'How will he eat curry from the market indeed! Does his mother wait for him with a princely stew each day?'

'Oh, what are you saying!' Jamila looked compassionately at Harish.

'I think of Bhabhi as my mother,' said Harish. 'Don't you go out in this cold. When we have jaggery and ghee, what else do we need? Come, Bhabhi, bring it quickly!'

Raking the coals in the stove, Jamila fetched some ghee from a clay vessel, put it in an enamel bowl, placed it on the stove and mixed some jaggery in it. Placing the bowl between her husband and Harish, she said, 'The rotis have turned cold, let me warm them up for you.' Then she put the hot rotis in front of the two men on a clay dish.

Taking a morsel of a roti, Harish asked, 'Bhabhi, what will you eat? The two of us will easily finish these!'

'Oh Allah! How little you eat! You eat, there is plenty for me. There is enough flour at home.' Then, looking at Harish, she said, 'Just see, how your face has shrivelled! Where have you been wandering?'

'Don't even ask, Bhabhi, far and wide!' Harish responded.

'He makes bombs and wanders around in search of suraaj!* How can rich gentlemen like you ever attain suraaj? You have your properties to worry about! Now if it were up to us labourers and rural folks, we would topple the rulers in a day!'

'Then why don't you? Get up and topple them!' Harish shot right back.

'Should we topple them? . . . But then people like the mistri would rule. He is a black Hindustani, after all. But see what a bloodsucker he is!'

'And you too are a black Hindustani! . . . Why would people like the mistri rule? Why not people like you? Whoever strives for it will rule!' Harish responded.

---

* Akhtar says 'suraaj', literally good rule, instead of swaraj, though it is probably just a more colloquial version of the term.

'As if we would ever rule! Our lot is to die now, and it will be to die then! We can't even get better wages, and you say we will rule the land!' Akhtar taunted.

'And your only concern is better wages!'

'So what should we do: wave the flag of the Congress?'

'If you all were to unite and carry the flag of the Congress, the Congress would be yours. You tell me, who is in the majority: you or the rich gentlemen? If you were to unite, they would dance to your tune!'

'But we have no money, Boss!' Akhtar cocked his thumb at Harish. 'What can we do without money?'

'It is you who produce money, and yet you beg from them . . .'

'Yes, this is the name of the game,' Akhtar interrupted. 'Now you talk differently, Sardar . . . like Rafiq. Rafiq also talks like this.'

'Does Rafiq come here?' Harish asked.

'Yes, Brother, he does come here. I feel terrified of him,' Jamila spoke up. 'That little fistful of a man, and snip-snip, his tongue moves, like a pair of scissors. They gather in fours and fives, those men, talking about strikes, and furiously smoking bidis. "Unite," he says, "unite," and tells stories about strikes. Brother, I am really very scared of that fellow. Earlier, we got our twenty annas daily in the railways . . . that was eleven years ago. But we lost that job during the strike. Now we barely make ends meet. Where will we go if there's another strike? You explain this to him, Brother! Akhtar will follow anyone who impresses him with a few words!'

'Stop this nonsense!' Akhtar said with mock anger. 'You're so wise, aren't you?'

Placing a finger on her chin, Jamila complained to Harish, 'Look, how easily he scolds me . . . he doesn't even let me talk!'

'Ok, listen,' Akhtar addressed Harish. 'Will you sleep here?'

'Where else would I go now?' Harish responded.

'In that case, we will surely freeze to death! There is only one quilt, and that too is torn. The two of us manage somehow . . .'

'A curse be upon you!' Jamila flung her hand in the air. 'Have you lost all shame?'

Harish laughed and said, 'You manage as you do. I will just lie here with your blanket.'

'Is this even a blanket! . . . Not even good enough for bundling straw!' Akhtar said, pointing towards the blanket. 'What do you say, Jamila?'

'The two of you take care of yourselves, and stop worrying about me!' Harish replied, looking away.

Shaking his knees, Akhtar said, 'Well, it seems your brother will be the death of us today!'

'I am telling you, I will leave everything and go away, if you talk like this again!' Jamila glared at him in embarrassment and mock anger, then covered her face with her dupatta.

'Yes, indeed, you will smash through the wall, won't you? Ok, listen, Sardar! Let's take a swig each from this bottle, then who cares even if we lie in the dew outside . . . What do you say?' Akhtar suggested.

'Again the bottle! It's the bottle that is destroying you all!'

'Yes, indeed!' Jamila agreed.

Harish continued, 'Instead of drinking each night through the winter, couldn't one get a new quilt made?'

'Here you go again with your Congress preaching!' Akhtar responded irritably. 'You would learn if you had to suffer through each night here! The worker spends four paise to get through the night. A quilt costs five rupees. In the time it takes for him to save five rupees, he would have already gone to hell!' Akhtar kept trying to convince Harish. 'Now it would be a feat if you could persuade Kartar Singh to quit! The bastard makes ten annas a day and has four brats to feed!'

'Will you eat your food or just keep blathering?' Jamila interrupted.

'And then his wretched wife, each year she gives birth! He always owes a few months' rent for his quarter. And on top of that moneylenders have sucked the blood out of him. But he is a true tiger! No matter what happens, as soon as he returns from the factory, he downs a bottle of liquor and passes out! One day over—Allah will see to the next!'

'But why does he keep producing children?' Harish asked in exasperation.

'Does *he* produce children?' Akhtar said. 'You tell me, what should he do? How should I explain this to you!' Pointing towards Jamila he said, 'Now what can I say in front of her . . . what's a man to do once he returns home after labouring like a beast for ten hours . . . except to forget himself somehow! If I had my way, I would give poison to the wives of all these bloody workers, and instead bring a hundred whores to live in this row.'

'What blasphemy you spew!' Jamila stopped him.

'Blasphemy indeed!' Akhtar scolded her. 'You would learn if you had a brood of brats gnawing away at you! We have but two, and you have left one of them with Amma so he can be fed and raised. Now you tell me: if you had any more, where would you keep them?' Akhtar looked at Harish. 'And do you know, a Kashmiri here has kept a few bedraggled women—as sorry-looking as cast-off shoes! The bastard rents them out for twenty-five paise a go and easily earns fifteen—twenty rupees a night! Every six months he sells off the old ones and brings in a few more wretches. Because of him, syphilis has spread through the entire *line* of houses. And we can't find anyone to put a bullet through that bastard's head!

'Listen, you have a pistol, don't you? I want to kill just three men. First, the engineer; second, this bastard, the Kashmiri; and third, that treacherous jobber!* The entire *line* has been ruined because of them. That jobber takes a cut from the salary of each worker for months on end. He has a moneylending business on the side . . . charges an anna per rupee as daily interest, and as soon as the workers start to band together, he pulls out a few, sends them packing, and brings in new ones. The bastard—he has put dozens of

---

* Jaabar (a jobber) is the contractor who hires workers for the factory. [Footnote in original.]

spies to work. I swear, he has hired thugs to beat up Rafiq. If I could only put these three to rest, thousands would rest easy!'

Jamila cupped both hands over her ears. 'My god! Brother, just look at what has happened to him! How he talks!'

Akhtar became even more irritated. 'So what am I saying? It is you who could be turned into a whore*—they have already created thousands! Then you too would go and sit in someone's home . . .'

Jamila interrupted him again, 'Heaven save us, what evil-tongued words you utter! God punishes us for such thoughts!'

Akhtar's anger rose. 'Indeed, He punishes! Is He asleep then? . . . Can He not see anything? These bastards are sucking the blood of thousands!'

'Why are you speaking such nonsense? Be quiet!' Harish scolded him. 'Let's say you kill them, then what? . . . Another engineer, another Kashmiri and another jobber will arrive tomorrow, what will you be able to do? . . . Here you are, angling to be a martyr! You give him bribes yourself, yet you want to kill the jobber!'

'So should I die instead of giving him a bribe? One way or another, one dies after all!'

'Talk some sense! If you must die, then die in a way that makes a difference!'

'What can I do? I worry because of this woman!'

---

* 'Raand'—a word that could mean either a whore or a widow.

'And if she had not been around, you would have become a drunken ass!'

For some time, both fell silent. Akhtar picked his teeth with a matchstick. The troubles of his past and future life appeared before him in their individual as well as their class-related aspect. Harish was wondering what path he could pursue now that his disagreement with his comrades had become evident. Until now, only his attachment to his ideas and to his comrades had held him in check.

Among the three of them, if anyone was content, it was only Jamila. Having fed her portion of the rotis to Harish, she was now contentedly kneading dough for herself.

Akhtar broke the silence that filled the room. Lighting a bidi, he said, 'Wherever you look, there's a fight . . .'

'It is precisely to end such fights that we want Swarajya. But you call this Congress preaching,' Harish said, finishing his food and washing his hands.

'When Suraaj comes, do you think all this will end? If you can just explain this to me, I will be ready to lay down my life for your Suraaj. Come, let's start right away!' Akhtar responded heatedly.

'Ok, you tell me then, what is the cure?' Harish asked.

'There is no cure, we will simply die . . . and you wait and see, in ten years, there will be so many unemployed labourers that we won't find work for even four annas!'

'And what if the labourers themselves become rulers? . . . But even if labourers start earning three–four rupees a day, if they still keep producing children at this rate, unemployed people will inevitably line up and wages will fall again!' Harish said.

'Oh, but then the labourers will become gentlemen! And gentlemen don't produce children like this,' Akhtar replied.

'Then he is right, isn't he?' Harish said.

'Who, Rafiq?' asked Akhtar. Then he said, 'Good!' and rose. Spreading sackcloth on a mat near the stove, they both lay down and covered themselves by joining the two blankets together. Jamila went to lie down on the cot.

Lying next to Akhtar, Harish asked, 'You've kept my European clothes safely, haven't you?'

'Yes, they are on the clothesline. Jamila wrapped them in her new dupatta.'

'I will leave in the morning. Listen, my friend, please arrange a meeting with Rafiq.'

'But you are a bomb-guy! . . . What will you gain from meeting him? . . . No, you have changed your stance now, you talk differently. Have you left off the bomb-games then?'

'No, no more bombs now . . . It is Rafiq whom I want to meet. And about how many men would you say are on your side?'

'If I open the bottle, they are all on my side, otherwise none,' Akhtar burst into a laugh. 'When lay-offs are in sight, they are all ready to kiss the jobber's feet . . . and that bastard, every fifth or sixth month, he cracks the whip and announces that lay-offs are imminent.'

In just a few minutes, Akhtar started snoring. Lying quite still in the dark, Harish thought about himself. He wanted to wake up Akhtar and seek his advice, but what advice could Akhtar give? Akhtar and his friends knew only two paths: either despair or blood!

Forgetting his own dilemma, Harish started thinking: How can the strength of labourers, indomitable like the lightning that thunders across the sky, be unified and used for revolution?

Three Forms

Shailbala was sitting in her room writing an urgent letter. A servant informed her that two men had come to meet her. Continuing to write, she said, 'Ask them for their names.'

The servant returned with a piece of paper. As soon as she saw it, she came outside. Joining her palms together, she greeted the two men and took them inside. Seating them on the cushioned armchairs, she looked at BM and asked with a smile, 'You have graced us with your presence after a long time—I hope all is well.'

She looked at BM's companion with a cursory glance. The gravity of physical strength was manifest in the face of the powerful, well-built man. Not tenderness, but determination shone in his large eyes. Shail addressed BM again in a low voice: 'When did you come? How is Harish?'

Pointing towards the window on the wall behind him, BM asked, 'Can we talk here?'

In place of a smile, a serious expression came over Shail's face. 'Yes,' she said, bowing her head, then she rose and went to the adjoining room behind the curtain, closed the door from inside, dragged her chair close to BM and sat down.

Gesturing towards his companion, BM introduced him in a low voice, 'This is Dada.'

Looking at Dada, Shailbala greeted him again, and smiling respectfully, she said, 'I've heard so much about you, now finally I meet you.'

BM said, 'Dada wants to ask you something.'

Dada suddenly asked, 'Where is Harish?'

With some surprise and apprehension Shailbala replied, 'Why? . . . I do not know. He came here about three weeks ago. He had to meet someone here. Then he left—I think to meet you all. Since then he has not come here.'

'So in the past three weeks Harish has not met you?' BM asked.

'Do you know where he may be found?' Dada's question had sparked a fear in Shailbala's mind that Harish may have been arrested again, but BM's question suggested that it might be something else altogether.

Looking at Shailbala's chair, Dada said, 'You should tell us where he is.'

As though Dada's words were not clear enough, BM immediately coughed and said, 'It is something very important.'

Shail looked at both of them with surprise. Neither the anger in Dada's tone nor BM's attempt to control the situation had escaped her notice. She asked in a surprised voice, 'What are you both saying? I'm afraid I don't understand.'

'The fact is that we can't find him, and due to this the party is suffering several losses. It is astonishing that he would come here and not meet you!' BM continued the conversation, 'because often our messages are received and dispatched from here.'

Without even looking at Dada, Shailbala could sense his growing disquiet. As if in accordance with her wish, Dada said, 'Look, the blunt question is whether for you the party is more important, or Harish.'

With the apprehension of not knowing what lies ahead, Shailbala looked at Dada, eyes wide with surprise, and responded, 'For me the party is indeed more important, but I am not able to understand the import of your question.'

Dada asked in an even more severe tone, 'What is your relation with Harish?'

With increasing astonishment, Shailbala responded, 'Why? . . . He is my *friend.*'

The red lining in Dada's eyes expanded. Restraining himself, he said, '*Friend* . . . what does *friend* mean? What does *friendship* between boys and girls mean?'

Shailbala was stunned. Unable to give any answer, she kept looking at the floor for a few moments. Her wheatish face turned rosy. Addressing Dada she said, 'I have immense respect for you in my heart. I used to think that you people are very liberal in your thinking . . . but now I see something else altogether. BM had spoken in a very different way about women's independence and old traditions . . . but let it be. I can't understand why you are concerned about my personal relations.' When she began, Shail was speaking in a humble voice, but her tone had sharpened by the time she reached these last words. She turned her face towards the window and in the same agitated tone, addressing BM, she continued, 'I want to help you people as far as I am able to, but I won't hear any criticism of my personal conduct from anyone but Father.'

The ground gave way under Dada's feet—he was taken aback. Thinking he should be civil to a woman, he swallowed his humiliation. Holding his breath, he bit his moustache ruminatively, then asked, 'Why, are you not a member of the party? As a member of the party, you will have to remain *disciplined*. Do you know how much loss you have caused us?'

Shailbala, holding her breath in astonishment, and BM, with trepidation, looked at Dada, but he did not pay attention to any of this, and continued, 'You have rendered useless the right hand of the party. The man who earlier carried his head in the palm of his hand, today uses the excuse of public unity just to save his own life, all because of this friendship of yours. . . . You came to help us, but you have destroyed us, and even now, disregarding the party's *discipline*, you refuse to tell us about his location.'

Shame, agitation and humiliation constricted Shailbala's throat. Tears came to her eyes, but ignoring them, she said, 'Look, you are humiliating me needlessly . . . Mindful of the respect due to you, I have listened, but you have gone too far. Who says I am a member of the party? I don't even know it, and I am a member of the party!' With all her strength, she tried not to let her tears become visible. A tremor ran through her body and her tears spilled on to her hands. Ashamed of her tears, she was wiping them with her aanchal, face turned towards the wall, when footsteps were heard outside. In an authoritative tone she said, 'Wait!'

A voice came from outside, 'Bibiji!'

Shail wiped her tears, gestured to her guests with one hand to remain seated and went outside.

In her absence, Dada looked at BM and said, 'You told me she is a party member . . . that she wants to leave her home to work for the party.'

With a wry laugh, BM responded, 'You see her manner?'

Dada slapped his hand against his forehead in irritation and said, 'Oh, I can't understand anything . . . how I've been humiliated!'

When she came outside, the servant gave Shailbala a piece of paper and an envelope. On the paper was written just one letter in English, 'H.' Mad with anger, Shailbala took a step towards the room so she could say, look, here comes your Harish, for whom you have been hounding me, but an inarticulate fear stopped her in her tracks. Envelope in hand, she went outside. Seeing her, Harish got off the horse-carriage.

Shailbala asked, 'Where have you come from?'

Seeing her red eyes, Harish asked, 'What is it?'

'Nothing,' Shailbala said. 'Please leave immediately. Do you have a safe place to go to?'

Sensing her agitation, Harish said in a carefree way, 'Now there is no safe place for me . . . but why?'

Shailbala twisted the envelope in her hand, and not seeing any other option she said, 'Go, go to Yashoda's place.'

'How can I go there?' Harish asked helplessly.

'I beg you, please go there. I will come to fetch you in half an hour—now go, quickly!' She shouted, '*Driver! Driver!* Please take him.'

Harish got in, and the car sped off. While returning to the room, she opened the envelope in her hand. Inside, there was a paper with just one line typed in English: *Dada and BM want to shoot Harish save him—a friend of the party.* Flames of fire danced before Shail's eyes. Her step faltered. Then she breathed a sigh of relief, 'Oh God!'

Calling the servant, Shail asked, 'Who gave you this envelope?'

The servant told her that just five minutes after the two gentlemen had arrived, another gentleman came on a bicycle, gave him the envelope and asked him to promptly hand it to her.

Taking a deep breath, she lifted her head proudly and entered the room. Looking at Dada, she said, 'You speak of the discipline of your party? You say, I have destroyed your party? Here, look at the discipline of your party!' So saying she placed the piece of paper in front of Dada.

Dada paused to read what was written on the paper. The paper shook with the force of his breath. Extending his hand, BM wanted to take it. Shailbala leapt, grabbed the paper, twisted it and shoved it inside her blouse.

BM said, 'Please give me the paper!'

Shailbala responded in a dry tone, 'Excuse me, I made a mistake. I can't commit any further treachery.'

Dada stood up. Cracking the knuckles of both hands behind his back, he spoke, looking at the wall, 'Forgive me,

I was uncivil. I was told you are a member of the party. Under that impression, I said so much to you, otherwise I had no right to criticize you . . . I am sorry.'

Saying this, Dada started to leave. With a '*Good-bye!*' BM too started walking behind Dada. Following them, Shailbala also took a few steps. She wanted to ask Dada for forgiveness. She had not been able to refrain from responding to his harsh statements, but in the face of his helplessness, she melted. Her self-respect and shame, which were but two forms of the same substance, rendered her body motionless. She wished she could just stand and weep, but a lightning bolt flashed through her mind: Yashoda!

Yashoda's home was not far from Shailbala's. It took Harish barely four minutes to reach there by car. But in this interval, what a lot went through his mind! . . . If Yashoda's husband, Amarnath, was not at home at this time, his life would be safe, but what if he happened to be there . . . of course he would be there. How would he spend half an hour with him? What would he say, why had he come to Yashoda's at this time? What if Yashoda got into trouble because of this? It would have been better not to come. At that moment, Shailbala's intensely agitated face rose before his eyes—'Go, go quickly! I beg of you. I will come to fetch you in half an hour.' Her anxiety, her intense proximity, her low but forceful tone, the black border of her sari, the hint of fragrance she carried. . . . Harish could not reach any decision by the time the car stopped in front of Yashoda's home. He did not even know Amarnath well enough to recognize him. What will he do . . . what will he say?

The driver opened the door of the car. Now there was no opportunity to retreat. Harish got down. The car left. He slowly climbed the two steps to the door. Felt the pistol in his pocket. Coughed a little, then straightened his necktie. The door to the drawing room was open, he lifted the bamboo curtain and entered.

A robust man of medium build, dressed in khaddar clothing, was sitting in a cushioned armchair in one corner of the room, writing something on the three-legged table in front of him. When Harish entered, he had just laid his fountain pen on the table and was about to take a sip of water from the glass in his hand. Seeing a gentleman enter, he put down the glass of water, and in a welcoming way said, 'Please come in,' and motioned to Harish to sit on the sofa.

Greeting him, Harish sat down with an easy air and said, 'My name is J.R. Shukla. I'm a travelling engineer in the Jeremy and Johnson Company. My house is here in Lahore but I have to travel frequently . . . If you don't mind . . . *may I have a smoke?*'

'I will ask for one,' Amarnath said, preparing to rise.

'No, no, see, I have one already.' Taking out an inexpensive cigarette case of the modern kind, Harish presented it before Amarnath and said, 'Please have one too.'

Joining his palms, Amarnath spoke politely, 'Please go ahead, I am not in the habit of smoking.'

'Oh, but you won't mind my smoking?' Harish looked at him and smiled.

'No, no, not at all. You please go ahead,' Amarnath assured him.

Lighting a matchstick, Harish lit the cigarette and turning aside, blew out a long line of smoke. During all this, he was trying to decide what to say.

'So, I have come here because,' he said, sitting back comfortably on the sofa, 'I have to travel a lot for my work . . . Almost two weeks a month at the very least . . . and sometimes three weeks.' Taking another long puff at the cigarette, he said, 'There is always some danger in travel. Last month my suitcase was stolen from the train, and today I barely escaped an accident.' He inhaled deeply again. 'Agents of companies have approached me for insurance, but I am a rather careless man, and then, you know, when someone approaches you, you try to escape.' Harish laughed. 'Although I too have to approach engineering firms or those that sell machinery.'

Joining in his laughter, Amarnath said, '*Good, that's nice.*' Picking up the glass of water he said, 'Please have some water.'

'You go ahead, I'll have some later,' Harish said. 'You drink this water, I am not thirsty right now.' Amarnath drank the water.

'So, as I was saying,' Harish said, 'today I escaped by the skin of my teeth. You see, I was going on Hospital Road in a friend's car—the same car that brought me here—when a lorry turned the corner in front and a horse carriage came from the left. I don't know how my life was saved. The *mudguards* of both the car and the lorry were broken. I reached my friend's home. He counselled me: life and death are fated, but you should get insurance before tonight.' Harish again puffed deeply on the cigarette and exhaled towards the clock on the wall—almost eleven minutes had passed.

Amarnath laughed and said, 'All right, where argument couldn't convince you, experience did. It is not my habit to pursue people. As you remarked, people become suspicious, but actually this is a *service*. Society and the government should provide it. Do you know, in Russia everyone is insured, every single person? This is, after all, a social necessity. I will make all arrangements for you. Please don't worry.'

With half-closed eyes, Harish was smoking his cigarette and looking contentedly at Amarnath, pleased that this kind man himself was providing assistance in the difficult task of passing time. As soon as Amarnath fell silent, Harish said again, 'And I have recently got married. My salary too is not much, 250 in all. There is also expense while travelling, and I want a policy for accident and theft insurance. All companies don't offer such policies. Your company is swadeshi. That is also an attraction for me. Please arrange something so I can get the best deal for a low price.' Harish laughed. 'I came because I heard about your company from a friend.'

'That is very kind of you,' Amarnath said, 'Our company's service is indeed unmatched. I will bring the rates and the necessary papers to you in a minute. I have to go somewhere right now for an extremely urgent task.

Please look over the papers, and then tomorrow or this evening perhaps I will come to your home. We will need a medical examination . . . nothing to worry about . . . I am just coming.'

Amarnath was about to leave, when Harish said, 'If it's no trouble, may I have a glass of water?'

'Of course, right away . . . Should I call for some *lemonade*?' Amarnath asked warmly.

'*No, no, plain water,*' Harish said with a laugh.

'Very good.'

Amarnath went to the other room and called, 'Please send another glass of water quickly.'

'Yes, we are sending,' Maaji's voice came from upstairs, and then she called to the servant, 'Bishan!' Receiving no answer, she looked at Yashoda and said, 'Daughter, you take the water, he probably has to go somewhere.'

Yashoda was stitching. Laying aside her work she said in an irritated tone, 'Once this boy goes to the market, it never takes him less than three hours to return!'

Taking the glass of water she went downstairs. Adjusting the aanchal of her sari, she thought, who could be in the drawing room at this time? 'He' was about to leave. On lifting the curtain to the sitting room, she saw a stranger and was startled. When he saw Yashoda bringing the water, Harish quickly rose. Gathering her aanchal, Yashoda said in surprise, 'You!'

At that very moment, Amarnath came from the other room with the papers. He saw Yashoda's surprise, heard her saying 'you!' and noted Harish's embarrassment.

He cast a quick glance over both of them. Putting his hand in his pocket, Harish tried to save the situation and asked Yashoda, 'Are you all right? I just came here to talk about insurance.' Then turning to Amarnath he made an attempt to explain, 'There's someone here who does some work for the Congress, I saw your wife at her house once.' In the meantime, Yashoda had left.

Amarnath was still trying to understand the situation when Shailbala glanced through the bamboo curtain at the entrance. 'Come, I am ready,' Harish said, and then, looking at Amarnath, 'It was at her place that I met your wife.'

Shailbala was agitated and in a hurry. With a brief greeting to Amarnath, she said, 'Come!'

Taking the papers from Amarnath's hand, Harish said, 'Namaste, I will come again.' And he sat in the car with Shailbala.

After Harish's departure, Amarnath remained thoughtful for a few moments. Then, forgetting that he had to go out, he ran up the stairs. 'Look here,' he called to Yashoda, 'what was that man's name?'

Yashoda blinked her large, surprised eyes and responded, 'They call him Harish.'

Scratching his head, Amarnath repeated, 'Harish!' Still pondering over something, he descended the stairs, and putting on his jacket, he went where he had to go, but Yashoda's surprise, J.R. Shukla's embarrassment, and the name Harish—these three elements starting flashing in his mind, one after another. Repeatedly, he kept thinking: J.R. Shukla—Harish!

Shailbala had not brought the driver with her. She drove the car herself. They had gone just a short distance when Harish said in a worried tone, 'Now there's another problem!'

Shailbala's gaze was on the road ahead. She asked, 'What?'

Harish said, 'To her husband I said I was called J.R. Shukla. How could I have guessed that Yashoda herself will come downstairs with a glass of water? Amarnath saw her recognize me. Now when he asks her, she will say that my name is Harish.'

'Let that be,' Shailbala said. 'You open my purse and take a look.'

'What is it?' Harish asked and opened her purse. 'This piece of paper?'

Harish read it and frowning in anxiety, he asked, 'What is this!'

'I just received it. When you arrived, Dada and BM were sitting inside, that's why I sent you here,' Shailbala said, her eyes fixed on the road.

'Now where are they? I will meet them,' said Harish angrily.

'What has happened to you, Harish? What good will come out of that?' Distressed, Shailbala kept her gaze ahead.

'Do you think I am running in fear for my life? . . . I must reach a decision with these people, once and for all,' Harish spoke forcefully.

The bazaar was extremely crowded. Shailbala said, 'Be quiet, don't disturb me or I will get into an accident.'

She signalled to the policeman at the crossing that she was about to turn right.

Once the crowd lessened, Harish said in a hurt voice, 'Shail, don't you hear me?'

'I hear you,' Shail turned the car towards Mall Road. From there they reached the deserted Firozepur Road in two minutes. Slowing down, she asked Harish, 'Now tell me. Do you want to fight? . . . Do you want to shoot them? . . . Will you take revenge?'

'No!' Harish responded. 'I want to talk to them.'

'And what if they shoot you before you can talk? Then there will surely be a fight. That will be very good for your party, won't it? The person who sent you this message will be seen as a traitor, I will be seen as a traitor. What good will come of that?' Shail asked.

Harish kept looking at the dashboard of the car in silence.

Shailbala again spoke, 'What do you think, what is the reason for all this?'

Harish said without raising his head, 'This is all BM's mischief. The reason is: envy! He wants to become more important in the party, and moreover, I think, you too are a reason.'

'There must be some people who agree with you—why don't you ask them for advice? Who do you think has sent this paper? You could consult with him! Just wait for a few days,' Shailbala counselled. Without a word Harish laid his head on Shailbala's shoulder. With her right hand on the steering wheel, Shailbala held his head with her left hand.

They had left the city behind and were now on Bahavalpur Road. In an impatient, childlike voice Harish asked, 'Where are you taking me, Shail?' 'That's exactly what I'm trying to decide,' Shail responded. 'There is a bungalow of a friend of mine close by. You will be safe there and comfortable too.'

Harish asked, 'Will I have to perform a role there as well?'

'They are Christians—brother and sister! You will definitely have to act in front of the girl. As for the man, you may be more frank with him, but I can't say whether or not we will find him there at this time . . . but let's go anyway. We will turn here.'

'But who is this—the recipient of such trust?' Harish asked.

'I told you he's a friend,' Shail said with a smile. 'I would not entrust anyone with you if I couldn't entrust them with my own life, you understand?'

'Innumerable are your friends!' Harish said in astonishment.

'So you too are going to talk like this?' Shail looked at him. 'But Hari, now everything else has come to an end. Now there's only he and you.'

'I too am one?' Harish asked. 'Is he just like me?'

'No,' Shail said with some embarrassment. 'You are you, and he is he. Hari, I now want my life's ship to reach the shore. I have been through enough storms. I thought I'd heard it all, and now I heard from your revolutionaries too!' Sadness filled Shail's voice.

'How?'

'Don't ask. Your Dada said: how can there be friendship between a boy and a girl?'

'Forget about what he said, he's Dada. He can see only one thing. But who is this Christian?'

'His name is Robert,' Shail said with a deep sigh. 'If it is in my destiny, I will marry him. Would you object?'

'No, why would I object, I am not a suitor. But your father!'

'We'll see,' Shail responded, drawing a deep breath. 'But I've had enough of those who trade in human beings. I'd rather join my lot to a true man.'

Entering the enclosure of a bungalow, she stopped the car in the driveway. They could see light behind the curtains of a room in the centre of the house. The darkness of twilight had settled around it. Shail asked, 'So, what name should I say?'

'G.M. Mirajkar*, Maharashtra.'

'Nancy! Nancy!' Shail called and pressed the horn of the car.

The clicking of a woman's shoes was heard from the room. A girl of about twenty emerged and responded, 'Hello, Shail?'

'Yes,' Shail said, 'Is Ruby in?'

'What are you saying? This evening he called you four times on the phone—where were you? He has been gone since five o'clock. He had to buy some things. We're going to Mussoorie tomorrow.'

---

* Probably a covert textual reference to S. S. Mirajkar (1899–1980), trade-unionist, general secretary of the Workers and Peasants Party, and one of the convicts in the Meerut Conspiracy Case (1929–1933).

'Mussoorie? In this weather? Do you want to die?' Shail asked, entering the room.

'How would you know? We got a telegram, there's a lot of snow. We'll *enjoy*, have fun!'

'Anyway,' Shail gestured towards Harish. 'My friend Mr G.M. Mirajkar. An engineer in the Jeremy and Johnson Company.'

Nancy held out her hand. Harish promptly took his hand out of his pocket and shook hers.

Shail said, 'Nancy, he will be your guest for a couple of days. He will not be very comfortable at my place, so I brought him here.'

'Of course,' Nancy said, 'we have a colossal palace, after all!' Then looking at Harish, 'You are welcome. *A friend's friend is a better friend.*'

'His luggage is at my place. I won't be able to bring it now, but please see that he is comfortable,' Shail again insisted.

'Why don't you also stay here?' Nancy said, laughing. 'We won't need anything!'

Inviting them to sit on the sofa and chairs, Nancy said, 'Shail, you must eat with us before going; it'll be about half an hour. Robert will also return.'

'All right, then may I call home?' Shail asked.

Shail returned after making a phone call from the other room. Nancy asked Harish in English, 'Will you have something to drink? You must be thirsty.'

'I could certainly have a glass of water,' Harish also responded in English.

'Water? Have a soda whiskey . . . or a little brandy! It'll be good before dinner,' Nancy said.

'No, I'm not in the mood for anything else at this time. Just give me some water—God's gift to us.'

Shail objected, 'Why don't you have half a peg of brandy? It will ease your worry.'

Harish shook his head to refuse. Shail joked, 'An old-fashioned gentleman after all! Are you afraid?'

Harish accepted—'Yes, new things do scare me. If you took some, I would too.' But Shail shook her head to decline.

When Nancy returned, Shail said, 'Mirajkar, I did not tell you that Naina—I call her Naina—is a very talented artist. When she plays the violin even stones are moved, and I have no words to describe her dance! Moreover, she has a voice so haunting it surpasses even the koel's. Naina, please sing something, Mirajkar loves music. Please sing, I really want to hear something at this time. It will ease the troubles of my mind.'

Nancy shook her head. 'Everything was packed and sent off by train this morning.'

'Where?'

'I told you, to Mussoorie. Won't you come with us? That's why Robert was trying to reach you on the phone. Come with us, Shail, everything is ready, we have a bungalow too. Really, come with us!'

'Should I go? Will you come, Mirajkar?'

Harish spread out his hands as if he were free of all worries and said, 'I have leave for a month. Gaurishankar, Kanchenjunga, Nanga Parbat—I can go wherever you say.'

'But what can I say to Father?'

'Oh, tell your father that it will be very good for your health. And it will be! Your father would pluck the very stars from the sky for the sake of your health,' Nancy replied.

'But alone?'

'Oh, is she not a total baby!' Nancy mocked. 'Just tell him that I am going. All the arrangements have been made. Father will never object.'

Shail laughed and looked at Harish. 'Let's go, it will be good, a bit of a change.'

Nancy said eagerly, 'Make your preparations tonight. We will leave in the morning by car; there is room for four people, and it will truly be a lot of fun.'

The sound of shoes was heard outside and Robert entered the room. He spoke joyfully, 'Wonderful! You are here, and I have just come from your place.'

Nancy said happily, 'Ruby, Shail will come to Mussoorie.'

'I have not yet agreed . . . I was only talking about my guest so far.'

Shail introduced Mirajkar to Robert. Finally, it was decided that they would all go to Mussoorie the next day to see the snow.

Human Being!

It had snowed through the previous day and night and till the following evening. Then the clouds parted at night and frost settled. Now, since morning, the sun had been shining in the clean blue sky. The brightness of the sun reflected in the vast whiteness spread below dazzled the eye. The bungalow was at the crest of the hill. When one looked around, one saw white everywhere. An amazing white, as if the colour of milk were mingled with the brightness of silver! Minor undulations had disappeared in the expanse of this whiteness. Only far below, in the deep valley, from between the snow-laden trees, one could glimpse the shadow of greenery. The branches of the huge deodar trees on the higher slopes of the mountain had sunk low beneath the weight of the snow. They looked like white skeletons of giant misshapen devils. It was only the greenery one occasionally glimpsed through the snow that reminded one of the almost invisible flora. The leaves of the oak had also turned white under cover of snow. The trunks and branches of trees that had lost their leaves in the autumn were covered with white patches. All human endeavours were lost in this immense play of nature, as if, in mockery of the powers of the human-child, nature had hidden his carefully planned dwellings beneath her white veil.

Robert, Shail, Nancy and Harish stood on the snow that had risen to the veranda of the bungalow and looked at the scenery in amazement. The frost that had settled overnight had hardened the surface of the snow. They could stand on it without much trouble and admire the scene around them. The snow, frozen on the roof of the bungalow, was melting in the sunshine and dripping down in thousands of little streams, and wherever the water had melted, garlands like large glass horns had formed. An expanse of white sprinkled with drops of diamond spread from beneath their feet and reached as far as the perennial wall of snow of the Himalayas on the far horizon. The crests of the mountains stood against the blue sky like shining mounds of silver. If there were any intervals in this expanse, they were of the brownish lines of the valleys in the far mountain ranges or of the greenery on the low-lying land of the valleys closer below.

There was no similarity between the bustling Mussoorie of the summer and rainy season, when one could see dense greenery from the red roofs of bungalows, and this silent Mussoorie covered with radiant white cotton wool. In the whiteness of the snow, it was difficult to recognize from afar the snow-covered houses and bungalows. With a hand shielding her dazzled eyes, Nancy stood with an outstretched arm, pointing her finger at this riddle-like, enigmatic Mussoorie: 'That is Charlie Villa, and there, Mailakaf! And above that, there is Highland . . .' Clapping her hands in rapture and astonishment she said, 'Ruby, look! Nothing at all is recognizable on the Depot Hill!'

Even in this dense snow, one did not feel the cold because the sun was intense and the wind, still. On the contrary, it felt good to walk on the snow and to feel the ice-crust crackle beneath one's feet as they sank a little in the clean white snow. Climbing a slope close to the house, the four friends could see far into the distance. As their feet dug into the snow while climbing, Nancy and Shail started panting. Robert supported Shail and helped her climb. Shail now held on to his arm, now his shoulder. Looking at Harish ahead, Nancy called out without embarrassment, 'Mr Mirajkar, won't you help me?'

'*I am sorry*, of course!' Harish returned. Looking at Robert and Shail, he was wondering what would be the proper way to hold Nancy so he could help her.

In just a few hours, the intensity of this wonder dimmed. The north-east wind caught speed, and even in the sun they started to feel a chill. Piercing through the warm, thick clothes, the wind struck their bodies like a lance. They returned and sat inside. The fire was lit, but they could not stop trembling. The only comfort was in sitting close to the fire. The rest of the room remained cold, so dragging the sofa and chairs very close to the fire, they sat together.

Nancy felt the cold the most, but she felt even more discomfort in sitting close to everyone. She felt alienated—a kind of restlessness whose cause was not clear even to her. Robert and Shail were lost in the self-forgetfulness of joy. Mirajkar was so immersed in his own thoughts that he seemed unaware of the presence of others. At times, drawn towards some point in the conversation, or on meeting Shail's glance, he would wake up from his reverie and smile. His eyes would sparkle, but the next moment he would sink in his thoughts again.

Nancy looked at Mirajkar several times, but found him lost in thought. Wounded by neglect from all sides, she wanted to run to a faraway place. The flood of delight that the amazing landscape and the elation of the journey had brought to her river-like heart subsided, and the pebbles and stones sitting at the bottom became visible. These were signs of the lacks and deficiencies of her life. She saw that Robert and Shail were in a state close to intoxication. There was no room for a third in their thoughts. And Mirajkar? He seemed to look upon everyone as part of material nature. Nancy looked at him several times, talked to him of related–unrelated things. With great politeness and more courtesy than required, Mirajkar gave a brief response and ended the conversation, as though they were unacquainted and he had no desire to become acquainted. The sadness of solitude made Nancy anxious. Her mind became restless, feeling an unfamiliar lack whose shape she could not delineate.

Harish was like a boy lost in his games or thoughts, who was not even concerned about his own state. Shail's loving glance was often directed at him. Even while gratefully accepting Robert's claim, how could she neglect Harish? She saw Harish as a wounded child.

Drawing the window curtain aside, Nancy looked at the snow-covered ranges of the north-east. The rays of the sun setting behind snowy peaks were spreading like the feathers of a peacock. Like the still flames of a radiant vermilion fire, the mountain peaks stood with heads aloft in the blue sky. Some parts that were hidden from the rays of the sun were covered in a blue-green fog. Looking at that and addressing Shail, Robert said, 'Uff! What splendour!'

Nancy felt as though the remark had been uttered just to provoke the anguish in her heart. Letting go of the curtain, she moved away. Shail made a request: 'Naina, please play something!'

Nancy received Shail's request as a new blow to an aching limb. Without responding, she kept looking at the wall with both hands in her coat pockets.

Shail asked Harish: 'Mirajkar, would you like to listen to something?'

Waking from his meditative slumber, he responded, 'Absolutely!' And looking at Nancy with a smile, he repeated, 'You must play!'

Nancy, falling in the depths of anguish, suddenly found support in Harish's smile. Digging her hands deeper in her pockets, she asked Harish, 'What would you like to hear?'

There was no despair now in Nancy's tone. It was Shail who replied, 'What you had played at Devi's place the other day . . . Moonlight Sonata! Please play that.'

'Yes, indeed, please play,' Robert agreed.

Smiling, Nancy spoke, 'Mirajkar is a connoisseur of Indian ragas. I should play something from our own country for him. Would you like to listen to Vihaag?'

'Absolutely,' Mirajkar agreed.

Taking the violin, Nancy started to draw the bow across its strings; her hand and the bow moving in rhythm. Waves of sound began to rise from the strings of the violin. After a little while, her head started moving to the rhythm. Her face became flushed. Departing from its natural rhythm, her breath began riding the waves of Vihaag. After playing for a few minutes, she stood up and switched from a slower to a faster scale. From the waist upwards, her body started swaying to the music. All three had their eyes fastened on her. Robert's head was swaying too. Closing his eyes, he became lost in the music. Once he uttered, 'Beautiful!' Shail too was looking at her as though spellbound. Ending the raga, Nancy drew an exhausted breath and looking towards Harish, she asked, 'So, did you like it?'

'Beautiful! You have a lot of practice,' Harish smiled and praised her.

'Listen to some more,' Nancy said enthusiastically and picking up the violin, she started playing Shyamakalyana. When the music ended all three praised her unstintingly. Nancy forgot her weariness. Shail made a request: 'Naina, please sing something for us.'

Spreading out both hands, Nancy replied, 'How can I sing without instruments? Here sits a Maharashtrian Pandit of classical music, he will immediately point out my mistakes!'

Harish laughed and said, 'One doesn't learn music just by being a Maharashtrian! I won't even understand your mistakes, let alone point them out!'

Nancy winked at Shail. 'Some people's heroism lies in not understanding anything. So, what shall I sing?' She asked Harish.

'Something apt for this occasion,' Robert responded.

Nancy again winked at Shail and teased her, 'The occasion is yours, not everyone's!'

Shail and Robert looked at each other and laughed. Humming a little, Nancy started singing:

My heart is forlorn, the land desolate—
Who has ever found joy in the mortal state.

Tell this throng of desires to find another home
For a despairing heart it is too heavy a freight.

The nightingale blames not gardener or hunter
Captivity in springtime was writ in its fate.

Four days of life I had borrowed and brought—
Two passed in longing, and two in wait.*

With her eyes raised to the ceiling, Nancy was singing passionately in a full voice. The sound resounded through the room. When the ghazal ended, the silence of that isolated place seemed all the more harsh. Shail asked her to sing something else.

---

* A popular ghazal by Bahadur Shah Zafar, India's last Mughal emperor (1775–1862).

'Great! Have I come here as a paid performer?' Nancy reproached Shail playfully. 'You should also sing!' At that moment her heart was in transports of joy from pride in her voice and art.

'If I knew how to sing, would I have asked you?' Shail said.

'Come, shall we sing a Punjabi dholak song together?' Nancy proposed. Shail agreed. Just then Nancy looked at Mirajkar and asked, 'But what will he understand?'

'I understand, I understand enough,' Harish responded. 'You sing, at least I will hear the music.'

Nancy picked up Robert's hat-case and holding it tight between her knees like a dholak began to drum on it:

'I am yours and you are mine, O flower of mine, O Moon of mine . . .' She paused her song and looking at Harish, she asked, 'Do you understand the meaning?'

Harish said, 'I understand. I am yours, you are mine, you are a flower.'

Addressing Shail, Nancy said, 'It's fine, but he doesn't know *grammar* very well.'

All three laughed. Harish smiled in embarrassment. Nancy was intoxicated with enthusiasm. Finishing one song, she started another with Shail

'*Chichi wala chhalla mainu de ja nishaani . . .*'

(Give me a ring for my small finger as a memento . . .)

In the midst of all this, Harish's thoughts had wandered off. He was thinking that this Miss Sahib, who lived an upper-class life and spoke English, was now wearing a salwar kameez and singing a Punjabi song with a dholak pressed between her knees. Despite all the gloss of western civilization, her Indianness and Punjabiat evidently persisted in her blood.

Suddenly pausing, Nancy again asked Harish, 'Tell us the meaning—what did you understand?'

'Yes, yes,' Harish said, 'she wants a ring as a memento.'

'What does chichi mean? If you are able to answer this, I will give you whatever you ask for.'

Shail said, 'This is your opportunity, Mirajkar. You may ask for her!'

Robert laughed and said, 'In ancient India this is exactly how Svayamvaras were conducted.'

Nancy challenged him without embarrassment, 'But he has to answer first . . . What does chichi mean, Sahib? Does it mean chachi?' She asked with her finger on her chin.

Pretending to be worried, Harish answered, 'Look, it means . . . a jewel . . . a jewelled ring, is that not so?'

Looking at Shail and Robert, Nancy said, 'Ah, so you've won the Svayamvara!'

Shail collapsed into laughter. She couldn't help it. Rising from her seat near Robert, she caught Harish's hand and pulled him towards the wall. Softly she said, 'What acting! Wonderful.'

And just as softly laughing, Harish responded, 'If I did not act, our secret would be immediately revealed.'

Still laughing, Shail returned to her seat. Acting embarrassed, Mirajkar had just sat down when Nancy addressed him, 'O Sir! Chichi doesn't mean chachi nor does it mean a jewelled ring. It means this finger!' She shook her small finger at him. 'Did you understand? But you don't understand anything!'

Robert and Shail were talking among themselves. Gesturing towards them, Nancy said to Mirajkar, 'You should understand the situation. Let them talk. Come, let me show you the moon. Are you feeling cold? It's because you don't have an overcoat. Here, you can wear this.' She took off her own overcoat.

Despite Harish's remonstrations, she wore a shawl instead and then looking at Harish she said, 'How nice you look! Should I give you a sari as well? . . . Oh come now!'

Shail started laughing.

Nancy and Harish stood looking at the moonlight on the snow from behind the glass doors of the veranda. 'How peaceful it is,' said Harish.

Nancy responded, 'Frighteningly quiet! . . . and cold!'

For about ten minutes they bore the peace, quiet and cold. Harish felt an emptiness in his mind. Nancy felt an emptiness in her heart. Despair enveloped her again. Leaving Mirajkar on the veranda, she went inside to lie down.

'Ruby, when one does not experience any obstacle in life then life flows like water down a slope. We don't even realize that we are living, or that there may be a question about life's problems or about one's rights. But when desires and wishes are not fulfilled in life, then one begins to think of everything. The disorder of society becomes visible.' Who knew what Shail imagined as she spoke with eyes half-closed.

Placing his right arm on Shail's shoulder, Robert took a deep breath in a calm, steady manner and responded, 'Society and the world start with the individual. Only when a person experiences obstacles in his life does he begin to experience concern about social problems, begin to think about personal and social rights.'

'But this is not true of Harish . . . I mean Mirajkar's life . . . after all what is his personal life . . . he just can't hope to attain anything for himself in life!' Shail said.

Robert looked at Shail and smiled. 'The man who wishes to erase himself for his country and society, he too is selfish in a way. He is like the mother who adores her child and cannot live without the child. There are some people who may want to lay down their lives for the good of humankind. In fact, instead of calling them selfless, we should call them wise, because they understand that their own ends lie in collective welfare. This is what I have seen in my life.'

Placing her hand on Robert's arm, Shail glanced at the veranda through the glass door and asked, 'Ruby, shall I call Mirajkar? Look at him, head lifted like a mad man, he is pacing back and forth as if he were an ox in a mill.'

Robert nodded to give permission. Shail called Mirajkar inside.

Coming inside Mirajkar asked, 'What is it?'

Shail said, 'Nothing, come and sit among human beings! What are you doing, pacing in circles like a caged animal! . . . You go around shouting about the revolution, don't you see the social oppression people face in their daily lives? I have found all of life's paths barred by society, and it is society that causes me the greatest vexation . . .'

Robert helped her. 'Just as a building cannot be made without bricks, society cannot be made without people. Society makes structures for its own protection or for the progress of people. But the life of a person changes, their needs change and they begin to feel obstructed by the old structure. If a cloth is sewn upon the body in childhood, it will begin to suffocate the person as they grow older. This is how it is with our social structures too . . . Look at my own experience! How can I blame my wife? At the time when I passed college with an MA degree, I was so deeply influenced by the Bible that I was not concerned about anything except bringing the world to the feet of the Lord Jesus. Even though I was not particularly inclined towards a job, seeing my religious faith, the Mission College gave me work. I was in such a state that morning and evening, leaving aside all other work, I would go among labourers and bhangis, sing hymns of Jesus and tell them about His teaching. Unless I did this, I was not at peace.

'It was at that time that I met Flora. My religious sermons seemed a stream of nectar to her. She would often come with me to sing hymns and stay during my discourses. I began to respect her because of her love of religion. I did not know when that respect took the form of love. The limits of intellectual love and physical attraction are not far from each other. On one side are reverence, love and devotion, and on the other the search for fulfillment—and moreover, this limit is not a tangible substance. This limit exists only in feelings and thoughts. Therefore, a wave of feelings, thoughts or desires can transport it somewhere, or even erase it.

'I myself proposed marriage to Flora. Her reverence and love for me—and these are simply other names for desire and inclination—were so powerful that it was not possible for her to refuse. I think, if at that time either of us had died, the other, finding life impossible to live, would have died too, or attempted to die, but when the 'cause' of love and attraction died, the love and attraction between us did not survive either.

'When I no longer remained in Flora's eyes what she had earlier imagined me to be, how could she not become alienated from me? In those days I was enamoured of Gandhism. Gandhi seemed to me to be the greatest active devotee of Christ. Many a time I enthusiastically contemplated converting Gandhiji to Christianity. His conduct is exemplary according to the Christian faith; I was pained to think that merely because he did not believe in God's son the Messiah, he would not find heaven and salvation. I could not bear his reverence for Ram, Krishna and other mythic gods. Only in non-violence and love did I see the essence of all religions, and the essence of non-violence and love I saw in Jesus, the son of God. At that time, a professor friend of mine—may he be well!—gave me a book by Bukharin to read, *Historical Materialism*. I read that book twice. Then I read a book by Haeckel, *Riddle of the Universe*. After that, despite making an effort, I could not touch the Bible.

'My atheism was unbearable for Flora. I tried to explain my thoughts to her, but to argue about religion was itself a sin in her eyes. It was a torment for her to accept an atheist for a husband and to eat with him at the table. She would fast in misery when I did not go to the Church. For many days I went with her to the Church, like a pet dog, just for her tranquility, but I found this mentally disgusting. I felt it was cowardice.

'One day we reached our limit. Under my table lay a black leather-bound book. When Flora saw it, she picked it up, kissed it and touched it to her head. Then addressing me in anger, she said—"Now you have fallen to such an extent that you kick the Bible with your feet!"

'Seeing tears in her eyes, I laughed and said—this is not the Bible, this is something whose truth cannot be tarnished even when kicked by shoes. This is *Capital* by Karl Marx! Her lips trembled in anger. "That atheist Marx!" she said, "and I touched this to my head and kissed it?"

'"This must have been your god's wish," I responded merrily.

'"Not God's, but the Devil's. You are the Devil! . . . Taking the form of the innocent lamb of Jesus Christ, you have deceived me." Stamping her feet in fury she went into the kitchen with the book. From there she called, "Look at this!"

'I went and saw that the pot had been taken off the stove and the book placed on the fire; flames were rising from it.

Looking at me with revulsion, Flora taunted me—"Look at this, the soul of your Marx is burning in the fire of hell."

'Flora's intolerance and bigotry became unbearable for me as the days passed. I could not say anything. My own religious blindness from just a few days past would rear its head in my memory. That day I became angry because of that incident. I tried to remain silent, but could not. I said, because your god wished it, once in the court of Nero, Christian saints were burnt just like this. Muhammad Ghori also burnt the Vedas in this country, but both Christianity and the Vedas are still alive and Marx's thoughts will also remain alive. What has been burnt today is just our mutual sympathy. Now we cannot live together. That very day she packed up her clothes and belongings and left the house.

'I heard that she has gone to a Mission in the Kangra district that preaches Christianity among untouchables. She leads a hard life as a nurse in a hospital. I thought, if she suffers hardship because of her pride, how am I to blame? Then I thought—would I have respected her if she had conformed to my will for the sake of food and clothing? I wrote a letter to her: Legally, you have a claim on my income. You don't need to suffer unnecessary economic hardship. . . . But the one-hundred-rupee money order I had sent with the letter was returned to me with this response: I have no reverence for an atheist's money.

'At that time, I was severely criticized in Christian society. People started saying that I had pretended to be religious for the sake of a wife and a job. Frightened by this criticism, I resigned from my job. Perhaps I would not have resigned, had I not known that somehow I would manage. My father had been a contractor and had built many houses. It is a recognized rule in society that by means of a father's wealth or by accumulating wealth oneself, one can live comfortably without lifting a finger.

'If this rule had not been made at some point, people would never have accumulated wealth nor would any development of the major means of production have taken place. And this rule continues even today. In my personal life I benefit from it. However, I also see that when, in order to maximize profit, resources as well as means of production are accumulated on an individual level, millions of people are left without any means of sustenance whatsoever. These people can only become objects of use for those who own capital and the means of production . . . just look at our two servants! If we did not need them for our own comfort, and if other rich people did not think alike, how would people of this class survive? . . . If we did not need their service, they would have no other means of survival. But don't think, Sir, that I'm going to embark on preaching Marxism now. Now, I just want to spend my life in comfort and ease. . . .

'It so happened that last August I got a registered letter from Flora. She wants me to convert to Hinduism so that our marriage can end. It has been a year and a half since we separated. I wrote to her that she can divorce me in court. But she considers that humiliating. She wants to be rid of me, but in a way that preserves her honour. This is the second rule of society—that a woman should form a bond with only one man for her entire life. Tell me, isn't this rule a problem for my life, Flora's life, as well as the lives of the man she wishes to marry and the woman I wish to marry? As long as a woman was considered the property of a man, it was necessary for her to remain attached to just one man, but today when you talk of giving a woman rights equal to a man, then what is the need for such rules and laws? . . . Society makes rules and laws only so that men and women can live in comfort and peace. You can't deny that marriage is a fetter. Fetters are put in place when there is fear of chaos. I am amazed that there is so much respect for this bond in society! Like other kinds of bondage, this one should also be considered an enemy of freedom. But the funny thing is that people are eager to be bound by this bond.'

'No, no, marriage is not a fetter,' Harish interrupted. 'Marriage is a license or an authorizing note. The real fetter is that in society no man can have a relation with any woman, but when this does not work, one man is given a license for one woman so that they may establish mutual relations.'

Robert and Shail laughed. Robert accepted this. 'Yes, you put it in a better way, or one could also say, just as it is a sin to take another's property, it is likewise a sin to touch another's woman, but a woman is a kind of property that has hands and feet and a head, so she has been taught that her salvation lies in sticking to her master, she should be a dutiful wife.'

Letting his body relax on the chair and lighting a cigarette, Harish said, 'Full freedom for women means, doing away with the tradition of marriage . . .'

'Amazing! So then, what should happen in its stead?' Shail asked in astonishment.

'Why not?' Harish responded with excitement. 'If the repressive laws of your country are abolished, what will happen? In the same way, by doing away with the repressive relations of marriage, man and woman will live in their natural state.'

'I don't agree with this,' Shail objected. 'There has to be a limit.'

'I know why you disagree,' Harish responded with a smile. 'Don't mind my saying this, but you want to make a man your husband to exploit him, to make him work for you. You want your husband to earn so you can spend the earnings. I ask— if a woman wants a child, why does she fear taking responsibility for its upbringing?'

'How rude he is!' Addressing Robert, Shail spoke in an affectionate tone, as if speaking of a child, and then raising her eyebrows, she asked Harish, 'And should the father not bear any responsibility towards the offspring?'

'Yes, why not, he must bear some responsibility, but only as much as the mother bears. Man produces a child, but this does not mean that for the rest of his life he should be responsible for feeding the mother and the child,' Harish answered.

'So, women do nothing?' Shail asked a new question.

'Women are of three kinds,' Harish leaned forward in his chair. 'There are women of the farmer—labourer class who work as much as their husbands, and on top of that, they are slaves to their husbands. The second are the women of white-collar workers. These women attend to the housework, which could be done very well by a servant at a pay of eight or ten rupees a month. Yes, the work of producing progeny is certainly apart from this.'

Placing a hand on her mouth in embarrassment, Shail looked at Robert and asked, 'So is that no work at all?'

'It is certainly work,' Robert accepted, 'But nowadays so many people in our society marry only because they want a child. Once the child is born, natural love compels the parents to look after it. In this country marriages commonly take place because it is considered essential. Sometimes marriage happens even before one feels a need for it, just as in government buildings, red buckets of sand are hung for extinguishing fires even before there is a fire, only because of fear. Similarly, at night, before going to sleep, one might place a glass of water by the bed. In the same way, marriage takes place in society. In moments when people forget themselves in order to satisfy their love or infatuation, they do not see before them the image of a moon-like child laughing and playing in the cradle. It is only later that the child jumps into the picture. The reality is that today's civilized society fears progeny, but nature deceives it, exactly as the bird-catcher deceives birds by using bait to lay a trap. Lovers see only the bait of physical attraction, not the trap of progeny hidden in it!'

'Let me say what I think,' Harish spoke restlessly, moving further towards the edge of his chair. 'So, the third kind are women of the rich class. They do nothing besides entertaining the man and going through the labour of childbirth. Rich men play with them for their own pleasure and prestige, just as one plays with a parrot, a starling or a lapdog. You tell me, what does such a woman do for society, and why should society look after her? She is a burden on society, so she remains dependent on a man's generosity, becomes his slave. If women of this society gain the freedom to go shopping for saris and jewels with an umbrella and a purse, they consider themselves free, but if they want to freely set up their home, or freely produce a child, then, are they free to do that?'

'I cannot accept that women of the wealthy class do nothing,' Shail objected, and then she laughed and said, 'but of course you will say so, since you are becoming a socialist.'

Robert stretched his limbs and joked, 'Of course they work—they rule over the servants, they manage the household, they quarrel with their husband and they shake the hands of their husband's friends. In this age, it is most profitable to be a woman, provided the husband is kind, wealthy and reasonably good-looking,' he looked pointedly at Shail.

Robert's joke dispelled the agitation of the argument. Harish laughed and said, 'All right, so you tell me, is it appropriate that four–five men should serve one man? This would imply that his life is more important than the lives of the men who serve him. If there were equal opportunities for education for all men in our society, no one would be ready to live their entire life serving others for bread alone. What would be the condition of women in such a situation? Why shouldn't a woman also work like a man, and if she wants to live with him after marriage, she should earn and help the family.'

To silence Harish, Shail spoke in a somewhat mocking tone, 'And what about the family's meals?'

'Arrange that as you wish,' Harish responded without paying attention to the mockery. 'Eat in a hotel or both can cook together and clean the dishes. I ask you—if each servant were to be paid a hundred rupees a month, how many servants would you be able to afford?'

'How can this happen anywhere?' Shail asked in an indifferent way.

'Why can't this happen? You may not want it to happen, but it will surely happen,' Harish responded. 'Imagine, if there were several opportunities for employment in the country, and if labourers were given a part of the profits that increased their income, how would you find servants for your whims? How many upper-class people in England have servants at home?'

'Oh, your glorious socialism!' Shail smiled and mocked him.

Robert scratched his head to keep sleep at bay. 'Socialist thought is of two kinds. One form of socialism says that rich folks should pity the poor and think of improving their situation while keeping their own position intact. And the second says that the poor should take control of the government and of their own rights. The former is the socialism of the saints, or Gandhian-socialism, and the second is Marxist-socialism. Your 'Dada' is now becoming a 'comrade', save him if you can!'

'Listen, Harish,' Shail spoke. 'You continue with your earlier revolution. Two bullets here, two bombs there. People will praise your courage and sing songs of martyrdom. If you start this new revolution, inciting servants against masters and women against men, there will be no place for you in polite society.'

'Yes, the Congress people will certainly not support you,' Robert laughed and agreed.

Hearing Robert say this, Shail's mocking and taunting tone changed. 'Ruby, what a life he leads! The government hunts him like a wild animal. His comrades are out to kill him,' she looked steadfastly at Harish.

Harish rose from his chair. 'So, you too feel mere pity for me, you have no sympathy for my ideas.'

'No, no!' Robert objected. 'Not pity, I have full sympathy with your ideas, but what can I do! I keep thinking but I can't do anything.'

Harish smiled and gestured towards Shail. 'No, I was talking about her.'

'If women became so rational, men would stop loving them and start fearing them,' saying this, Robert laughed heartily and stood up.

'So, did you hear him?' Harish said and started walking towards his room.

'Will you be able to sleep or shall I pat your back to lull you to sleep?' Shail called.

Harish returned to respond. To avenge all the mockery, he said, 'Till women don't become fit for anything else, they should continue to preserve their attraction.'

Before Shail could answer, he left, taking long strides. He was still on the veranda when he heard Shail saying to Robert, 'Look, how he attacks and bites.' Harish heard Shail's words, but he could not recognize the warmth and affection in her tone.

As she spoke, Shail's feelings changed completely. She was overwhelmed by indebtedness and gratitude as she thought about her freedom to express affection for another man in front of Robert. She began to think, would this be appropriate, would it be wise . . . even after marriage?

By the fourth day the snow had melted a little. The mountains surrounding Mussoorie became visible—they were bereft of vegetation, sheer cliffs all the way from the valley below to the peaks above. One could also see the extent of grass with frost on it. Nancy was anxious to return to Lahore. On Robert's request she stayed for another two days. Then Robert had to prepare to leave for her sake. Shail was sad that Robert was going away so soon, but she decided to stay back for a few more days with Harish.

When Nancy and Robert had piled their luggage on to the heads of the coolies at the bungalow and departed, Shail could not hold back her tears, however much she tried. Harish tried to wipe away her tears with a handkerchief, but the more he wiped, the more they flowed. Suddenly Harish understood that he was being unjust in trying to stop these tears. He felt a deep anguish in his heart. Leaving Shail alone by the devdar tree, he went to the other side of the bungalow and sat on a rock. His gaze was fixed on a distant, deep hollow in the twilight-reddened slopes of the mountains. Finding no aim, his gaze was suspended there. Breaking off blades of the tall dry grass, he chewed and tossed them, distracted, lost.

No human behaviour is meaningless. Behaviour is the manifest form of the inner life. Just as Harish's teeth were gnawing on blades of grass, so was memory relentlessly gnawing at his heart. A memory buried for years had awakened in his mind . . . after all, he too is a human being! In his human body too lies a heart: though suppressed, its existence has not been erased. Harish's open eyes were at that moment unseeing, but the forgotten memory was coming alive before his mind's eye. Just as Robert had left today. In the same way, one day he too had . . .

He felt a weight on his shoulder and he heard, 'Get up, why are you sitting here? . . . What are you thinking about?'

'Nothing,' Harish shook his head.

'How can it be nothing?' Shail nudged him. 'Why don't you tell me?'

'What were you thinking about?' Harish asked. 'Only in thoughts is the human free; everywhere else circumstances bind them . . . so I did not think it wise to interrupt your thinking.'

'Yes . . . so you came here and started thinking as well.'

'Yes.'

'Tell me the truth, what were you thinking about? . . . Was it about BM, Dada . . . how this work will continue in the future?'

'No . . . what were you thinking about?'

Taking a deep breath Shail said, 'I was thinking about past wounds and future obstacles.'

'I was thinking about something like that too,' Harish responded.

'Tell me . . . you must tell me,' Shail pulled at his arm and pleaded.

Harish got up and started walking. Shail walked beside him silently. Every now and then she would interrupt his reverie by pointing to something on this or that mountain. Harish would look and make a monosyllabic response. After a while, Shail said reproachfully, 'What kind of a man are you, you don't even respond to what one says.'

'Look Shail, in front of the world, I have to hide myself and become whatever people want me to be. But today with you, I am not forced to hide myself, so without any pretense I am thinking my own thoughts.'

'What?' Shail asked taking his hand in both her hands.

'Just this—a person's life is also something. You know that Harish is not my real name.'

'Yes, earlier you were a Sikh. This has been your name since you escaped from prison . . . BM told me.'

'Yes, see, seven years ago on just such a wintry night I had quietly left my home in the village. My wedding had taken place two years earlier and the bride was to arrive the next day for the gauna.'*

---

* In the case of child marriages, the bride would stay in her natal home after the wedding. The marriage would be consummated much later, after she reached puberty and was brought to her husband's home. This latter ceremony is called gauna.

'You are very cruel!'

'Cruel . . . perhaps . . .'

'Do you remember her?'

'This is just what I was thinking about. Sometimes I remember her and sometimes I don't. When I think that a woman has a natural place in the life of a man, then I remember I too had one. In those moments I think of her a lot . . . otherwise I don't . . .'

'All right . . . so how would you have treated her?' Shail asked after some thought.

'You are mad!'

'No, tell me.'

'I can't say with any accuracy . . . perhaps I would have seen that she is beautiful.'

'And if she were not beautiful?'

'Does it ever happen that a woman is not beautiful?'

'Are all women beautiful . . . look here!'

'But I can't see.'

Harish was looking at the crests of the far ranges in the last light of the sun. They were ablaze like still flames of fire. A bitter wind was blowing, but he did not care.

Shail asked him to come inside. Without looking at her, Harish answered, 'You go.'

Shail kept standing close to him. As they watched, the sun's rays vanished from the mountain crests and a dark blueness descended. Shail again said, 'Do come now.'

'You go!'

'Now what is left? . . . That beauty has vanished.'

'Yes, objects bereft of attraction turn unworthy.'

'Like?'

'Myself.'

Shail remained quiet for some time, then repeated, 'Come, you will catch a chill. The servant is waiting to give us dinner.'

Harish's silence began to weigh on Shail's heart. She was thinking, who knows what anguish pierces his heart. After dinner Harish strolled silently on the veranda for some time, then went in to go to bed, but Shail brought him to her own room. She said, 'Shall I tell you something? . . . You have offended Nancy. She told me, "He is very proud! So many times I tried to talk to him, but he always speaks as though he is doing me a great favour. When I lost my balance on the snow, he held my arm in such a way as though I had some contagious disease."'

'Oh, so this is what she said!' Harish responded. 'I did not give it much attention. Actually, I was thinking of you.'

'What?' Shail asked, looking at his eyes.

'Yes,' Harish looked at the wall and spoke, 'I envy Robert . . . it's not enmity . . . I hope you will not misunderstand me! Look, Shail, you too have loved someone. When you like someone you start to desire them, and when you desire someone you try to attain them. You have experienced all this. You know the despair as well that comes when one faces obstacles . . . Well, I will go now.'

Shail clasped Harish's hand and pulled him to a seat, 'No, sit.' Seeing him silent, she pleaded, 'Speak! . . . Please go on!'

'There is nothing to say,' Harish said. 'I wonder, is desire a necessary part of life?'

'Perhaps . . .' Shail responded. 'Look, last time when I was hurt, I told myself, now I will not let the seed of desire grow in my heart. When Robert resigned from college, I went to express my sympathy. There I heard about Flora. Robert's generosity and large-heartedness made such an impression on my mind that I started to see him every day. Whenever I thought of his sadness, I could not resist seeing him. When I wondered why I went, I found this answer: only with the peaceful pace of this calm, steady person will the defeated train of my life be able to move. This was another addition to my list of sins. I made him alone my goal. But then, who knows from where that unfortunate BM brought you. Once I came to know you, I felt I had been waiting for you for a long time. As though I had found some long-lost companion. I could not understand what our relation was: were you a brother, friend, son or husband? I don't think it is possible for me to follow BM when he says, "Make someone your own, or become someone's." Can all the goodness of the world be contained in one person? When one sees goodness elsewhere, how does one turn away from it? Must the love of the human heart limit itself to just one person? . . . Hari, you have fallen silent, why? Why are you sad?' Shail placed her cheek on his head and asked.

'My head feels a little heavy,' Harish said, running his fingers through his hair. 'I will lie down with my head in your lap.'

'Yes, lie down.' Shail placed her hand on his forehead.

'Look, if seven years ago it had been you in her place, and I had come to know you in this way, would I have left you and gone away?' Harish closed his eyes and asked.

'Of course! Otherwise, you would not have been you.'

Harish opened his eyes and saw two teardrops falling from Shail's eyes.

'You are crying?' Harish asked.

Shail shook her head in refusal.

Harish lifted both his arms and put them around her neck. He pulled her head down and placed his lips against her brow. Shail did not stop him. Feeling Shail's tears on his face, Harish lifted her head and said, 'What is this? . . . You are indeed crying.'

Shail again shook her head.

Filled with yearning, Harish kissed her lips. It was as though lightning streaked through Shail's body, she trembled.

Harish became embarrassed and sat up. Lowering his eyes in shame he said, 'Please forgive me . . . that was wrong of me . . . I did not mean to hurt you.'

Tears were falling from Shail's eyes. Her cheeks turned red. Looking at Shail, Harish felt constricted by shame and went to his room.

In a state of agitation and anxiety, Harish lay down on his bed without changing his clothes. In the sharp electric light he lay looking fixedly at the white wall before him. In the silence that stretched for miles around, he could hear only the blood coursing through the veins of his head.

He did not even hear the sound of Shail's footsteps on the veranda. When he heard the door opening, he looked and saw Shail coming in, smiling. In an intensely sweet tone, she asked, 'Are you upset?'

'I?' Harish expressed surprise. He felt as if his feet had suddenly touched earth while he was drowning in a bottomless current of water.

'Why did you leave?' Shail sat down on his bed.

'You were frightened!'

'You crazy man!' Shail started stroking his hair.

Harish looked at her face and asked, 'Why do women fear men?'

'Who says so? . . . But perhaps there is indeed fear, when a man becomes an animal.'

'Had I become an animal?'

'You're crazy! . . . Then why would I come here?'

Harish took a breath of comfort. 'You see, Shail, it seems as though seven years ago I had left you and now I have returned to you. I mean . . . for me, you are the form of woman . . .' Feeling embarrassed, he gathered himself. 'As if I had returned, not as a husband . . . but a companion. You had asked me, do I think of her. Indeed, I think of her—as a very beautiful woman who stands before me like a vermilion flame of fire, and I want to lose myself in her. Perhaps this is what woman is . . . and you are its symbol.'

Shail's cheeks and eyes were flushed, it was difficult for her to speak. She looked at Harish with a smile, and her glance alone communicated how overwhelmed she was.

So as to escape a frightening confusion, Harish asked, 'Listen, Shail, does a woman always push a man behind, even if their path is the same, if their aim is the same?'

'Why, she may also take him forward,' Shail responded.

'A woman should fulfill a man's life. Both should move forward together. Is that not true?'

'Certainly!' Shail agreed.

'If attraction to a woman was destructive for the progress of a man's life, why would nature create this attraction? A man fears and flees from those objects that are harmful for his life, but he is attracted to a woman as though there was a void in his life, which he hoped to fill. Doesn't a woman feel the same way about a man?' Harish asked. In his tone tremulous emotion receded as the conviction of thought grew. His attitude changed from the personal to the theoretical.

'Who knows,' Shail responded with lowered eyes. Her response changed Harish's theoretical argument into personal feeling again.

'You don't feel this . . . that is why I think I may not be a good man,' Harish fell silent in despair.

When Shail saw sadness where she had expected strength, she gathered all her courage in compassion, as is the natural tendency of woman, lowered her eyes, and said hesitantly, 'Perhaps, women don't say this.'

Finding support, Harish said, 'Would you mind if I said something?'

Shail shook her head. In a trembling voice Harish said, 'If I said that I felt attracted to you, you wouldn't be upset, would you? . . . Tell me!'

Tears welled up in Shail's eyes again, but she did not want to show this to a man who could not distinguish between tears of anger and tears of joy, so she bit her lip and said, 'Is anyone ever upset by honour?'

Harish's eyes shone with the exultation of victory. 'Shail, will you agree to a request?'

'What?'

'First, you must promise me.'

Shail bent her head in assent.

Harish said, 'Look, Shail.' His voice trembled. 'I will not do anything . . . I only want to know, want to see, how beautiful a woman is. Just once, I want to see a woman's beauty fully.'

Shail asked in a thrilled voice, 'How?'

Harish, breathless, hesitant, said, 'You . . . I want to see you without clothes.'

Shail covered her face with both hands.

In a choked voice Harish said, 'For once in my life, I want to see for myself, what is 'that' powerful attraction. In my life I will have neither the opportunity nor the courage to make such a request to another woman.'

Shail was hiding her face in both hands.

In a trembling voice, Harish asked, 'Are you offended?'

With her face still buried in her hands, Shail shook her head.

Harish moved forward and started to take her hands away from her face.

Shail wrapped her arms around his neck.

Harish pleaded, 'Can't you do this?'

Shail turned her face away. 'How shall I do it?' And looking at Harish she said, 'It's very difficult, I won't be able to do it.'

Harish bowed his head in disappointment, 'As you wish.'

'But how should I do it?' Shail bent her head. She held her arms clasped, as if to gather strength. Then she recalled Harish's words that he would never be able to ask another woman . . . 'But you are sitting here before me.' She said helplessly.

Harish replied, 'I will go to the veranda. When you call me, I will come.' He got up and left.

Harish went to the veranda. Shail found it extremely difficult to take off her clothes; it felt as though she were taking off her skin, but as she thought about Harish hanging his head in disappointment, she felt compelled to force herself. How could she disregard the words of this boy, who was caught in the mouth of death? She took off all her clothes, one by one, and wrapped herself in a shawl, but how could she call Harish? She switched off the light.

Harish understood the signal and came with slow steps towards the switch. On turning on the light he saw that Shail's clothes were lying on the bed and with her head bent low, she was sitting against the wall wrapped in a shawl.

Standing near Shail, Harish said, 'This shawl is not made of glass.'

Shail's closed her eyes, let go of one end of the shawl, exposing her naked back.

'Please stand up,' Harish pleaded.

When he made the request twice, Shail stood up, bowing a little like a sinuous stream of smoke, her eyes still closed.

'Just once . . . open your eyes,' Harish said.

Shail looked at Harish through half-closed eyes and then quickly sitting down, she wrapped herself in the shawl and said, 'Go out!'

Harish went out.

Quickly Shail wore her clothes and returned to her room. Harish followed her. She lay down on her bed as though she were very tired.

Standing near her pillow, Harish said, 'Look, Shail, I feel as though I have received a lot. A kind of satiety . . . As if you were mine, and I yours. With this trust I will keep walking on my thorny path, otherwise I would become a criminal in your eyes.'

Shail clasped his hand and seated him on the bed. She placed her head in his lap.

Harish said softly, 'Now, even if no one understands me, you will remain sympathetic to me, won't you?'

Feeling fulfilled and peaceful in each other's presence, they both sat quietly.

Harish placed his hand on Shail's head and asked, 'I know what I have gained . . . What did you gain?'

'What shall I say? . . . Perhaps everything, whatever can be desired . . . the satisfaction of experiencing my being . . . a path for suppressed feelings.' Shail sighed deeply. 'See, you want revolution only in government—why don't you think about the tormented fluttering of lives trapped in the meshes of family and society? Doesn't a person want the right to fulfill her desires in life? . . . More than anything else, this is what I feel.'

Household

'J.R. Shukla' and 'Harish'—these two names alternately flashed across Amarnath's mind. He just could not doubt his memory. He remembered with certainty that the man had said his name was J.R. Shukla, and Yashoda said his name was Harish. He kept thinking—this man is acquainted with Yashoda, and they met at Shailbala's home. Why did Yashoda never mention before that she visits Shailbala's home? In the entire city, Yashoda visited only a few families, and he knew them all. What was her relation to Shailbala, how did she become acquainted with her? Shailbala participates in Congress processions, takes part in other public works. Whatever her qualities might be as a public worker, it didn't seem quite right for her to be frequenting familial spaces. And then, why didn't Yashoda mention this to him? Why was she so taken aback when she saw Harish or Shukla?

Some four–five days had passed since this incident. J.R. Shukla had promised to come to Amarnath's home for insurance, but he did not come. He had been evasive when Amarnath had asked about his address. It was also the first time that someone had come on their own accord to Amarnath's place to get an insurance policy. He tried asking Yashoda three or four times—'Since when do you know him? How many times have you met him at Shailbala's place?'

'Once,' Yashoda answered briefly.

'How long ago was it?'

'It must have been about a month ago.'

'What was the conversation about?'

'Oh, about Congress work.'

Amarnath was surprised. In this city, there was no Congress worker whom he did not know. He knew all the men of his own party and also the boys of the socialist and extremist groups. Shailbala lived in the same area where eight or ten of these young lads lived. He also knew most of the loafers, but he had never laid eyes on this youth—this Congress worker, wearing a suit and tie! He said he was a travelling engineer for Jeremy and Johnson.

Amarnath asked Yashoda again one day, 'So, you too work for the Congress, but you are not a member of the Congress!'

'I am,' Yashoda responded.

'Since when?'

'Since a few days.'

Yashoda's responses were very brief, and she kept her eyes lowered. In the last eight years he had never seen this side of her. Yashoda's conduct suggested that she might be carrying a mental weight; that she had started thinking of herself as someone who meant something too. Amarnath often remained dejected these days because of his mental confusion. He asked his neighbour Girdharilal about the Jeremy and Johnson Company, since he worked in a bank and knew the names of most of the big companies. Girdharilal reeled off the names of several engineering companies and said, 'I have never heard of Jeremy and Johnson.' Amarnath asked many of his other acquaintances about Jeremy and Johnson. He even looked up the name in the telephone directory but could not find this name anywhere.

It was in Yashoda's nature to speak sparingly, though her eyes would always smile when speaking to Amarnath. But since the day Amarnath started asking searching questions about Harish, a troubled expression came over Yashoda's face when she spoke, and she kept her eyes lowered. Amarnath also spoke as little as possible. An invisible distance had appeared between them.

After another week had passed, Amarnath asked again, 'His name is Harish, but to me he said it's J.R. Shukla!'

'It may be, but he and Shail told me it was Harish,' Yashoda answered in a guilty tone, like a criminal.

'What kind of Congress work did you all talk about?' Amarnath asked.

'Oh, just the work Congress does—about Swarajya.' Yashoda lowered her head.

What else could Amarnath ask? Nevertheless, his sadness and the embarrassment in his tone revealed to Yashoda the deep anxiety hidden behind these questions. With her chin resting on the fist of her right hand, Yashoda sat thinking— there is now a suspicion in his mind about me. . . . Her

lips trembled with fear and remorse at the very thought of
suspicion, but anger, arising from a perception of injustice,
suppressed her tears: After all, why this suspicion? What
have I done? What does he suspect? Looking at the ceiling
for hours, she would ponder—why is he humiliating me?
Why is he being so harsh? . . . After all, what have I done? Is
it just this that he has come to know about my acquaintance
with a man! That I did not tell him I have had conversations
pertaining to Congress work! . . . He has been working for
the Congress for eight years. I have never asked him what
he has been doing and why . . . And now this suspicion
because of a trivial matter! Is it because I am a woman? Can
a woman do nothing but engage in suspicious activity? Her
mind recalled the time when she had let Harish spend the
night downstairs in her home, but Amarnath didn't know
of that, and if he did, who knows what he might think!
After all, what evil deed did I commit?

Yashoda wept bitterly for days; silently, so no one
would see. She felt an injustice, and there was no recourse
but endurance. What other solution could there be? She
could ask for forgiveness—but for what? This was in her
fate, so it was unfolding. Just like other events—marriage,
childbirth—had happened, this too had to happen, and so
it was happening. She was just sad: in eight years she had
never given him a reason to suspect her, so what has he seen
now to make him suspicious?

Yashoda was not used to going out of her home.
Sometimes in the course of a month or two, she would
go out for a couple of hours only if someone had invited

her. But now she wanted to leave this home and go away somewhere, or perhaps wait for death to release her from this cruelty. Why shouldn't she simply die? What loss could her death cause to anyone? What is life and death for women? As long as the husband is happy, they live; as soon as the husband is displeased, they die. Her mother-in-law asked about her lassitude several times. Time and again she advised her to eat dried ginger or some other hot food or cooling food. Once she was almost ready to take her to the doctor, but Yashoda put her off saying she had no ailment.

Uday would come and cling to her. She would take her son in her arms. Earlier, when Uday obstinately insisted on something senseless, she would take him in her lap and explain, but now to get rid of the trouble she either simply gave in or told him in a distressed tone, 'Son, look, you are not a baby anymore, why are you pestering me?' She no longer found satisfaction in cajoling Uday, but when he asserted stubbornly that he would go to his father, she took him in her lap and caressed his head.

Yashoda would ask Uday, 'Son, will you be a brave man?' Trying to slip out of his mother's lap, Uday would say, 'Yes, let me get my gun.' He had an air-pistol. Yashoda, remembering the pistol in Harish's hand, had bought one for Uday. Sometimes Yashoda wished she could go to see Shail. But afraid that her husband would be even more displeased, she would stifle the wish. She turned pallid. She was convinced that she would just waste away in grief.

Amarnath had begun to find his domestic life entirely joyless. He spent all his time in his insurance work. He went upstairs only to eat and sleep. Even while working, he often gazed out of the window, his fountain pen clenched between his teeth. Harish, wearing a suit, smoking a cigarette, would dance before his eyes. Who is this person? He would begin to ponder. The way he laughingly made up stories, sat with Shail in the car and vanished—for Amarnath, all this appeared proof of his utter depravity.

Amarnath thought—for eight years I trusted Yashoda blindly. After all, she just met Harish once. Then why is she so sad, so lost in thinking about him? I am nothing to her even after eight years, and he has become so significant in just one day! He felt humiliated and debased in his own eyes. The man whose wife finds him useless—what kind of a life can he lead? He should send her to her parents and never call her back, or turn her out of the house. Let her taste the pleasures of being friends with other men. He would recall stories about various unfaithful women who had been punished, but finally, even in her punishment lay his own disgrace.

If the woman is an unfaithful wife, the husband's disgrace is a hundred times more than the woman's. He thought—a woman is restless by nature. Yashoda had never seemed restless, but how could one trust a woman! Woman is the root of all misconduct, all degradation, she should never be trusted! Earlier he did not believe such things, but now it seemed a mistake to him. This incident has opened his eyes and he has seen the world for what it is. He had himself seen many beautiful women from time to time. Even if he felt attracted to one—so what? He always kept his mind in check—but what of woman? The mere sight of one youth, not very good-looking either, rather garrulous—and she is smitten!

At times Amarnath thought that whatever has happened has happened, now he should make Yashoda understand that she must forget about that youth. Then he thought: who knows how far they've gone in their relationship? If it is purely platonic, that's different, but if they've gone further . . . The very thought of a strange man in a physical relationship with his wife made his head spin . . . he saw red. After that he could only see death . . . Yashoda's . . . his own . . . and both their deaths.

When he imagined a physical or a mental relation between Harish and Yashoda, he thought: which of these two would be a greater sin? His Reason answered: Why worry about a mental connection, thoughts come and go, but the body is a material thing. Whatever happens to a body cannot be wiped out. Again, Reason would argue— why worry about the body; we touch so many objects and we then clean our hands. What we touch does not become a part of our body. The human is a puppet of feelings and thoughts. When feelings and thoughts change, the person changes. Sitting alone, Amarnath would sigh deeply, but as far as possible, he did not let this change his behaviour. He thought: why not talk to Yashoda about this someday, but at the same time he would think: will she tell me the truth? If she were still true to me, why would she be attracted to another man?

Amarnath and Yashoda would lie in the darkness on their beds, eyes to the ceiling. Neither could fall asleep till late, but they could not talk to one another. Many times the words rose to Amarnath's lips but he could not utter them. Once or twice, in order to start a conversation, he called out, 'Look! . . .' And Yashoda responded, 'Yes?' but then Amarnath lost courage. He thought: what will I gain by speaking? He put it off.

'We should put Uday in school now,' Amarnath said.

'As you say,' Yashoda responded.

With no enthusiasm or interest in anything, Yashoda lay on a cot, wrapped in a shawl, her gaze fixed on the kite-filled sky. She thought—what will become of this life?

Bishan informed her: 'Bibiji, a bibiji has come to meet you.'

'Which bibiji?' Yashoda asked lazily, still lying. She thought of Shail, but assuming there was no possibility of her coming, she was thinking of her other acquaintances when Shail arrived upstairs and asked, 'So, why are you lying down?'

Yashoda promptly sat up. 'No reason—it's nothing. Come!'

Yashoda gladly made room on the cot for Shail. 'After so many days, a glimpse of you! I thought of going to your place many times but could not go. Are you well? You seem well.'

Shail sat close to Yashoda. 'I had gone to the hills for a while. How are you? You have become so pale! What is it?' Seeing Yashoda silent, Shail took her hand in her own and pleaded, 'Tell me!'

The anguish in Yashoda's despairing heart rose to flow out as tears from her eyes, but with feigned laughter she held her heart in check. Shail put a hand on her shoulder and asked, 'Did something happen that day when you brought water?'

Without saying a word, Yashoda kept her head bent and tried to muster a smile. When Shail repeated her question, she said, 'What could have happened? Why, what made you think of that?'

'Just that men become suspicious very quickly,' Shail said. 'Harish was very worried. He asked me many times to meet you and ask, but I was so entangled I could not come. Tell me; consider it was my fault that day. Harish was not ready to come to your place. In a way it was I who sent him here for half an hour, and then you entered! . . . Did something happen? Harish told Amarnathji that his name is J.R. Shukla. He must have asked you later?'

Yashoda took a deep breath. 'Yes.'

'And you said "Harish". . . . Then?'

'Then what?' Yashoda turned her face away. 'You have already said, men look for an excuse to be suspicious.'

'He didn't ask you anything else? . . . What kind of suspicion? Did he ask you, "Who is Harish?" Has he understood that he is a revolutionary?' Shail asked anxiously.

'No . . . He just keeps brooding over it,' Yashoda averted her eyes. 'He understands only one thing—that Harish is a young man.'

'So, this is the sorrow that has reduced you to this state? If he thinks you are in the wrong, what fault is it of yours?' Shail asked sadly. 'You are wasting away because of this.'

'But to think so wrong about me . . .!'

'Sister, is there nothing in the world besides a man's pleasure and displeasure? What if the man is unjust?'

'Shail, indeed this is an injustice but I just don't know what I should do.' Tears came to Yashoda's eyes.

Shail took her hand in her lap and said, 'I would say, either don't care or tell him who Harish is. The quarrel will end.'

Tears fell from Yashoda's eyes. She said, 'If he could not understand who I am in eight years, what shall I explain to him in one day? You say I should tell him . . . now that his suspicion and jealousy have been aroused, what if he decides to take revenge once he knows about Harish! And what would I tell him? . . . Maybe Harish hasn't told you, the night that he escaped from jail, he suddenly came here. He stayed hidden all night in the room downstairs. If I also tell him this, will it not increase his suspicion?'

Shail was stunned to hear this. To express her devotion to Yashoda, she took her hand and placed it over her own heart. 'Sister, you are older than I am, but let me say this, if you care so much about men's suspicion and needless displeasure, then either live like a handkerchief in their pocket—stop thinking and talking about your life— or let them think what they will! They will eventually understand!. . . . There is no dearth of the nasty things I've heard about myself. If I had become anxious like you, I would have died a long time ago, but I alone know how much of truth there is in such talk. Till now women have remained objects of personal use for men. If women make even the smallest attempt to establish their separate individuality, fingers will certainly be pointed at them initially, but not after some days . . . Try to be courageous. Men should get used to the idea that women have their own individuality. They don't simply become a part of someone who sees them or touches them . . . Just step out of your home. Consider the other side, then you will not be forced to give up your life just because of a man's suspicion. Whatever he understands—is that right? You too must understand something!'

'What should I do?' Yashoda asked helplessly.

'Just this—don't worry so much about senseless things. Let's talk about sensible things! It should be clear that you too are someone! One should worry about things other than the displeasure of men!' Shail laughed.

'But tell me, what should I do?'

'Come with me today! We are going to ask in a public meeting that the economic demands of the people be placed on the agenda of the Congress. I have a speech prepared, you read it out! Read it a couple of times in advance . . . Don't hesitate. One always begins like this. I will also speak.'

'But what will he think of this?' Yashoda asked anxiously.

'This is just what we want. Listen, if two women are speaking at the meeting, five hundred men will show up instead of fifty. This is how we will gain our objective.'

Yashoda smiled in embarrassment and said, 'How wicked you are! Taking me along to drag men to the meeting!'

'So what? They are not going to eat you up. They will look at you, you too can look at them. We are concerned about being heard. If a hundred listen, ten will understand, and one will start acting . . . What will you lose? After all, how will you achieve anything? . . . Today, tomorrow, the day after, whenever you pass before men, they will stare, but what can we do?'

'Sister, I will not be able to do this,' Yashoda laughed and waving her hand, refused.

'I am determined to take you . . . Harish also told me to.'

'I am very scared of him.'

'Why? After all, you are not going to steal anything. This is the only way to cure him.'

When Shail insisted, Yashoda had to agree—but on this condition that she would not speak at the meeting, only come along. Amarnath was not at home. Shail spoke to Yashoda's mother-in-law on her behalf, 'Maaji, I'm just taking her with me for some time, I will bring her back.'

Yashoda was changing her sari to go out with Shail, but her body trembled from time to time, as though she were planning a dreadful rebellion against her husband . . . but what could she do? At that moment it seemed she had entrusted the raft of her life to Shail. As she was leaving, she wrapped a shawl over her sari as she always did.

Shail said, 'So, you're going to become a granny at the very outset. This sari is enough to cover the body. If you have to wear a shawl, at least don't become a wrapped-up bundle!' Yashoda did not agree. She went out in her usual style.

Having embarked on her journey of rebellion, Yashoda was descending the stairs at the threshold of the house when she saw Amarnath asking Shail's car driver questions. Yashoda felt as if she would fall. At that moment she heard Shail's unembarrassed voice. Without formality, she was saying to Amarnath, 'Bhai Sahib, I am just taking her with me. I will myself bring her back.'

Before Amarnath could say a word, Shail pushed Yashoda in the car and sitting beside her, she ordered the driver to start the car, while saying 'Namaste' to Amarnath.

When Yashoda gathered herself, she felt as though her raft had broken from its anchor and was being carried away by the current to another world, which had no relation to her old, familiar world. Now what would become of her? . . . There was no path of return. Nor did she have any desire to return.

On reaching her home, Shail gave Yashoda the speech she had written. Just like an accused, who, upon hearing the death sentence from a judge is no longer attentive to minor discomforts, Yashoda had become insensible and unaware to some extent. After reading the speech a few times, she began to think that all these statements are correct; she must indeed lend her voice to them. Since she had been brave enough to leave her house right in front of her husband, she must do something now.

When Yashoda stood up in the assembly to read the speech, she felt that the eyes of the people gathered there were attacking her, but she was determined to endure it. She read out the speech. Her body and mind were so agitated that she could not hear the words that came out of her own mouth. Only when she sat down after reading the speech did she begin to understand what others were saying. She also understood now the arguments that others proposed. She felt that something else should also be said in response, but that was beyond her capability. When she saw Shail speaking freely, she felt content that at least she had not suffered a terrifying meltdown.

After the meeting, when Shail was taking her home in the car, Yashoda felt that the biggest difficulty was yet to confront her, but now there was no question of escaping it. Now that she had already spoken at the meeting, what would her husband say? . . . What was the most that he could say? Yashoda wanted him to speak the harshest of harsh words to her, and she wanted to endure them. Now there is no option for her but to endure.

On reaching the drawing room, Yashoda saw that Amarnath was sitting in a chair. As though he had been waiting for hours for her to return. Actually, Amarnath had become quite agitated when he saw Yashoda leave with Shail. Is Yashoda going to meet Harish? This thought had aroused intense feelings of revenge in his mind. He could not wait. To clarify matters he went to Shail's home. After pacing in front of the house for a long time he went inside. On inquiring he found out that Shail had gone to a meeting in Ganga Hall. Amarnath reached the hall in an agitated state and he saw and heard Yashoda reading her speech.

He thought: what will people say when they recognize me? He immediately returned. On arriving home, he began to think about how far Yashoda had moved away from him. At Harish's mere behest, she was performing the kind of task that was extremely difficult even for him. How insignificant he had become! Then, this feeling of insignificance changed to anger—if she wants to stay in this house, then she will have to do as I say.

How could Yashoda go upstairs without saying anything to her husband? That would have been an insult to him, a declaration of revolt and hostility, but she had neither revolted nor declared hostility. She had handled everything courageously today. Once again, she took courage. Looking at her husband, she asked, 'Have you been sitting here since then? Come upstairs! You look very tired. . . . Shall I warm up some milk for you?'

After almost three months, Yashoda had spoken to her husband in this way. Amarnath had been sitting, waiting for her, ready to say a lot of things, but once Yashoda said this, he weakened. Then, trying to take the initiative again, he accepted and said, 'Yes, let's go.'

While Yashoda was heating the milk, Amarnath sat on the bed, trying to prepare his speech with firm resolve. Yashoda brought the glass of milk. To keep his resolve intact Amarnath kept the glass on the table near him and clasping both hands, he said, 'I want to say something to you.'

Yashoda was waiting for just this instant. She responded, 'Yes.'

'Sit down,' said Amarnath. With lowered gaze, Yashoda sat facing him.

'Where did you go?'

'To an event with Shailbala.'

'What kind of event?'

'These people had organized it.'

'Hmm . . . You didn't go to events before.'

'Yes. Now I think I should go . . . I should do something,' Yashoda responded, still with her head lowered.

'Hmm . . . this J.R. Shukla . . . Harish . . . must also have come there?' Looking obliquely at Yashoda's face, Amarnath asked.

'I can't say . . . I didn't see him,' Yashoda answered, and bit her lips to quell the rising tide in her heart.

'I think,' Amarnath again clasped his hands in determination, 'women's place is within the home. Everything goes well if one stays within a limit. And especially this girl, Shailbala, you perhaps don't know how notorious she is in the city . . . I don't want to say anything else, but I know how our society behaves. If women take part in public affairs, what is said about them, how many fingers are pointed at them—all this should also be kept in mind. I don't like hearing and seeing such things with regard to my wife.'

When Amarnath became silent, Yashoda said, 'I am mindful that there should be no lapse in the household work. I consider Shailbala to be a good person. In any case, people needlessly suspect any woman . . . men always distrust women . . . If someone points a finger or makes up stories without cause, what can one do? . . . When Father started sending me to school to study, even then so many people talked about it. You used to praise the women who work for the Congress. If you have noticed something particular in me, then please tell me. However, if you wish that the wives of others should work for the Congress, but that I shouldn't, then please tell me what I lack. Everyone has the same honour. . . . If you believe that women can't be trusted outside the home, then how can you trust them within the home? If you don't trust me, then tell me the reason . . .!'

If after this argument Amarnath placed restrictions on Yashoda, these restrictions could only be physical ones. And that would mean that he accepted his fear of Yashoda, that he had fallen in her eyes and that he was not confident of himself. There was only one path available. He said, 'No, that is not what I meant. I meant, you should consider the fact that our—your and my—welfare lies in the same direction.'

As long as Yashoda was sitting in front of her husband she held back her tears by biting her lips. But later she went to the bathroom and wept for a long time. She decided that having taken this step she would not retreat, otherwise all the work she had done so far would only be seen as sinful behaviour.

Amarnath began to think, was his suspicion regarding Harish baseless after all! . . . Though he tried to convince himself in various ways, he was not successful. The one thing he could not deny was that he was no longer the sole lord of Yashoda's heart. Whatever else might be the case, now Yashoda no longer considered herself the mere dust at her husband's feet. Instead, she was thinking of how she herself could become a human being in her own right . . . Though he could not find any fault in her, Yashoda no longer remained his personal object. He alone was no longer everything for her. Now when this 'event-attending' and 'procession-participating' Yashoda stepped into the home, he would not be able to gather the courage to pet her, to treat her merely as material for his comfort. It seemed to him that now he faced his wife not as her master, but as just an ordinary person.

Riddle

In the garden in front of their bungalow, Robert and Shail sat on a wicker sofa. In one hand Robert held a cigarette and in the other a letter. After many days he has received a letter from Flora. Robert read the letter aloud to Shail:

'Even though I have placed my life as an offering at the feet of Jesus, I cannot ignore God's will. You have placed me in a religious crisis. In my past two letters I have written to you that if you no longer have faith in God and in the teachings of his Son the Messiah, then for you to continue as a Christian is simply deceitful. Your physical and spiritual relations with me have broken; there is nothing to be gained from the pretense of preserving them. By ceasing to believe in the Bible, you have already broken the vow we both took, with Bible in hand, to spend our lives together. Six months ago, I had pleaded with you to become a Hindu and thus end our marital relationship. Though you have no reverence for Jesus, you did not accept my plea because you wanted to keep your legal rights over me. This obstinacy of yours has produced a life-crisis for me. Though the goal of my life is religion, I am also a woman. I have not cared about financial difficulties—for me a far greater difficulty is to hurt the emotions of a companion who has dedicated his life to the service of God's beloved ones, the impoverished and the unhappy. I too need a companion in life. Even with Christ as one's companion, there is much that remains on this earth from which one cannot turn away, for the heart's inclinations render one helpless.

'You may call me a culprit and a sinner, but in fact the fault is yours. If six months ago you had accepted my prayer and become a Hindu, I would have peacefully married again, but you were unkind. Today I am three months pregnant. You have written that I can divorce you. You know that in this condition it may not be possible for me even to remain here. My companion and I will be so disgraced that in future it will not be possible for my companion to stay in this society and to serve religion. I am not particularly worried about my own life. I am not afraid of death either, but I don't want to commit suicide and burn eternally in the fires of hell. More than this, I am concerned about that dear beloved of God, who will have to bear disgrace and difficulty for all these reasons. He has dedicated his life to the service of Jesus. He does not have enough wealth to help me today.

'I cannot bear the thought of people calling the child of my womb illegitimate, the child of sin. All this has happened because of your stubborn refusal to become a Hindu. My soul, my companion's soul, and the Lord Jesus know that the child is innocent. It is not to be blamed for our conditions and difficulties. Then why should I take upon myself the sin of killing it? Till the child is born, I want the legal right to call myself your wife, and I would like you to arrange for me to live in some secluded place at this difficult time. After the birth of the child, we will get divorced. I will not ask for any kind of help in raising the child. Earlier, you wanted to help me financially, but I had not accepted your help. Today, I myself am begging you for a loan, only to protect this innocent child in my womb. I hope you will not disappoint me. May Jesus awaken kindness in your heart . . .'

Robert suddenly felt his finger burning as the cigarette had burnt to the end. Throwing it away, he looked at his finger.

Shail asked, 'You burnt your finger? Uff . . .!' Holding his hand, she put his finger in her mouth, and asked, 'Does that give some relief?'

Robert laughed. 'But it's the heart that's been burnt.'

Placing her arm around Robert's neck, and resting her head on his shoulder, Shail asked, 'Ruby, now what will you do?'

'What should be done?' he asked, lifting her chin. 'Just think, what a crisis she is in at this time.'

'Yes . . . but this means that we cannot think of our marriage for another eight or ten months,' Shail said in a sad voice.

'Yes, if I agree to what she says, then we can't think of it,' Robert responded, lighting another cigarette.

'But Ruby, what is your fault in all this? You had advised her to divorce you at that very moment,' Shail said, raising her eyebrows.

'Shail, after all, what is a fault?' Robert replied, exhaling slowly. 'To see someone in trouble and not to care is also a fault. If Flora were in my place, and I in Flora's, she would have said, you have committed a sin, you must bear the punishment, and she herself would have prayed to God—O God, you are merciful and just, save me from this crisis, and her duty would have ended. Her mind and soul would have been appeased, but what should I do? I cannot deny the fact that she is in a terrible crisis. If you speak of legal justice—from the perspective of justice, no one has anything to do with another person's crisis. Justice exists only to protect selfishness.'

'Some obstruction or the other will always appear in my life,' Shail became sad. 'All right, so what will you do?'

'I could do this: rent a home for Flora in Mussoorie or Nainital or Shimla and regularly pay for her expenses, but Nancy should not know of this or she would create a storm. She has not yet seen the difficulties of life, so she has a very harsh notion of what is appropriate and inappropriate. She is also not a little upset with Flora because we have been quite severely humiliated on her account.'

Taking Robert's right hand in her own hands, Shail said, 'When I think of you, I am amazed . . . how large-hearted you are.'

'Just ask Flora!' Robert laughed.

'*Damn Flora!*' Shail tossed her head. Then after a few moments of silence she said, 'Ruby, is suicide really a sin?'

'What sin is, I have not been able to understand so far. If one starts hating one's own life, why should one live? At least as far as I am concerned, if I find no enthusiasm in life, I don't want to live.'

'And Ruby, abortion?' Shail asked.

'It is cruel to end any life. Think of this: when Flora's child plays in her lap, how much enthusiasm and contentment she will find in life; but think also of this—if that child only makes Flora's life difficult, and if there is no place in society for the child's own life, how unjust it is to bring the child into the world to receive only hatred and rejection! Everything depends on society. Society may worship Jesus Christ, but it cannot bear the birth of another Christ because there is no place in society for him. I believe that in the present scenario, there is no option but *birth control*.

'If the state of society were as it was earlier, meaning that one man kept many women, then, as in the early civilizations of Greece, India and other countries, there would be armies of beautiful women for the amusement of men. If there were no fear of unemployment, all children born would simply be considered gifts of God, but now that situation does not prevail. A human being's condition should not be such that all day long he finds no opportunity for anything except trying to fill his stomach. Nature pushes him towards sexual pleasure. If a human being has means and time, why should he not go towards it? Don't be needlessly shy. Tell me—if a healthy young woman were to become pregnant each time, how often would she have the opportunity for sexual enjoyment in her life? Either she would produce a child each year, for whom there is no space on earth, or she

would not think about sex more than two or three times
in her life. Of those great souls who preach celibacy, how
many would be able to pass such a test? It is to fulfill this
very need that civilization has given birth to prostitutes.

'In this era of new civilization when there is talk of
giving a woman the right to full equality, how can her
natural inclination for pleasure be obstructed? In our
society, becoming pregnant is indeed a woman's biggest
dependence and weakness. The man walks away, dusting
his hands, smoking a cigarette, but the woman lands in deep
trouble! . . . What should she do! The desire for sexual
pleasure is a powerful natural inclination. All the religions
of the world have prohibited it, but it has remained strong.
As long as life courses, it cannot be stopped. Whatever
consequences we have to bear because of this, they are a
result of our social conditions. Whenever there is desire for
pleasure, there isn't a corresponding desire for progeny, so
why should there always be progeny? It is an injustice to
bring a child into the world whom its circumstances cannot
welcome. A time also comes in life when one wants a
child—that is the time when the child should come. Many
people say that contraception is against nature. I ask them,
when nature produces such intense desire, is it not against
nature to obstruct it? And is it not against nature to give
birth to beings for whom there is no place in society . . .?'

Feeling embarrassed by Robert's words and trying not
to meet his eye, Shail opened his cigarette case. Taking
out a cigarette, she put it in her mouth. Robert said, 'Just
light it!'

Shaking her head Shail said, 'No, you keep talking . . . so what is the path? You have surrounded us on all sides with nature.'

Robert said in a pleading tone, 'No, first you light the cigarette. It feels very nice to see a beautiful woman smoking a cigarette.'

'I am beautiful!' Shail raised her eyebrows to show her surprise.

'You know that I find you very beautiful.'

'I will feel dizzy,' Shail said somewhat helplessly. 'You continue what you were saying. I myself sometimes think . . .'

'You light your cigarette. Don't breathe in the smoke. You won't feel dizzy. Now that the wish to see you smoking has gripped me, you will have to indulge my obstinacy.'

Embarrassed, Shail lit her cigarette. A thin circle of smoke spread around her face. Robert said, 'This is lovely, please continue. There's a contentment in being seen as beautiful, isn't there? That's why women get their nose and ears pierced.'

Shaking her head, Shail said, 'You continue talking about nature.'

'Yes; so, what was I saying? Yes, nature forces us to make an arrangement and find a path such that sexual pleasure can be separated from its consequences. When we don't want a child, a child should not be born. A child, rather than being a cause for sadness, should only be a cause for happiness. You must believe that without facing necessity, humans do nothing. Contraception is a natural necessity. In nature, this task is carried out by other means. A she-snake lays a thousand eggs, but when a thousand offspring are born, she herself wraps her tail around them and eats them. Only the one or two that are left survive to become a terror for other creatures. If all of them survived, other beings in nature would die. It is the same with fish and other living things. Some decrease their numbers themselves, some are decreased by other predators, but who will decrease the number of human beings? Diseases break out, but the human being finds a cure. Although the human being has not yet been able to find a cure for the disease of war, war too starts only when tribes and nations begin to die of starvation because of increased population; or when they make a pretense of such starvation deaths. Since it limits the population of human beings, contraception is also a way of making their lives happy.'

Fearful of the smoke, Shail said, 'I am going to throw this cigarette.'

Tossing his own cigarette stub, Robert said, 'Here, give it to me.'

'What, this used one!'

'Not used, call it sweet. Otherwise, you always keep your lips far from mine. Let it be via this cigarette then!'

With smiling eyes, Shail placed her head on Robert's shoulder. In a low voice, Robert asked, 'Is this acceptance?'

'You are full of mischief!' Shail said and was moving back, when Robert kissed her.

Hearing the horn of a car at the door, Shail looked in that direction.

'It must be Nancy,' Robert told her. 'She had gone to the market. It won't be long before Harish and his companions come. It is almost six-thirty.'

Nancy was going towards the steps of the veranda when Shail called to her, 'Come here, Naina!' And she asked Robert, 'Naina is very quiet these days!'

'She has her own problems,' Robert responded. 'She is twenty years old. When the mind enters the world of hope and imagination, obviously alienation and silence ensue. She asked me for Mirajkar's address many times. She asked you too, didn't she? I thought before matters go any further, I should explain to her, so I told her what is Mirajkar's actual state. One can't write a letter to him. He simply turns up in the course of his wanderings now and then.'

'You explained it all clearly, didn't you? Lest she say something!' Shail asked worriedly.

'Very well. She knows that if Mirajkar is in danger, we will also be in danger. But the consequence has been quite different from what I had imagined. Now she thinks about his bravery and sacrifice. Earlier her friendship was with David. Now she has stopped meeting him. These days she doesn't play the violin either. And do you know, this is the phrase that is on her lips these days: "That which couldn't be of use to anyone, I am that handful of dust!"*

---

* A line from a popular ghazal usually attributed to Bahadur Shah Zafar, the last Mughal emperor (1775–1862), though it may have been written by Muztar Khairabadi.

Nancy arrived in two or three minutes. Since a few days she had stopped wearing a gown and wore a sari all the time, with its end carelessly thrown around her neck as if she were very busy with housework. Addressing her, Shail said, 'Nancy, your sweet peas have turned out wonderfully!'

'Oh yes, poor things, they're good,' Nancy said carelessly.

'I have asked for tea, Nain. We didn't have any either, we were waiting for you,' Robert said.

'Let's wait for another five–ten minutes; Mirajkar is probably about to reach,' Shail advised. 'Didn't he say he would reach by a quarter to six?'

'What's the hurry?' Nancy sat down on the chair facing them.

Just then, they saw Harish coming on his bicycle. Keeping the bicycle at the entrance, he came towards them. As soon as he came, he asked Nancy, 'So, are you well?'

'Yes, indeed, very well.'

Harish then asked Robert and Shail how they were. Nancy rose and said, 'I will ask for tea.'

Looking at Shail and Robert, Harish said, 'Those people will come after seven. Mr Robert, I wanted to come a little early so that I could tell you my thoughts. Rafiq is only focused on raising economic questions among the labourers and other people. If the labouring folk take this path, national consciousness will never awaken among them and their protest will remain very restricted. I want that some middle-class men should also join the central committee of the labourers of different professions so that their protest may be given a national form. Isn't that right, Shail?'

'Yes, of course this is right, and we have started your work already. We have held three of your events. We have ensured that proposals expressing sympathy with the labourers of the cloth-mills and power sector were passed. Yashoda also attends these events now, and so does Nancy. Scores of college boys have started attending. You tell us about yourself. Have you settled in your new home?'

'Yes,' Harish took out a piece of paper from his pocket and started looking at it.

Shail looked at Robert with smiling eyes and said, 'Oh, Naina . . .'

With his eyes, Robert signalled to her to remain quiet, and himself finished the sentence, 'Naina is taking a long time . . . She must be just coming. Have you seen these sweet peas?'

Keeping the paper in his pocket, Harish said, 'I saw them as soon as I entered. It is amazing how fragrant they are.' Harish got up and picking two very beautiful flowers, he gave one to Robert and one to Shail. Shail put the flower in her hair.

Nancy came with the server carrying the tea-tray. As soon as she came, Robert complained, 'Naina, look, Mirajkar has plucked two of your flowers.'

'Is it forbidden to pluck flowers?' Harish looked at Nancy.

'Here, let me make tea,' Shail pulled the tray towards herself.

Nancy went towards the sweet pea tendrils. She asked Harish, 'Which colour do you like?'

'They are all nice,' Harish replied.

Seeing Nancy crestfallen Robert said, 'Of course he will like the red colour, isn't that right, Mirajkar?'

Hesitating a little, Nancy plucked some red flowers with long stalks, made a bouquet and silently placed it before Harish.

'Thank you!' Taking the flowers respectfully in one hand, Harish kept drinking his tea. When he finished, he addressed Nancy: 'May I place these flowers wherever I wish?'

'Why not?' Nancy said, taking a sip from her cup.

Harish arose and going behind Nancy he placed the flowers one by one in her hair. They looked like a peacock's plume. Nancy sat quietly, but her wheat-coloured face turned pink. Harish thought: this arrogant Mussoorie girl will say something. But Nancy remained quiet.

When Harish returned to his place, Nancy said, 'How well you know how to return things.'

'Everything looks good in its own place,' Harish responded.

Shail looked at Nancy and said, 'Mirajkar has made you a queen. You will see if you just take a look in the mirror . . . Mirajkar, you are a man of taste!'

Without responding, Harish merely laughed. Robert got up, went near the flowerbeds, lit another cigarette and wandered away. From a distance he called, 'Shail, have you seen these dianthuses?' Shail went towards him. Seeing

Harish extend his hand towards the teapot for his third cup
of tea, Nancy started preparing it.

Harish looked at Nancy and asked, 'Why are you so
quiet?'

'Not at all,' Nancy replied. 'Perhaps you fear that I am
not worthy of trust. Are you Harish or Mirajkar these days?
You acted so well in Mussoorie!' Nancy spoke without
looking at him.

'You are offended. It had nothing to do with not
trusting you.'

'No, what right do I have to be offended?' Nancy said,
giving the cup to Harish.

'You tell me, what right do I have to burden someone
with my secrets without permission?' Harish said, as though
asking for forgiveness.

Offering him the plate of biscuits Nancy said, 'You
have not eaten anything.' Looking around towards the
flowerbeds, Harish finished his tea and biscuits. Nancy
opened Robert's cigarette case and offered him a cigarette.
When he took one, she lit a match and held it for him.

'Thank you,' Harish bent to light the cigarette. His
head touched Nancy's.

'Forgive me,' Harish apologized in embarrassment.

'It's nothing,' Nancy was quiet again.

'Why are you so quiet today?' Harish asked again.

'If one speaks, people assume one is shallow,' Nancy
said, cracking her knuckles. Looking at her long, slim, fair
fingers, Harish looked at her body. Her hair was exceedingly
fine and soft; not greasy, but naturally smooth. A fan of red

sweet pea flowers in her bun, a long and thin face, a long neck, the shape of her body dimly perceptible through her sari, the slight curve of her breast, a slim waist, and then like the flow of a stream of water, her calves below the knees, and her soft fair feet encased in sandals. The sari gathered all around her feet was spread out like the petals of a flower surrounding the pollen-centre. Her arms, smooth and soft like yellow ivory, were settled in her lap. On each wrist lay a very fine black bangle. An obscure fragrance came from her body. Nancy was like a flower bud; she had not yet fully opened and spread out, but was on the verge of blossoming. She was complaining about Harish's neglect. Harish felt that an incomparable beauty was facing him, it was the most beautiful and radiant figure he had ever seen, but like the statue of Urvashi in a museum, it was meant only to be seen and praised. It may be far more beautiful than the reality that Shail had generously revealed to him, but he had a claim over Shail that he did not have here. Harish's mind filled with passion and gratitude for Shail. For a moment he saw Shail sitting in Nancy's place. He alerted his mind—this is not Shail! Everyone is not Shail, for whom his transgression wasn't a crime.

To escape that difficult silence, Harish said, 'Shail has dragged you too in this work.'

'No one can drag another person against their will,' Nancy objected, her head still bent.

The way Harish's question gestured towards Shail's primacy and the spark of jealousy it provoked in Nancy's mind—Harish did not pay attention to that. Not finding anything else to say, he said, 'Your flowers are really very beautiful. One wishes one could look at them forever.'

Nancy did not respond. She kept cracking her knuckles, but her proud heart thought—I am fit only for diversion and superficial conversation. As if no serious or responsible conversation could be had with me! Acting out her mental unrest on her soft fingers she said without raising her head, 'You cannot be concerned about such petty things. These are for people like us, who are of no use.'

Harish's mind was stung by this sharp distortion. Not comprehending that it had been made in order to seek a claim, he began to defend himself, 'This is a matter of circumstance, but a human being does desire life, does experience beauty.'

Seeing that her words had not reached their mark, Nancy looked sadly at Harish. She hoped that the gaze would make clear what words had been unable to, but Harish was looking elsewhere. Nancy spoke again, 'Your life is in such danger here, why don't you go abroad?'

'How should I go?' Harish's answer was a question.

'It is not so difficult for you. You will be able to gain so much experience there and when the time comes, it will be easier for you to return to your work here. It is just a matter of money, is it not? Sometimes I too think of going to Europe for a while.'

Taking a drag on his cigarette, Harish answered, 'By going abroad I will escape danger, but I did not leave my home to run away from danger. The work for which I put myself in danger will be left behind.'

'Then you should stay back, not put yourself in danger. You should give instructions so others can do the work,' Nancy said.

'Whoever comes forward to work will be in risk of danger. If I don't, why should others?' Harish asked.

'Haven't you been doing enough work? Will it not affect your health—neither eating on time, nor sleeping? Why don't you stay here? There can be no suspicion here,' Nancy said warmly.

'It is not a matter of suspicion . . . Now when you go forward and start working among the people, you too will come under suspicion. You too will not be free of danger. I want to live where the labourers live. I am trying to get a job in some mill, I think that would be good. It does not seem good to continually burden others for one's subsistence.'

'What kind of burden? . . . Do you need money?' Nancy asked.

'No, not yet.'

'If you don't have money, please take it, I have some . . . You don't need to tell anyone,' Nancy said.

'When I need it, I will surely take it. I have no hesitation with you . . . you are like my sister.'

Although she had come close to Harish, Nancy was not at peace. 'I will just return,' she said, and went inside. She opened her box and saw that she had sixty rupees. Folding the notes in her hand, she came outside. She had just reached close to Harish when a police sergeant and some constables entered from the door on the other side of the house. Harish said softly, 'You move aside. I will have to fire.'

Instead of moving aside Nancy came closer. Harish said again, 'Move aside, you will needlessly be hurt.'

Determined to bear the coming assault on Harish, Nancy stood in front of him. In order to go in front of her, Harish moved towards the police sergeant with his hand on the trigger of the pistol in his pocket. Seeing that the sergeant's hand was not placed on his revolver, he kept his hand still. After a long silence, the sergeant said, 'Good evening, please forgive me for entering without permission. What is the number of your car? . . . May I please see your car?'

Telling him the number of the car, Nancy pointed towards it. Harish asked the sergeant, 'Why, what is the matter?'

The sergeant responded, 'About an hour ago, a car hit the mudguard of the Governor's car on the Mall Road and sped on to this road. We can't locate it.' Apologizing, the sergeant and the constables left.

On seeing the police enter the house, Shail and Robert's hearts had started beating fast. When they saw the police leave, and Nancy and Harish laughing, they came close. Upon hearing the reason for the police visit, they all started laughing.

Nancy smiled and said to Harish, 'You think everyone is a coward.' It was the first time that day that Nancy's face was lit up with laughter.

Harish looked into her eyes and said, 'You stepped forward as if determined to embrace death!'

Flitting like a sparrow on to the other flowerbed, Nancy said, 'Aha! You have not yet seen this nargis.'

Harish failed to understand both Nancy's readiness to make herself the target of a bullet for his protection and her carelessness in responding to his observation. Nancy was leading him from one flowerbed to the next. Harish felt something rustling in his pocket, he put his hand in and felt something paper-like. Taking it out, he saw there were a few notes. Harish looked at Nancy, but she was saying, '. . . You have no discernment; neither of flowers nor of anything else.'

Earlier Harish had complained about Nancy's silence, but now he could not understand her chirping.

When Rafiq and his companion arrived, Robert, Harish and Rafiq argued for a long time. Harish called Shail to participate in the discussion too. On not being invited to that gathering, Nancy, humiliated and disappointed, took a shawl and went to lie down on her bed; it was barely seven-thirty. When, even after risking one's life, one receives nothing but indifference, then what can one do but weep and wish for death.

Harish insisted that though the question of the economic improvement of the labourers and other workers must be raised, yet the main question facing them should be of uniting with a nationalist aim. And through this path they should raise their demands. Their struggle should be conducted through the organization of the Congress. He claimed that only after achieving political power would it be possible to remove the difficulties faced by Dalits and other oppressed groups.

Disagreeing with Harish, Rafiq said that to talk with Dalits and other oppressed people, it was necessary to first raise the question of their daily troubles. It is not possible to unite them or to raise their consciousness on the basis of political questions. They will only gain strength and political consciousness from attempting to solve the problems that are present before them in their own lives. They cannot understand ponderous political slogans like 'Complete Independence' and 'Freedom from Colonialism'. The people who form the Congress come from a class that generally neither understands the difficulties of the labouring class nor sympathizes with it. The interests of the people who control the Congress and the interests of the labourers are opposed. The Congress follows the ethics of Mahatma Gandhi. The basis of this ethics is that because of God's wish masters became masters and labourers, labourers. Masters will remain masters and labourers will remain labourers. Only the kindness of masters can bring about an improvement in the condition of workers. But we want to erase the very difference between master and labourer. When we simply don't want to preserve the master as master, how can the master class in the Congress tolerate us, how can it allow us to become strong?

Robert tried to explain, 'We have to take the Congress itself from the hands of this class and deliver it into the hands of the labourers and the farmers.'

Rafiq objected, 'This is a dream. The Congress is in the hands of a class that cannot let go of its control. You want to increase the number of your own people in Congress and thus to capture it. You don't know that the Congress will pass such laws that it will not be possible for your majority to even be visible. Let us suppose, if the condition for membership were changed from four annas to the weaving of cloth again . . .! You are a very strange man, you want to create a workers' organization in the stronghold of the capitalists. It would be a different matter if the labourers and farmers had their own organization and they captured the Congress, but to think that they can form their own organization only by entering the Congress—this is just not practical. There is no other basis for uniting the labourers but their hunger. The labourers can come to know their own strength only by means of a strike. Labourers can gain political power only after uniting. First the labourers, the labourers of all professions, must be united on an economic basis, then we should try to seize political power on the strength of their united front—this is our *line*. You want: first political consciousness and later the economic demand! How is that possible? Whoever has the economic means will be the master of political power.

'Neither you nor the Congress can change this sequence. In the cloth mill there is such a situation now that we can unite the labourers. We can convince them to fight. Their success will become the basis for uniting all other labourers. It is all right to make labourers members of the Congress, but their independent united representation in the Congress is also essential.'

Robert said again, 'I agree with everything you have said in terms of principle and policy, but as far as this strike is concerned, I want the Congress to lead it. I agree that there is a conflict between the interests of those who control the Congress and the interests of the labourers, but in the name of humanity we can carry the Congress with us.'

Harish said, 'Let's dispense with this quarrel. We must strike, and Robert, we will place you and Shail both in the strike committee. Apart from this, we must have four or five other people from the city, so that those members of the Congress who are concerned about their public image may not deceive us at the last minute.'

Rafiq said to Harish, 'I, you, Kriparam, Akhtar and all others, we should start making committees for all the departments of the mills. If we want to give notice to the manager of the mill on 15 April, all the arrangements should be made before that. Their own condition should be placed before the labourers, along with this question: what do we want? For now, only those who are undisputed members of our party should know about the strike. The men should be completely on board before the meeting that we will hold prior to giving notice. If the owners come to know of the strike in advance, they will surely stage a riot on some pretext or the other. This has already happened in the Laxmi Kamalam Mill in Madras.'

Along with many other matters, it was also decided that henceforth, Harish would stay only in the quarters of the

mill and would work as secretary in the cloth mill. Shail,
Robert and Rafiq were given the responsibility of raising
the required funds.

After the meeting ended, Harish stood in the veranda,
preparing to leave. Nancy, weeping, her face covered with
a shawl, was thinking in deep despair: can I be of no use
whatsoever? She could hear conversation from the veranda,
'. . . Harish, you leave your bicycle here, I will take you
wherever you want in the car.'

Harish's voice was heard, 'I will need the bicycle as
soon as I reach. I will ride back. . . . Has Nancy gone to
sleep already?'

Throwing aside the shawl, Nancy stood up. Wiping her
tears and casting one glance in the mirror to check her hair,
she gathered the end of her sari and went out. She saw that
Shail had linked arms with Robert on one side and Harish
on the other, who was walking his bicycle, as they slowly
walked towards the gate of the bungalow.

Nancy's heart filled with loathing for Shail. She
thought—her entire public work is just an excuse for
promiscuity. She has made our home a base to entice
Harish . . . Why should we care about this problem? It
seemed to her that Harish was entirely innocent, trapped
in Shail's deceit. But then—why care about Harish? . . .
Nancy thought, how stupidly she had acted just a few hours
ago! She had placed herself in front of Harish, ready to
be pierced by a bullet. Standing in the veranda, her mind
was engulfed in a fog. She could not understand what she
wanted. She had become a riddle facing herself.

Sultan?

The cloth mills of Punjab, Satara and Dalton* had been on strike for a month and a half. There was no sign of settlement between workers and owners. In the June heat, when the dusty Loo wind scorched the faces of people on the streets, Robert, Rafiq, Shail and their companions led processions through the streets of Lahore. In the evenings, they held protests outside Mori Gate and arranged for resolutions to be passed expressing sympathy for the strikers. Sometimes Nancy and Yashoda also came to the processions and the meetings. Images of the strikers' children, hungry for many days, were sketched before the public. Funds were collected for feeding the strikers. Many youths from the Market Workers Union as well as college students assisted in the strikers' campaign. Public sympathy was largely with them. The Congress also held several meetings in sympathy with the strikers, but the owners did not budge.

Robert was handling the correspondence with the mill owners on behalf of the strike committee. Nothing fruitful

---

* Probably Daltongunj, now Medinanagar in Jharkhand.

was yet in sight. There were ongoing pickets at the gates of the mills. All day long, Sultan, the secretary of the cloth mill's labour committee, went from one mill to another on a bicycle. Through their coercive means, the mill owners had brought over nearly a thousand new labourers from Amritsar, Dhariwal, Kanpur, Nagpur and other places. These newly arrived labourers were ready to work in the mills. Overseers and others who received higher wages also wanted to go back to work, but the labourers on strike lay down in front of the mill gates and prevented them from entering. Every four hours the striking labourers lying in front of the mills changed shifts. The labourers who came from outside tried to enter by walking over the bodies of the prone workers. Fights ensued. The police intervened, wielding their batons. Many workers were sent to prison. Others came in to replace them on the picket lines. The struggle continued.

The cloth workers committee said: the workers cannot retreat from even a single demand. The workers who had been discharged because of the economic slump must be reinstated. They will not tolerate any reduction in wages. A schedule of timely promotions must be announced. If a worker has to be punished, the decision must be taken in the 'job-*panchayat*' of the workers.

The mill owners were not ready to accept these demands. They said that the mills belonged to them, not to the workers. And workers who didn't accept the rules were free to leave. They didn't have the right to stop other workers from working. Sultan, Rafiq and Kriparam gave speeches at the gates of each mill twice a day. The police made reports of these speeches. They said:

'Brother-workers—these mills have been built with your hard work and the work of your brothers. Without you, these mills cannot function for even a second. Not a single strand of thread can be produced in them. The income from your labour enables the mill owners and shareholders to live in leisure, enjoying every worldly pleasure, and you, having produced everything, cannot make enough even to fill your stomach. The economic slump is being used as an excuse for massive lay offs. Tomorrow, you will also be laid off, and in your stead, other workers will be hired for lower wages. When thousands of your brothers are unemployed, how will they buy food and clothes? Such dearth of consumers will lead to further economic depression and become an excuse for dismissing more workers. Capital is created by constantly chipping away at the wages of your labour, and then new mills are opened, you are hired, and they simply suck your blood. Although these mills have been created by the hard work of the worker-brothers themselves, the workers don't ask for the entire profit. The workers only ask: where is the profit that was made from their labour when trade was brisk? During a depression, it is the profits of the owners that should decrease. They have plenty to live on. The workers earn barely enough to eat, they should not be subjected to cruelty. Brother-workers! We are asking for dry crusts of bread, and the owners are stubbornly holding on to their luxuries. We will die, but we will not retreat . . .'

In public it was said that the workers were adamant and would not budge, but the protest organizers knew the inner secret. They trembled as they saw the workers lose courage. Because they were unemployed, the workers couldn't even get loans. Those workers who had been starving for three days on end came to Sultan, Kriparam and Rafiq, weeping, and said: 'What should we do? You have wrecked us.' Volunteers went around begging for alms and flour to bring to the workers. Communal meals was prepared from the alms collected. Some workers were given flour and others some roasted chickpeas.

Sultan often got a nosebleed while walking around in the heat all day.

Living on just chickpeas and water had given him dysentery, but like a ghost, he still kept doing the rounds on his bicycle. Seeing no other way out, Robert mortgaged his house and handed over his loan money for the strike. The owners refused to budge. They tried to convince Robert that if the workers ended their strike without any demands, they would not be treated harshly, but Rafiq, Kriparam and Sultan were not ready for this.

Gradually, counter-protests began. In the meetings that were held to express sympathy for the striking workers and to collect alms for them, some people started raising doubts and questions, creating noise and disturbance. Others began to say that the strike was a communist conspiracy; that the striking workers were being incited—is it ever possible for servants to become masters? Some said that these were preparations to weaken the power of the Congress and to establish a united front to compete against it. Some said that an attack on the country's industry was national suicide. The mill owners sponsored a Ramayana *katha* in the mill quarters, where the audience was taught that it was a sin to oppose the master who feeds you. Some maulvis said that the strikers who went against God's dispensation were Russian agents. It was a crime to listen to them.

Because of strike-related troubles, Shail often reached home late. Her father would wait for her. It mortified her to see him waiting, but she was helpless, delays were inevitable. She had no control over this. He had explained to her many times that it was not right for her to get entangled in this matter. She also knew that her father's sympathy was not with the striking workers. Though kind and justice-loving by nature, his sympathy nevertheless was with the mill owners. This was not only because he was himself the Director of Punjab Cloth Mill, but also because, on principle, he found the workers' demand unjust. Once Shail had asked her father for some money. He understood why she wanted the money. At that time, he merely said, 'I will talk to you about this later.'

When she saw that her father was waiting for her, Shail said with embarrassment, 'Father, you should rest. Because of me, you have to suffer much hardship, but I am entangled in a particular kind of problem . . . From tomorrow I will try to return on time.'

Her father said, 'My child, ask to have your food served. You eat; I want to talk to you about something. You had asked for money. I know why you need money.

I understand your sympathy for the workers. I also know that they are suffering greatly, but, my child, they cannot be helped in the way in which you wish to help them. For me you are everything: son as well as daughter. I have never tried to restrict your ideas. I did not think it right to obstruct your intellectual progress in any way, but, my child, you are making a mistake in this matter. The workers are on a wrong and unjust path. If you help them to walk on this path, they will go even further and in the process hurt themselves as well as society. Society functions according to a rule. Just as the various parts of the body have different positions and tasks, in the same way the positions, duties and rights of people in a society are different. The striking workers want to become masters, but you must consider: those who have built these mills by spending money earned over several generations, don't they have any rights? Aren't those who manage these mills responsible to their shareholders? Aren't they also responsible to the public? Just a few select capitalists manage the economy of the country. You can understand their responsibility. They have to take into view the effect of one trade on another, balance production with the market, but the worker has no responsibility apart from filling his stomach. Are you ready to entrust the workers with running the economy of the entire society?'

'But if you snatch the fruit of their hard work from them and keep all rights for yourself, what are the workers to do? They too must protect their lives!' Shail spoke up.

'My child, rights or responsibilities cannot be snatched in a day. They have to be accumulated grain by grain and must be protected as well. Those who are masters today, did not become masters in a day. In a way it is the inheritance of their class, and it is their duty to protect this inheritance for their progeny and class. If I had not been in this position, would it have been possible for me to arrange for your education the way I did? Would I be able to run the charities I run now? We people are in this position today because we have worked very hard to take the key of the economy in our hands. Today, by raising the demand to determine their wages themselves, the workers are trying to snatch this key from us. This will mean that the wealth of society, its produce, will be distributed according to the wishes of workers. In such a situation, what will be the condition of our class? This is not about raising wages by one or two annas. It is about the key to the social structure being passed from one class to another. This is not about pity and sympathy. Why don't you try to think? For us, this is a matter of life and death—a matter of the life and death of our class, which has until now kept society in control. It is a matter of our responsibility towards society.

'It is we who have built this social structure. If we follow the wishes of the workers, that structure will be destroyed, and they will be destroyed with it. I have grown old, I will not live for long, but if I did not face the labourers' attack on our rights with strength and determination, I would be a traitor to my class and to our new generation, to you. My child, charity and pity is one thing, cutting off one's roots quite another. I have always given you freedom because you must decide your own path. All the wealth of this home is yours, but you must understand your duty towards yourself and towards society. I admire your compassion and pity. I am glad that you have pity in your heart, but this is not pity, this is erasing one's being. If you had no means, you would not even be able to express pity. You or I can make personal sacrifices, but we cannot betray our class and society. If you like, I could give ten or twenty thousand rupees for setting up a school or hospital for the children of these labourers, but this strike is a war. The labourers themselves have created their troubles in order to destroy us. Just as we have a duty towards the nation, in the same way we have a duty towards our own class . . .'

A plate of food lay in front of Shail. She had broken off several pieces of roti and put them in the little bowls on her plate so that her father would think she was eating, but it was not possible for her to swallow even a single morsel. Washing her hands, she went and lay down on her bed. Harish's image in the guise of Sultan that she had been observing for several days came before her eyes: unshaven beard and moustache, torn clothes, his face gaunt from weakness, an old, red Turkish cap on his head. She heard him saying: will you not be able to do anything, Shail? . . . Will we lose?

Shail wept for long. When the pillow became drenched in tears, she turned it over. What will she tell Harish tomorrow? She spent the night crying. If only she could bring some money from somewhere, she might have been able to give Harish some peace. Often, she thought that now it was a disgrace for her to live in this house. In the morning she rose and after her bath, got dressed to meet Robert, without eating any breakfast. She saw in the mirror that her eyes were red and swollen from crying. How could she go out with such eyes? She put on sunglasses. Seeing her go out of the gate the driver apologized, 'Bibiji, I will come in two minutes.'

'I don't need the car!' She responded.

She went on foot. She thought she would get a tonga later. Then she realized: how will I pay for the tonga? She had not brought her purse. Whatever two or four rupees were in it, it was her father's property. Anyway, Ruby would pay for the tonga.

Since two months, Robert had left all other work and was embroiled in the problems of the strike. All day long, in the dusty, hot wind, he would do the rounds of the city in his car or on foot. At the beginning of his youth, he had been impassioned by the preaching of Christianity. This passion had arisen from within his heart, but the struggle* for establishing the workers' rule had been thrust upon him from without. In his youth, he had entered the field of duty with passion and determination, and attempted to gather the entire world at the feet of Christ. But eventually, he had found that attempt meaningless and useless. Having experienced this, it was no longer possible for him to accept any single path as entirely true, or to walk upon it with eyes closed. He now considered any passion foolish that took

---

* *Jihad* in the original Hindi text—literally a struggle or an effort for a worthy cause.

one's own thought and decision as the sole truth, and thrust it forcefully upon others. He had become entirely inward-facing in his disposition. He wanted to think, to leave a space for doubt in each thought, to analyze it. Instead of walking himself, he wanted to observe others walking, and to study their disposition. He had been dragged into this campaign against his own nature and inclination. There was no opportunity to sit quietly for even a minute in this workers' struggle. Some message or the other would inevitably arrive: Sultan had sent for him; Rafiq had urgently called him; Shail was waiting for him. The most difficult task was to walk around asking people for donations. To escape from this burden, he had borrowed two thousand rupees and given it to the strikers. This was a mere drop in the task of feeding thirty-five thousand workers. Now he was helpless. He felt embarrassment and even shame while walking on the streets with workers as they screamed and shouted slogans from all sides. He was making desperate attempts to somehow reach an agreement and escape from this mess, but Rafiq and Sultan would not agree. At the end he began to consider this as excessive force on the part of the labour-leaders. He thought, this is their nature, how long can I stand by them?

The preparatory meeting for the strike had taken place in Robert's bungalow. Since that meeting, Nancy had not caught even a glimpse of Harish. Once strike-related processions and meetings began, Nancy went to them. It was Shail who had asked her to accompany her, but Nancy wanted to prove that she was working harder than

Shail. She believed that Harish would see all this from somewhere and would finally understand his mistake. At times she would hear a mention of Harish, but more often there was mention of Sultan and Rafiq. She even suspected that Shail might have stopped him from visiting their home, but he was not to be seen at processions and meetings either. Meanwhile, listening to Rafiq she thought that he was by far more learned and impressive than Harish, but she experienced this disparagement of Harish itself as a wound that in fact kept her focused on him. This was Nancy's defeat.

It was nine-thirty in the evening. Robert had not yet returned. As she waited for Robert to reach home for dinner, Nancy's hunger was slowly turning into anger. As soon as he entered, Robert flung the papers he was carrying on to the table and putting his hand to his head said, 'I've had enough of this trouble!'

'Where were you till so late?' Nancy asked.

'With Harish and Shail . . .' Robert responded.

Nancy was aflame with rage from head to foot. 'What do those people say?' she asked.

'They are not ready for any kind of agreement. They want the Soviet to be established today . . . and they want money!'

'Why doesn't Shail give money?' Nancy asked.

'What can Shail give? Without her father's consent, she can't get money even for petrol for the car. I am amazed—instead of trying to solve the problem, Shail and Sultan agree with Rafiq's stubborn insistence on continuing the strike!' Placing his head against the back of the chair, Robert expressed his helplessness.

'Who is this Sultan? Does he interfere?' Nancy asked.

Robert looked at Nancy. He thought, doesn't Nancy know the secret that Sultan is Harish? Without answering her question, he said, 'But for how long can I bear the responsibility for money? Our own situation is not very good.'

'Those who insist on continuing with the strike instead of reaching an agreement—they should bring the money themselves! Come, have some food now!' Nancy replied.

Robert did not like Nancy's words, but his own feelings were the same. While eating, both remained quiet. He had understood how Nancy felt about money. Robert thought: what should I do now? Nancy thought in anger: if Harish wants someone's help, why doesn't he himself come to talk about it? For two months there had been constant bickering about the strike and Nancy was weary of it. She thought of life before the strike! . . . An orderly life and its pleasures now seemed a tale of the past. When had all the old companions parted ways?

In the morning Robert got out of bed a little late. He lit a cigarette. He was standing on the veranda waiting for a cup of tea. He was used to having a cup of tea as soon as he woke up. Seeing Shail arrive so early in the morning he said, 'Come, come!' And expressed surprise, 'What brings you here so early today? All well?'

Shail sat down on the chair next to his bed, and answered, 'How can it be well with this strike!'

'You are right. I am also worn out. I've had enough. I was about to tell you today.'

Shail was stunned to hear this. Taking off her glasses, she asked, 'Ruby, what are you saying?'

Without looking at Shail, Robert yawned and lazily scratched his hairy arm. 'I have reached the limit of my ability. Rafiq and Hari, I mean Sultan, don't agree. I did as much as I could. Now no more.'

'Meaning?'

The tea arrived.

'Will you also have a cup?' Taking a cup in his hand, he asked Shail, 'And what happened to your eyes?'

'Nothing, yesterday some dust got in my eyes because of the strong summer wind,' Shail answered.

She had become so anxious after hearing Robert, she did not have the courage to tell him that she had wept from helplessness.

'What were you saying about the limit of your ability?' Shail asked.

'From the very beginning I was not in favour of this strike. You and Harish got me entangled in it, so I had to carry through. The most I've been able to do is to convince the Directors to consider the demands of the workers sympathetically, if they end their strike without any conditions. I admit this is not our victory, but we cannot win. If labourers had the power to win, they would have been successful even without the strike. The public is not helping them, nor will it help them in the future. Now these people are threatening to organize strikes in the electricity and water departments. If that happens, the government will invoke public distress and crush them. I took out a loan of two thousand that has already been used. I don't have the heart for more. You know, I have promised to help Flora. I will have to dedicate at least one thousand to her. Then Nancy also has a right to her share of Father's wealth. I don't know what has happened to her. What would I gain by hiding my weakness? I don't have it in me to follow the path that Harish and Rafiq are following. I have to set something aside for my subsistence. If I remain secretary of the strike committee, I will have a moral duty to put money into this cause, even if it means selling myself. That is not possible for me. In principle, Harish and Rafiq may be on the right path, but in terms of a practical course it doesn't sit well with me. I kept my pledge as far as I could. I have already told them to reach an agreement this time. But those people would rather die than agree, so I can only say farewell and wish them the best!'

'Ruby, what are you saying?' Shail asked in an anxious tone.

'Shail, what I say is right. I was already thinking that you might not agree with me. That may be either because of your attachment to Harish, or because, in fact, you think like them.'

Shail arose in silence and walked away.

Robert called, 'Listen!' But Shail did not turn to look back. Nor was it possible for her to do so.

The tonga driver on the road asked, 'Will you return?'

'Yes!' Shail answered. On the way back she thought: let me stop at Yashoda's place. She told the tonga driver to go through Gwalmandi.

The door of the house was closed. Shail knocked. The door opened after about two minutes. The servant opened the door and said, with hesitation, 'They said, please don't come here.'

Shail looked at him in astonishment, but gathering courage, she asked, 'Who said this, Yashoda madam, or sir?'

The servant was a little anxious. 'Yes, they said so.'

Shail understood. Taking a deep breath, she returned to the tonga. Even in her dreams she had never imagined that she would be turned away from every door in this manner.

Facing disappointment from all directions, Shail returned home and lay down on her bed. It was necessary to tell Harish that she could not do anything, but how could she face him? Her heart sank as she pictured Harish's immeasurably exhausted face, unshaven and ravaged by sickness. What would be the effect on him and his companions when they hear this disappointing news? She could not muster the courage to take this step, but she knew it was her duty to acquaint them with the real situation. The poor men should not lose because of a deception. What could she do in this predicament . . . evening fell as she remained lost in thought. At last, she got up. Though she did not want to do so, there was no option but to take the car. She drove towards the mills.

Gloom had descended everywhere. Groups of labourers were sitting here and there. Looking at their sad faces and weak bodies, she became even more dejected.

At the gate of one of the mills, Rafiq stood on a barrel and counselled the workers to stay firm. He reassured them that workers from other cities—Kanpur, Bombay and Ahmedabad—had sent them a message that they would assist them in all possible ways. The worker-brothers of the entire country are together in this protest. The workers of the world are united.

Shail realized that Harish was elsewhere. Going towards another mill she saw Kriparam. She said to him, 'Will you send Sultan for some time this evening?'

Kriparam responded, 'In fact, it would be better if you took him with you. He is in a bad state of health, but I don't know where to find him . . . All right, I'll tell him.'

'Please tell him to come at nine, the same way he came before.'

Shail went to lie down in her room. She called for her dinner and kept it there. A little before nine, she opened the garage door. Harish entered in about fifteen or twenty minutes. His eyes were red and his clothes drenched in sweat. Sitting on the chair facing the bed, Harish clasped his head in his hands and said, 'Robert too has left us; anyway, what can we do. People deceive you at the worst moments . . . Shail, I feel dizzy . . .'

Shail pointed towards the adjoining bathroom. 'Take a bath.'

'Take a bath? How will I wear these clothes after bathing, they stink.'

Shail took out a colourful silken *sleeping suit*. 'Wear this, it will be small for you, but it doesn't matter.'

Harish took a bath and came back. Placing the food in front of him, Shail said, 'Eat a little.'

Harish shook his head. 'I don't feel like eating. I have a bitter taste in my mouth.'

'No, you must eat a little. You will feel worse if you don't.' Placing a glass of milk in front of him, Shail said, 'At least, drink this.'

Harish shook his head.

Putting the glass next to his lips, Shail said, 'Please do as I say, you must drink this.'

Harish drank the milk.

'How many days has it been since you slept?'

'I don't find time, and when I find time, I can't fall asleep. The mistri in Dalton Mill beat up some of the striking workers yesterday. Akhtar and some of the other workers were ready to kill him. If they commit such a mistake, all that we have accomplished will be ruined. With great difficulty I begged and restrained them.'

'You should lie down . . . sleep.'

'You know, there's a buzzing in my head, like the sound of a millstone grinding away. I fear I'll go mad.'

'Hunger and sleeplessness have dried you up. You will not feel better till you sleep. Lie down, I'll help you sleep,' Shail said, helping him to lie down and caressing his head.

'But I can't forget the mad despair of the workers. How will it be possible to control thousands of men without any strength?' Harish responded in an agitated manner.

'Harish, for a little while, forget everything and close your eyes. I beg of you, please agree.'

'Shail, what can I do? It is not in my power.'

Tear drops fell on his brow. Feeling them with his hands, Harish asked, 'What is this, you are crying? . . . How can crying solve matters, Shail!' Lowering Shail's head towards himself, he held it in his embrace.

Shail wept even more. Pulling her on to the bed next to him, Harish tried to console her. Taking him in her arms, Shail pressed him to her heart. Her heartbeat resounded in Harish's ears. Caressing her body, Harish kissed her hair again and again. In some time, all his worries and distress were drowned in the excitement awakened by the touch of Shail's body. She was trembling. With every tremor Shail tried to move closer to Harish and clasp him tightly. She was afraid that Harish's wandering mind might once again become entangled in those worries. She wanted to drown all his conscious thoughts. Her own mind remained focused. She cared only about Harish, not about herself. Harish forgot himself. Shail kept making way for his desire. After a while, Harish, exhausted, fell asleep. Shail was still awake.

She looked steadfastly at Harish's face. His once beautiful face was now burnt and distorted. Shail found him more beautiful than ever. There was a smile in her eyes and on her lips. Overwhelmed with her success, she kissed Harish's closed eyes, brow and lips again and again.

Getting up, Shail washed his dirty, smelly clothes with her perfumed bathing soap. Turning the electric fan on high, she spread them to dry on a chair. Then she returned to lie down next to Harish. Her arms held him as if to protect him from all worry. Her eyes were on the shining radium hands of the clock. How long could she let him sleep peacefully—she was thinking only of this. She should have awakened Harish at three o'clock, but she could not. When it was three-thirty, she had no option. She tried to wake him up by kissing his lips, but he did not stir. Shail was sad to rouse him from sleep, but she had no choice. Kissing him over and over again, she called to him lovingly, 'Hari . . . do wake up now!'

Harish opened his eyes and said in surprise, 'Oh!' He could not understand anything.

'Now get up, it's three-thirty. Your clothes are here.'

Harish looked at the clothes, and then at the clock. He wore his clothes and got ready. The event of the previous night became vivid again. With hesitation he said, 'Shail, I do not feel like going yet.'

'You have to go, for it is your work,' Shail said, kissing his head. She felt no hesitation or embarrassment.

Dada

On the road bordering the right side of the large canal in Lahore, Dada was riding a bicycle. About twenty feet behind him, Jeevan followed on a bicycle. Crossing the Model Town bridge, they reached the left side of the stream. After covering some distance, Dada got off the bicycle. When he came up to Dada, Jeevan also got off. He held both the bicycles while Dada took a package tied in cloth and towel from the carrier of the bicycle and laid it carefully on the grass. The caution with which the package was placed on the grass made it evident that it wasn't simply a bundle of cloth and towel.

Jeevan tried to balance the two bicycles against each other. Looking at him, Dada said irritably, 'I've told you so often not to tangle bicycles together in this way. If one ever has to pick them up in a hurry, what would one do?'

'I forgot, Dada,' Jeevan replied and laid down the bicycles on the grass, on either side of the cloth and towel package. Both of them sat down with the package between them. Jeevan looked at the flowing water of the canal with a thirsty gaze and said, 'It would be nice to take a bath.'

'Are you mad?' Dada replied. 'Where will you throw the wet clothes?'

'I am not really going to bathe. I was just talking about how I feel. BM must be on his way.'

Turning towards Dada, Jeevan lay down and started to hum: 'Mother, bid us farewell / Today we go to unfurl the victory banner . . .'*

Dada interrupted him. 'I suspect BM won't come; I don't understand why he keeps postponing this *money-action*. The first time he had said that it was a good opportunity to shoot an informer, and the opportunity would be lost if the robbery was carried out. Later he said, the informer has suddenly left town. The second time he claimed that the police have their eye on their hideout in Lahore, it is not safe for anyone to come and go, and hence no preparations can be made from there . . .'

Jeevan looked at this wristwatch and said, 'What I don't understand is how the two men who were with him were killed just at that time. On the third occasion the man with him was arrested, but he always escapes danger. Oh, there he is! . . . But he is alone.'

As he turned on to the bridge, BM cast a backward glance. Reaching close to them, he propped up the bicycle against the bank of the canal and came to sit near Dada.

Looking at him with an inquiring gaze, Dada said, 'So?'

---

* "*Ma hamen vida do / Jaate hain hum vijay ketu lehraane aaj . . .*". Chandrashekhar Azad's favorite song, according to several accounts.

BM wiped the perspiration from his brow with his handkerchief, and responded, 'Dada, indeed I see difficulty. The number of policemen on the roads has increased greatly because of the strike in the cloth mills, and since the mills are closed, there's no money coming to that wholesale cloth shop these days. I've also heard that the Communist Party is going to stage a protest at this shop. In such a situation, nothing can be done yet.'

'But we promised in Delhi that we will definitely send money by the tenth, and it is already the sixteenth. If we act in this manner, how will anyone trust us?' Jeevan said, looking at Dada.

Biting his thumbnail BM said, 'Dada, there is one way we can obtain the money. We could easily get up to five thousand, if we assist in breaking the strike here.'

'What?' Dada asked in astonishment. 'What do you mean?'

'I mean, if we arrange for pamphlets to be distributed on behalf of our party saying that this strike is a conspiracy organized by the Communist Party and against national interest . . .,' BM responded.

Keeping his gaze on the water current in the canal, Dada asked, 'You mean we betray these starving and dying labourers? Cut the feet out from under those who are struggling for their daily bread?'

'But what is to be gained from these strikes? This is mere mischief. What a blow these strikes are to the new, growing industries of the country. If mills continue to operate peacefully, the profit from these very mills can build more mills in the country. Do you know that in order to strengthen their party, the communists are taking money from Japanese firms and causing harm to the mills of their own country? This is an opportunity for us too. We can improve the condition of our own party with the help of Indian capitalists. These days our mills are losing sixty, seventy thousand every day . . . It is not at all difficult to break this strike. Not only will this benefit the industry of the country, it will also save us from the trouble of a *money-action*.'

'Hmm . . .' Dada said, raising his gaze from the canal to the treetops, 'nothing can be said about this without consulting other comrades. At the very least we'll have to ask Ali.'

To emphasize his point, BM said, 'We don't have much time, we should act quickly. The strike is going to break in a couple of days anyway. This is an advantageous opportunity for us. I could make arrangements elsewhere for a *money-action* if you say so.'

'Hmm . . .' Dada responded, looking at Jeevan. 'Yes, make arrangements, but your plans are *failing*, what's the matter? Be careful and be quick. All right, then we should go.'

All three got up. BM went from the bridge towards Central Jail. Dada and Jeevan tied their cloth bundle to the bicycle carrier and started walking back on the path by which they had come. Suddenly Dada stopped and said, 'Jeevan, you heard what BM said. What kind of a game is this? . . . Will we support the workers or the mill owners? . . . This damned politics is beyond me—changing from one day to the next! One day *socialism*, the next, patriotism. Any bastard who comes along starts conning us. Every day, a new *theory* is produced. What I heard about Japan was news to me. My heart breaks at having to pretend in front of my own comrades, but what should I do? . . . No one can be forced here. If all of them agreed, we could have *discipline*, but everyone thinks of himself as a bandit hero. What is your opinion? Tell me, how do you make sense of this? What should we do?'

Jeevan said, 'Dada, yesterday I was passing through Anarkali Bazar. I saw volunteers from among the strikers and two girls, including Shailbala, collecting donations. Some ruffians were throwing pebbles at them, some were clapping and calling them Japanese agents and some were calling them Russian agents. One ruffian soaked a cloth in gutter water and threw it at Shailbala's head. A worker swore and leapt towards that boy. The communist Rafiq was also there. He caught that worker by the scruff of the neck. Truly, Bhaiya, I felt like shooting that scoundrel who had attacked Shailbala. I restrained myself with great difficulty. Do you recall how BM would talk about Shailbala and the communists? Dada, do you know who the secretary of the cloth-mills strike is?—Sultan. He is our own Harish. After being cast out of the party, he has joined them.'

'What rubbish are you talking!' Dada interrupted.

'Dada, I swear by you. Do you know what he has done? . . . He has taken out two of his lower front teeth, so that even his voice is not recognizable. His face is pockmarked and leathery. He may have used some acid to burn the skin. His face has become very ugly and repulsive. He has grown a slight beard and moustache. He looked sickly. His face has changed so much that he cannot be recognized at all, and nor can his voice be recognized. I was on my bicycle. He was returning from the mill, also on a bicycle. On the way we came face to face. He smiled at me, so we talked a little. He said, "Dada must be annoyed, but do give him my regards." When I think of Harish, tears well up . . .'

'Your tears always well up! . . . As for me, I feel extremely ashamed. What must the Delhi folks think of us? Who will trust us? We needlessly wasted two thousand on these weapons. It is not as though they produce milk for us! Whom can we trust? Hari turned out better than all of us—and we were trying to kill him! How many men in such a situation would have resisted cooperating with the police? And here comes the great scholar of politics, advising us to make money by selling the blood of workers!'

Seeing Dada fall silent, Jeevan said, rattling the bicycle brake, 'Dada, why not do this? Why don't I go to that wholesale shop and see for myself? Let's leave these people, our third man from Delhi is with us. We must send money to Delhi, otherwise our word will have no value.'

'Jeevan, I tell you truly, I am ready to die of shame. Even if we can't accomplish anything, at least we should not be tarnished as liars. My own honour is at stake here. Whatever the danger may be, I will undertake this task today itself. Let's leave BM alone,' Dada said, biting his moustache.

Next morning, the front page of the newspapers carried this headline in bold letters: 'Armed Robbery in Lahore Bazar. Bandits Snatched Twenty-seven Thousand at Gunpoint.' Underneath, in small letters, there was a detailed description:

'There was an armed robbery in the Jivaram–Bholaram wholesale store. A little before closing time, two dacoits came in the guise of merchants, asking to buy some bales of cloth. When the servants in the shop were sent to the warehouse to bring samples, the dacoits took out knives and guns hidden in their clothes and asked the owner and the clerks for the key to the safe. In the meantime, other dacoits had entered the shop. The owner of the shop was either drugged or rendered unconscious from a blow to the head with a heavy object. No sign of injury was found on the body. The medical report says that his death was caused either by a severe injury to the brain or by heart failure. The clerks' hands were tied behind their backs and their mouths gagged. The telephone wire was cut. The dacoits took twenty-seven thousand in notes and some change from the safe and disappeared. By the time the servants returned with the bales, the dacoits had vanished. The owner was found sitting propped up against a cushion, but he was lifeless. When the servants shouted for help, the police were informed. The exact number of dacoits could not be determined. The police are intent on investigating this matter.'

Those who were not sympathetic to the strikers suspected that it was they who were responsible for the robbery.

Rafiq, Sultan and their friends too were afraid that the mill owners might hatch a conspiracy and get them entangled with the police. At the same time, they were confident that when the robbery took place, they were conducting a meeting with the strikers and the police were also present. Hence, the police already had proof of their non-involvement in the robbery.

Two weeks passed by. People forgot about the robbery. Talk of the strike and its outcome occupied everyone in the city. The newspapers reported only news related to the strike. People's speculations were concerned only with the strike.

Taking with her a couple of girls and some boys, Shailbala was busy collecting donations for the strikers and organizing resolutions expressing solidarity. She was both praised and criticized. Some people called her a dedicated and self-sacrificing worker. Some said she enjoyed meeting new boys. Shailbala was no longer concerned with either criticism or praise. Till now she had valued her father's opinion, had feared him, but now she no longer cared even about him. Her father too was silent. He had given her freedom, but gave her no money except for her personal needs. When she didn't have money for petrol, she would walk around on foot. One evening, at eight, she was returning on foot from a meeting and had just stepped inside the gate of her bungalow when someone called from behind, 'Sister Shailbala!'

Shail turned to look: a tall man in a close-collared coat and trousers, wearing a turban and glasses, was looking at her. Shailbala could not recognize him, but said, 'Yes?'

The visitor came closer and taking off his glasses, asked her, 'You didn't recognize me. You used to call me Dada.'

'Dada!' Shail looked at him in surprise. Now she recognized him. She took him inside and seating him on a chair in a room, she said, 'Dada, you simply forgot about us. We are caught in a terrible situation. When did you come? Is BM well . . .?'

'I have been here for two weeks,' Dada said, 'and I have learnt quite a lot. Harish has become Sultan. How he has disfigured his face. That day when I found out, I went to see him from afar . . .' Dada bit his lip and fell silent. He found it difficult to speak because of the constriction in his throat.

Shailbala did not pay attention to that. With a finger on her chin, she said, 'He burnt his face with acid, Dada, and had two front teeth extracted; when I asked, why are you disfiguring your face like this, he responded, "what's in a face; I can't work in public without changing my face. If I no longer believe in carrying guns and working in secret, I will have to work openly among people."'

Dada held his glasses in his hand and looking at the floor, he said, 'I am sorry. Whatever I said about you and Harish that day, please don't think about it . . . I had to trust my men. So, how's your strike?'

'Dada, it will *fail*,' said Shail, taking a deep breath. 'Somehow, we managed to keep faith for so many days.

Asked for assistance from Kanpur, Bombay, Ahmedabad. I don't know what has happened to the people of this city. Instead of helping us, they call us Japanese agents. The mill owners are spending thousands of rupees daily—the newspapers print false news about us, and when we hold a meeting, their men come and create chaos. The owners are now anxious, so they are making every attempt to break the strike. If we can hold fast for another seven days, the workers would win. If the workers lose now, they will be suppressed for many years to come. Actually, the situation is so bad that the strike would have broken a long time ago. It is because of what Rafiq and Harish say, that the workers think about their own future and remain steadfast.'

'Will money alone make your strike successful? How much money do you need at this time?' Dada asked, clasping both hands.

'At this time, Dada, if we could get ten thousand, we could keep the workers fighting for twenty days. You know that workers can live on a handful of parched gram, but here they are surviving for three continuous days without any food at all.'

Opening the buttons of his coat, Dada took out various sized bundles of notes from several pockets and tossed them on to Shail's lap. He said, 'This is twenty thousand. Now your work can continue? I don't understand Harish's complicated talk of *technique* and *theory*. I am a soldier, and this is my tribute to Hari, because he is a true soldier . . . It is a matter of one's understanding.' Shaking his head in confusion, Dada said, 'Anyway, I don't care about money.

I have paid what I owed. The rest should go to those to whom it belongs. The ocean water back to the ocean! And yes, give Harish my love. Tell him to forget our quarrel. I will see if I can be of help again sometime. Now I will go.'

But Dada did not rise. Joining the fingers of both hands, he leaned forward in his chair. Looking at the floor, he bit his moustache, and said, 'How quickly time has changed. It seems as though we had barely started to push the boat across the river when the stream of water beneath the boat shifted course and we found ourselves on dry sand. The river has moved in a different direction . . . Hari is right, instead of trying to move the stream back under the boat, we should drag the boat to the stream . . .' Dada said, with his gaze still on the floor, as if he were speaking to it. 'I mean, the stream of people.' Then he fell silent.

Shail was looking at him silently and thinking: how straightforward this man is. He was not content to express himself metaphorically. He could not help but explain it in clear words.

Suddenly, Dada got up. 'Now I will go, Namaste!'

'No, Dada, if you give all this to him yourself, he will be very happy,' Shailbala said, her eyes shining with happiness.

'No, no, I don't want all this performance. You give it to him. As if I care about that bastard's happiness!'

'Dada, there's nothing to fear in this, is there?' Shail asked and then was embarrassed by her own doubt.

'Nothing to fear from me . . . but the work will have to be handled wisely. Hari is wise. I don't know about communists . . . they jabber a lot. The man who jabbers can't be trusted. All right, now I must go.'

After Dada left, Shail kept sitting with the wad of notes in her hand. She had read news of the armed robbery at Jivaram-Bholaram. She started to remember that. She also felt fearful about the consequences of robbery and murder. Clasping the stolen bundles of notes in both hands, she experienced in her body the thrill of a strange fear. She thought: this money was snatched by oppressing the poor. Then it was snatched from Jivaram-Bholaram perhaps after killing them. Now it will doubtless cause the murder of the person into whose hands it falls. She was afraid that this stolen money would put Harish in danger.

Dada had obtained the money through armed robbery, but had shoved it towards others without any greed, attachment or self-concern. He had thus freed himself from sin, but will the person who now uses this money be able to escape? She wanted to burn all these notes, but then recalled at what great risk the money was brought. She saw the fearful eyes of the striking workers for whom each grain of wheat was precious, begging for alms. Then she saw a smile on Harish's acid-burnt face. Hari was saying: how superstitious of you! What is money, after all? It is a means, a power, it can be put to good or bad use. We are not going to oppress anyone . . . At the same time, she saw her father's tear-filled eyes. In her childhood, he would seat her on his lap, and as she listened, her finger between her teeth, he would explain, 'My child, to lie or steal is a great sin. It always brings sorrow to the human being.'

Shail felt as if she would become dizzy and fall to the ground. She called out in a loud voice, 'Driver, take out the car!' She realized she was trembling with fear. Without drinking even a sip of water, she left the house to deliver the money.

There is a limit to the courage of a human being. He fights against circumstances, but sometimes he has to admit defeat. Rafiq, Sultan and Kriparam were also forced to admit defeat. In their despair, they were thinking of ways to end the strike. Their only concern was that this task should somehow be carried out in an honourable way. Just then Shail's car arrived. Calling Rafiq and Harish, Shail gave them the bundles of notes.

Within half an hour the news reached the workers' quarters as well as the bungalows of the mill owners that immense assistance from Bombay had reached the strikers. They could fight for months.

Justice

In the cloth mills strike, the workers had won. Enthused by this victory, the workers in other mills and factories started forming unions. In many mills and factory quarters, night schools started. Rafiq and Sultan were occupied with organizing the workers. Shail was quietly spending time at home. She did not visit Robert's place. And it was not easy to meet Harish. As Sultan, his appearance and his way of life stood out in respectable society.

Her father was also content to see Shail spending her days in peace. Regardless of whether the workers had won or lost, there was no longer any cause for quarrel between father and daughter. Once she got some rest, Shail experienced a slowness and languor in her body. She had understood its cause as well. She was fearful of the consequences, but determined to make arrangements for this difficulty . . . One day, a child will become manifest and appear in her lap: this image set her heart beating.

Society! . . . What is society? She would arrange things in a way that would satisfy the whims of social norms, and she too would gain control over her life. Now if she had any worry, it was only this.

Suddenly one day she got the news that the police had arrested Harish, Kriparam and Akhtar from Akhtar's quarters under Section 396. Upon inquiry, she learnt that Section 396 covers the crime of armed robbery and murder. Shail was terrified. Disregarding the heaviness of her body and her mental state, she started pursuing lawyers. The police did not give her the opportunity to meet the accused and get further information.

When the trial began in court, the police testimony revealed that the police had noted down the numbers of some large currency notes from the register at Jivaram-Bholaram store. One of these notes was found, and when the police pursued the man who had used it, they found out about cell number 38 at the cloth mill's quarters. When the quarters were raided, more notes worth one and a half thousand were found, whose numbers exactly matched those in the register at Jivaram-Bholaram. Sultan, Kriparam and Akhtar were arrested at the quarters, and they were being tried for armed robbery and the murder of Lala Jivaram. The public believed that the strikers had attained success by using stolen money to continue the strike.

Shail and Rafiq rushed around the city trying to find help for the accused, but who would be ready to help murderers and robbers? Shail pleaded with her father and begged him for help. From time to time he had given the Congress thousands of rupees in donation, but when he was convinced that the strike had been waged by robbing people of his own class, and in order to harm people of his own class, how could he be ready to help? Shail's sympathy for criminals filled him with such shame and sorrow that he stopped going out of his home. The elderly, respectable people who met him expressed grief at Shail's conduct and explained to him how freedom corrupts girls. Lala Dhyanchand Ishwarbhakt was a pious man. He thought, it must be because of some great sin in his past birth that he had to suffer such humiliation and censure in his old age. Constant sorrow and worry rendered him bedridden.

Shail understood the cause of her father's sorrow and trouble. There was deep reverence and love for her father in her heart. On the one hand she was pulled by her love and loyalty for Harish, and on the other by her duty towards her father. It was unbearable for her father that his daughter was sympathetic to dacoits and went to meet them in court. Often, he bade her sit close to him and explained that this behaviour would ruin her future, but Shail had just one response: 'Father, he is not a dacoit. He is bringing us a message about a new age for human society. He is suffering society's oppression for society's own benefit.'

Bhuaji would counsel Shail, 'My daughter, this obstinacy of yours will kill your father.'

Bhuaji's words would fill Shail with agitation. The father who gave birth to her, nurtured her and brought her up, had immense claim over her, but what could she do. Rafiq and Harish's words would appear before her: what a large part of humanity must watch its children die, crying of hunger, because of the prevailing conditions. How many poor people must see their old parents die in front of their eyes because they cannot afford two doses of medicine for them, cannot even arrange a doctor for them in their last moments. She remembered that Harish would call her 'the daughter of a dacoit' in jest. He used to say, "Has your father's house, in which scores of poor people could survive, and your father's immense wealth, been produced by the labour of his own hands? His wealth is but the stolen part of the labour of thousands of workers. Today if someone takes a handful of flour from your home, he becomes a thief, but your father, by investing his wealth in so many mills and banks, makes money he does not earn. Perhaps he does not know how many workers work in these mills, and how hard they work. This wealth is earned from the hard work of these same workers who cannot even cover their bodies, who cannot eat their fill. Isn't this theft? Your father and his friends have made laws according to their profit and convenience, such that their theft is legitimate but not that of others.'

Harish would argue, 'If your father has the right to capture a portion of the labour of thousands of workers in his companies, and if this is justice, then how can it be unjust for foreigners to keep this country subordinate and exploit it? They make loud noises about justice and religious duty in order to maintain this system in society for their own gain. They boast of giving employment to thousands of workers. Your father eats these workers in exactly the same way as the hen-keeper feeds hens in order to raise and eat them.'

Shail used to get irritated by these arguments. Now she felt guilty about carrying her father's name, like a criminal who has been unaware of his crime and who feels ashamed when he becomes aware of it.

Pushing aside these thoughts from her mind, Shail tried to recall moments from her childhood—wearing knee-length frocks she would play, and then, her hair and clothes filled with dust, she would put her arms around her father's neck, her feet trampling all over his clothes. Recalling this childhood memory, her eyes filled with tears. Then Harish's image would appear before her misty eyes. In police custody, chained and handcuffed, he would be brought to a court that would decide when he was to be hanged. As soon as he would enter the court, Harish's eyes would search for her. When their eyes met, his eyes would light up with joy.

Shail imagined that one day a little Harish would appear from her own body into her own lap and frolic. When she saw toddlers playing in the neighbourhood or in the street, a tiny form would leap into her imagination. Her childhood, her father's love, appeared to her as something from the past, and her own love, brimming forth for the baby laughing in her lap, as the present and the future. Sighing deeply at the memory of her father's tenderness, she thought, the chain of life has to continue. She would not survive if she kept turning to glance backward, she had to look forward.

For Shail it was not possible not to go to the court to listen to the trial. Tears filled her eyes whenever she left her father, who, hurt by her behaviour, lay silently in bed, but she was helpless.

The accused shouted slogans as soon as they entered the court: Workers of the World, Unite! Death to Capitalism! Victory to Socialism!

The lawyers asked Shail to explain to Harish that in his testimony he should only declare himself innocent and should say where he was at the time of the robbery, but Harish was committed to talking about his aims. Once the police had finished giving their testimony, the judge asked the accused for theirs.

Sultan spoke on behalf of the accused:

'. . . The police say stolen money was obtained from us. The court is accusing us of armed robbery, but the police know very well that at the time of the robbery my companions and I were at the Dalton Mill gate. It is not our job to explain the connection between the notes that have been obtained from us and the armed robbery. The public may also think of us as dacoits and hate us. Failing to find the people responsible for the robbery, the police are venting their anger on us. It is possible that the court will declare us guilty of murder and robbery and sentence us to death on the basis of the testimony presented by the police, but if there is such a thing as truth, then we say with utmost conviction that we did not commit the robbery.

'We do not believe in the method of armed robbery. We have dedicated our lives to opposing the relentless robbery of capitalist exploitation established in society. It is the purpose of the court to mete out justice, but what kind of justice is this! Some orders and rules have been issued by the capitalist class to maintain its rights and rule. In the eyes of this court and the government, the perpetuation of this system alone is justice. The duty of this court is to see that we conduct ourselves according to the capitalist system and its rules. And because our goal is to change the capitalist system, we are guilty in the eyes of this court, but we are not guilty of robbery and murder. The court is accusing us on the basis of the stolen money obtained from us. The police can obtain whatever it wants from anyone. We wish to turn the court's attention towards these four cloth mills' claim of having lost sixty thousand rupees during the three months of the strike. They suffered this loss because they were deprived of the opportunity of profiting from the workers' labour. These mills have digested crores of rupees generated by these workers. We want to know whether or not this robbery too will be noticed . . .'

The judge interrupted the accused and asked a question, 'What is the relation between what you are saying and this trial?'

Sultan answered, 'In your view we are accused of armed robbery. I am telling the court where and how the robbery is taking place in society. The testimonies presented before you have already proved that the three of us, the accused, do not spend our lives earning and accumulating money, and that we were under the watchful eyes of the police at the time of the robbery. We spend our lives ensuring that violence and robbery should not take place in any form. We spend our energy and time precisely to stop violence and robbery. It is astonishing that despite such testimonies, you are accusing us of robbery just because the police are trying to prove that someone else's money was found in our custody. Can't you consider that the police themselves might have brought this money to our place? I want to submit only the following to the court: when you see the money earned by the workers in the custody of capitalists, why don't you consider that as robbery . . .'

The public prosecutor objected and addressed the court, 'My Lord, the accused is not defending himself, he is trying to propagate his revolutionary ideas, which have no relation to the events of the case.'

Sultan looked at the public prosecutor and raised an objection, 'You know that our life or death depends on what I am saying. Then why don't you let me say what I have to?'

The public prosecutor: 'We have not come here to listen to your ideas.'

Sultan: 'Do you think ideas have no connection with the actions of a person?'

The public prosecutor looked at the court and said, 'I want the court's decision on this matter.'

The judge gave his decision, 'Whatever the accused is saying bears no relation to the events of the case. If the accused wishes to cross-examine the witnesses for the police, he may do so.'

Sultan agreed to cross-examine the police. The Deputy Superintendent of Police, who had conducted the raid on Akhtar's home and arrested the accused, appeared before the court.

The court said, 'The witness will take an oath to speak nothing but the truth.'

Following the court's order, the Deputy Superintendent said on oath that knowing God to be present and watchful, he will speak only the truth.

Sultan asked, 'Khan Sahib, have you ever seen God?'

The Superintendent said, 'No, I haven't really seen Him—who can see God?'

Sultan then asked, 'Then how can you say that God is present and watchful?'

The public prosecutor stood up and raised an objection. 'The criminal is only trying to harass the witness. The question should pertain to his testimony.'

The judge looked at Sultan and said, 'We are not sitting here to resolve spiritual questions about the existence of God. You may ask whatever you want to ask in relation to the testimony.'

Sultan responded, 'Sir, in all politeness I want to ask: how can the witness who speaks such a big lie at the very beginning, speak the truth later?'

The Judge pronounced, 'No, this cannot be called a lie. This is the custom of the court. If you wish to cross-examine further, you may ask questions.'

Sultan: 'Very well, as you say. Khan Sahib, how did you surmise that the money you found in our custody was stolen?'

'Because this money belonged to Jivaram-Bholaram. They have entered the numbers of these notes in their report.'

Sultan: 'But can you tell me, how did Jivaram-Bholaram get so much money? Is it possible that the money may not belong to them? That they might have somehow come to know that we had notes with such and such numbers? Why did you believe that so much money has been stolen from them?'

Deputy Superintendent: 'Everyone can believe that. They run a very large cloth business.'

Sultan: 'Do they weave cloth?'

Deputy Superintendent: 'No, they don't weave cloth, the weavers weave.'

Sultan: 'Then the money from the cloth business should be with the weavers. How did this business fall into Jivaram-Bholaram's hands?'

The Deputy Superintendent looked at the public prosecutor.

Sultan said, 'Please look at me—are you asking the public prosecutor for an answer?'

The public prosecutor objected, 'I wish to draw the court's attention to the fact that the criminal is conducting this cross-examination not for his own defense but to harass witnesses and waste the court's time. This can only mean that he has no defense against the charges laid upon him.'

The Judge looked at Sultan and said, 'I am sorry to see that you are unconcerned about the serious charges and the evidence against you, you are trying only to propagate your ideas. The court is not the appropriate place for that and nor can the court permit it.'

Akhtar said irritably from his place, 'Sir, if you wish to hang us, why don't you just do it? You won't even let us speak our mind! Why not just slaughter us?'

Sultan gestured towards him to stay quiet, and said, 'We are sorry that the court is not ready to hear our defense. If the court does not want to know about our ideas, how will it understand that we could never have committed such a heinous act as an armed robbery, that we have not committed this act, and that in fact we are sacrificing our lives precisely to oppose such acts? We believe that each person should have full rights to the fruits of his labour. When one person steals the fruits of labour from another— or one class from another, or one country from another— that is illegitimate, unjust and criminal. This is the terrifying violence and robbery ceaselessly taking place in society. The aim of our lives has been solely to bring an end to such violence and exploitation. We have strived to do just that. It is unjust to accuse us of violence and robbery, but we cannot even hope for justice from this court because it simply cannot think about justice and injustice from the perspective of humanity and ethics. This court's job is to agree with its police.

'It appears to be the duty and aim of this court to maintain the very conditions that we consider unjust and are attempting to change. Therefore, we may be culprits in the eyes of this court, but the justice that understands all humans as equal in their bare humanity, the justice that gives each human being rights over his own labour and does not give him the right to profit from the labour of another—in the eyes of such justice and human ethics we are innocent. We are fully convinced that the concept of justice that deprives ninety-nine point nine percent of the people of the rights and means of life, in order to protect the right to luxury of a few, will change one day, and our sacrifice will assist in that change!'

The Judge dismissed the court and determined the date when the verdict would be announced.

The testimony of the accused Sultan in the armed robbery case had created a sensation in the city and therefore a considerable crowd assembled in the court to hear the verdict. Shail's face had become pale from fear and apprehension. Yashoda and Akhtar's wife had also come to the court that day. Shail was sitting with them on one side.

Everyone had guessed what the court's judgment would be, but people were eager to hear it from the judge's mouth.

The judge made reference to the police testimony and declaring it to be entirely trustworthy, he said, 'There is no doubt that the accused are guilty of robbery and murder. According to the learned public prosecutor, the accused, having seen the powerful evidence of the testimonies, made no attempt to defend themselves. Instead, they only tried to propagate ideas of revolt against the social condition. Instead of trying to prove that they have not committed the crime, the accused tried to convince the court that their robbery is an act of public welfare. In such a situation, one simply cannot posit that this crime has been committed by the accused because of the immaturity of youth or because of particular circumstances, nor hope that, if given a chance, they will be able to live the life of peaceful citizens. On the contrary, the accused have tried to paint their heinous act as a sacrifice which increases, rather than decreasing, the seriousness of their crime.

'In this situation, the court is unable to accept the appeal of the defense counsel that considering the accused are youths and have never before participated in such a crime, they should be given the least possible sentence. When a crime is committed not because of circumstances or an unexpected event but on the basis of ideas and beliefs, its seriousness increases greatly. Hence, keeping in view its duty towards justice and order, the court, finding the accused definitively guilty of armed robbery and murder under Section 369, awards them the full punishment for this crime, death by hanging.'

It seemed that the accused had been waiting for this very decision. They shouted, 'Long Live Revolution! Long Live the Workers of the World!* Death to Imperialism! Death to the Exploitation of the World!'

The judge's last words left Shail sitting like a stone statue. She was roused by the sound of Akhtar's wife crying aloud. Yashoda, repeating God's name, had put her arm around her back in sympathy and compassion.

The court was dismissed. The lawyer, holding Akhtar's wife by the arm, took her to meet Akhtar for one last time. Shail and Yashoda went with her.

---

* *Duniya ke mehnat karne vaale zindabad*: literally, Long live those who are the hard workers of the world.

Surrounded by the police, the accused were raising slogans. Shail saw that Sultan's eyes were waiting for her alone. Akhtar's wife clasped Akhtar's knees and sat down with a piercing cry. Yashoda was trying to recognize Harish in Sultan. She could only recognize his eyes. Her own eyes filled with tears.

Harish looked at Yashoda and said with a smile, 'That day you saved me from death, but tell me, where is God now?'

Yashoda wiped her eyes and said, 'He is the Master, we depend only on Him.'

Harish's eyes met Shail's petrified eyes and he said, smiling, 'Oh Shail, will you be anxious? But it is to you that we entrust all responsibility as we go. Give my love to Dada and thank him for his help.'

Akhtar called Shail and placing his wife's hand in hers, he said, 'Sister, you must console this poor woman!'

Shail tried to console and support Akhtar's wife. At that moment the police took the accused away and locked them in the jail van. The van left the court compound. Akhtar's wife, tearing her hair called out, 'Allah, grant me refuge! Oh Allah!'

Yashoda was saying, 'God's will is powerful. What can a human being do.'

Shail was muttering in helpless rage, 'It is the cruel who are powerful even in God's court . . .'

Yashoda somehow escorted Shail home in that crazed state.

Dada and *Comrade*

Upon returning from court, Shail took to her bed with a high fever. The fever was so high that she fell into a delirium. Whenever she regained consciousness for a while, she would look around herself, think of something, then again fall unconscious. Bhuaji, sitting by her bedside, repeatedly placed an ice pack on her head and the maid massaged her feet. She drifted in and out of consciousness. While unconscious, she would start muttering in a low voice as if she were talking to someone. She would sometimes speak in Punjabi, sometimes in Hindi or in English. Neither Bhuaji nor the maid could understand anything. At times she would start screaming because of her headache. Sometimes she felt nauseous. For two weeks she remained in this state.

Shail's father was not in a condition to get out of bed, but he was so worried about his daughter that he would go upstairs many times to see her. The old family doctor came twice a day to check on her. She was being treated according to his instructions. Bhuaji proposed that some other experienced doctor be consulted.

When the new doctor came to see Shail, she was unconscious, but as the doctor was about to leave, she regained consciousness. Recognizing the doctor, she said, 'Doctor, nothing has happened to me, I am perfectly well.'

'That is just what I say, my daughter,' the doctor responded. 'Don't worry, you will soon be well.'

The maid told Shail that the doctor had put a rubber tube in his ears and examined her body carefully; he had explained everything to her father. Following the doctor's prescription, Shail was to be given a spoonful of medicine every three hours and another medicine to inhale whenever she fell unconscious. When Bhuaji came, Shail asked worriedly, 'What did the doctor tell Father?'

Bhuaji answered, 'Nothing, my daughter, the doctor said that you will soon be well.'

'No, what did the doctor tell Father, Bhuaji?' Shail insisted, Bhuaji herself did not know what the doctor had told her father. She only knew that the doctor had said that the patient should not be allowed to talk too much, and that nothing worrisome or upsetting should be said to her. Hence, she tried to distract Shail, but Shail, pale-faced and blinking her wide, restless eyes, would repeatedly ask, 'What did the doctor tell Father?'

The doctor had said that until the patient was able to remain consistently conscious and to sleep in a normal manner, nothing of import should be discussed with her. On the floor below, Lala Dhyanchandji lay in bed, his hand covering his eyes. News of Shail's condition was taken to him regularly. Only God's name could be heard on his lips.

On the fourth day, supporting himself on a cane, Lalaji slowly reached upstairs. Shail was astonished to see her father's face. She thought: he has indeed been ill and worried for many days, but what is this that has happened to him? His lips were dry and his eyes entirely lustreless.

Sitting on a chair close to Shail's bed, Dhyanchandji said, 'Are you well?'

He told everyone to leave the room.

When everyone had left, he again asked Shail, 'How are you feeling now?'

'I am well,' Shail said, and raising her eyes, looked at her father. She was frightened by the change in his tone. It seemed as though he were speaking from the depths of a cavernous pit.

Father again asked, 'Did you sleep well last night?'

'Yes,' Shail said apprehensively, her head bent.

Holding a handkerchief to his mouth, Dhyanchandji coughed and said, 'I want to talk briefly. My friends criticized me several times because I let you be free. I did not care about their words. I knew that after I am gone, you would have to take care of yourself in the world. I wanted you to become capable of facing the conditions of the world. Apart from that, I had faith in you, infinite faith; perhaps it was blind faith. I never paid attention to the difference in our ideas. I explained to myself—new ideas come with new times, and experience will change your ideas. Even if your ideas don't change, it is a part of being human to suffer for one's ideas, it is evidence of spiritual strength. Despite all this I had faith that you would remain firm on the path of truth. Just as you were ready to suffer for your ideas, and wished to sacrifice everything, in the same way,' he steadied his faltering voice, 'you would remain firm in your conduct . . .'

Shail's gaze was lowered.

Lala Dhyanchandji fell silent. Though it took a vast toll on his heart and mind, he began speaking again, 'After what the doctor has said . . . I don't have the capacity to bear any more. Perhaps this is the form in which I must finally confront the deeds of my past birth, but I will not be able to bear it while I am alive. Had it happened after my death, my soul would still have been agitated, but people would not have had a chance to spit on my face. Because of my love for you, I even considered committing suicide so as to set you free. Whatever honour is left to me in my old age, let it remain protected . . . This stain should not become manifest in this city and in this home . . . that is all I have to say.'

Shail was now face to face with the very danger she had feared when she repeatedly asked about the doctor's words. Tears did not come to her eyes. In a low but determined voice she said, 'Father, my path has always been distinct from the path of common custom. I will remain indebted to you for as long as I live. The greatest gift you gave me was the gift of freedom. In whatever I did, our difference remains one of ideas. In facing my intellect, I am not ashamed of any of my actions. I don't have any regret either. If I considered myself a fallen woman, I would kill myself rather than show my face to the world. In a day or two I will go somewhere. You will not have to be ashamed because of me . . .'

Lala Dhyanchand remained quiet for some time. Then sighing deeply and placing his hand on his lowered brow he said, 'Whatever I have is all yours. You may take whatever you need.'

'Father, I don't need anything,' Shail said looking out of the window. 'I need only your blessings. I still consider myself worthy of your blessings. I have done no more than has been granted me as my natural right as a woman. I am a human being and wish to remain one.'

Tapping his cane, Lalaji went downstairs.

Shail called for a glass of water, drank it, and sank into worry—in another kind of worry, not worry about what would happen, but worry about what must be done.

I will go, but where will I go? She thought. She had been lying down, she got up to sit. I have to go, she thought . . . perhaps I'll have to walk a lot, will I be able to walk? I am weak now . . . Harish, I will not be anxious. I am your companion, your *comrade*! . . . You smiled even when you heard the death sentence and I can't even walk? . . . Will I fear the spite of idiots?

Shail rose and started walking around the room. Her feet staggered a bit, but she continued walking . . . there's no fear, Hari, I will be able to walk.

Shail sat down on the chair . . . what do I need, I need only courage. Society will not be able to frighten me, to suppress me. Shail thought, where could she go? Robert was her friend, was exceedingly generous.

Shail turned away from this thought. I don't need help . . . I will walk on my own feet.

Shail called the maid. When the maid came, she asked for a glass of warm milk. She did not particularly want milk at this time, but she drank it to recover from the weakness. She asked the maid, 'I am well now, am I not? . . . Am I weak?'

The maid could not understand the storm rising in Shail's mind. She responded, 'Yes, Bibiji, you are well now.'

'Good, my sister, go and rest now. After three hours, please bring some more milk.'

When the maid left, Shail started thinking: I will go . . . I will go anywhere. This world is large. I will keep Harish alive . . . I will raise him . . . He will continue Harish's work. I must sleep to recover from weakness. She lay down and was really able to sleep. When the maid brought milk after three hours, Shail was sleeping.

Upon waking, Shail saw that the darkness of evening had descended. The clock showed eight. She thought about the dream she had just had. She remembered that Bhuaji believed in dreams and would say that dreams dreamt in the daytime are not true. Just then the servant came from downstairs and said, 'Dadaram has been sitting downstairs for a long time waiting to meet you.'

'Dadaram—who?' Shail asked in surprise and then, recalling, said, 'Please ask him to come here.'

In a minute Dada was before her.

'Dada, you? . . . I was just thinking of you,' Shail said eagerly.

'I have seen everything in the newspaper,' Dada said in a very sad and moist tone. 'Sister Shail, I am sorry that in an ill-fated moment I gave you that money.'

'No, Dada,' Shail said firmly. 'That is what led to the victory of the exploited in this battle. It will become the foundation of their liberation. Dada, the last thing he said was, "Give Dada my love and my gratitude."'

Dada's eyes brimmed with tears. Wiping his eyes, he took a deep breath and said, 'Harish is gone, but he made manifest the ideal of a revolutionary.'

'No, Dada, he will remain alive yet,' Shail lowered her eyes.

'What?' Dada asked in surprise. A blush of embarrassment spread over Shail's pale face.

'Dada, you have come to take me, haven't you?'

'Why, what is the matter?'

'I had fallen ill,' Shail said, scratching the threads of the bedsheet with her nails. 'I am his wife. Father has told me to leave. He can't bear the taint . . . I want to go to a place where I will not be considered a tainted woman.'

'All right . . . why?' Dada looked carefully at Shail's face and tried to understand.

'Dada, do you also consider me a tainted woman?'

'You? . . . Look, Shail, please don't make me embarrassed by recalling what I said that day. I warn you! . . . This is the natural path of your life. I am happy, indeed very happy . . . This is a very good thing. Sister, see, I don't really know how to say a lot . . .'

'Dada, please take me away . . . If I can take anyone's support, it is yours.'

'But Shail, the life you are used to living . . .'

'No, Dada, don't talk like this. With you, I will be able to spend my life even under a tree . . . Dada, really . . . I will place your Hari in your hands . . . Did you not say, I have stolen your Hari from you?'

Looking at the floor, Dada kept biting his moustache for some time, then clasping together the fingers of both hands, he looked into Shail's eyes and said, 'I thought that my life had become purposeless. Earlier I had shaped myself as the instrument of a particular task. Once that task was no longer needed, I became useless. Shail, you have prepared new work for me. I had believed the light of the lamp was fading, for whom will I live now . . .?'

'Dada, the light never fades. We will go, we will keep the flame alive. Take me with you.'

'Rise, *Comrade*!' Dada stood up, and Shail also stood up.

Shail's feet were faltering. Grasping her arm, Dada said, 'Are you afraid, *Comrade*?'

'No, Dada, let's go. We will go as we are.'

Glossary

aadaab	a common Urdu salutation
aanchal	the loose end of a woman's sari; figuratively also breast or bosom
Baisakh	the second month of the Hindu calendar (April–May)
Bhabhi	brother's wife, also used as an affectionate term of address for women
Bhangi	a caste associated with sweeping and sanitation work; here used as a name for Dalits in general
Bhai Sahib	respectful term of address for an elder brother.
Bhaiya	brother; commonly used as a term of address for men
Bhuaji	a term of address for one's father's sister
Bibiji	madam; a term of respect for a woman
chichi	the little finger of the hand
Chachi	the wife of the father's younger brother

datun	a twig of the neem tree, often used for cleaning one's teeth
dhoti	a garment worn around the waist by men, usually reaching to the knees or ankles
dholak	a drum
dupatta	a long scarf or veil worn by women
kameez	a shirt
Maaji	mother; a term of address for an older woman
mistri	a worker-overseer
salwar	loose trousers tied with a drawstring
Sardar	literally, the man at the head. Commonly used to refer to men of the Sikh community, or to a leader
Swaraj or Swarajya	literally, one's own rule; self-government
Swadeshi	made in one's own country
Swayamvara	the custom of a woman choosing her own husband from among several suitors

Translator's Acknowledgements

I began this translation many years ago, but was waylaid by events so shattering that all my writing projects had to be shelved. I am glad I was finally able to retrieve this one and finish it. I would like to thank my father, Sewak Singh Sawhney, and my sister, Sabina Sawhney, for their incomparable support, as well as all those whose interest in this translation encouraged me along the way, especially Ajay Skaria, Ania Loomba, Divya Karan, Gayathri Prabhu, Guy Pollio, Joe Allen, Kama Maclean, Nikhil Govind, Stuti Khanna, Vasudha Dalmia, and Vrinda Sharma. Stuti Khanna and Guy Pollio read drafts of the translation and gave me excellent suggestions, and Kama Maclean, Guy Pollio and Ajay Skaria provided helpful comments on a draft of the Introduction. I am deeply grateful to Anand, Yashpal's son, whose unflagging faith made this work possible as well as to Richa Burman, my editor at Penguin, Binita Roy, my copy editor, and indeed, the entire team for their attentive and thoughtful work. Finally, I must acknowledge my great debt to Sumitra and Raji for their laughter no less than their labour.